The King David Report

The King David Report

A Novel
by
STEFAN HEYM

HODDER AND STOUGHTON
LONDON SYDNEY AUCKLAND TORONTO

2

34604

I

PRAISED BE THE NAME of the Lord our God, who has allotted wisdom to the one, riches to another, soldierly virtues to a third.

I, Ethan the son of Hoshaiah, from the town of Ezrah, was called this day to King Solomon, and was brought in his presence by Elihoreph and Ahiah the sons of Shisha, scribes; and found with him Jehoshaphat the son of Ahilud, the recorder, and Zadok the priest, and Nathan the prophet, and Benaiah the son of Jehoiada, the captain of the host.

And I prostrated myself at the King's feet, and he bade me to rise. Thus it came to pass that I saw King Solomon as one man sees another, face to face; and though he sat upon his throne, between the Cherubim, he appeared smaller than I had thought him, smaller even than his late father, King David; but his countenance was of a yellowish colour. And the King gazed at me from beady eyes, saying, "You are Ethan ben Hoshaiah, from the town of Ezrah?"

"The same, my lord. And your servant."

"I hear it being said from Dan even unto Beer-sheba, Ethan, that you are one of the wisest men in Israel?"

But I replied, "Who may claim to be wiser than the Wisest of Kings, Solomon?"

At which his delicate lips curled peevishly, and he said, "I will tell you a dream, Ethan, which I had the other night after sacrificing and burning incense in the high place at Gibeon." And to Elihoreph and Ahiah, the scribes, and to

5

Jehoshaphat ben Ahilud, the recorder, "Mark this dream, for I want it entered into the annals."

Whereupon Elihoreph and Ahiah took from their gowns stylus and tablets of wax, and waited to take down the royal words. And this is the dream of King Solomon.

"In Gibeon Yahveh appeared to me by night, and Yahveh said, Ask what I shall give you. And I said, You have shown unto your servant David my father great mercy, according as he walked before you in truth, and in righteousness, and in uprightness of heart; and you have kept for him this great kindness, that you have given him a son to sit on his throne, as it is this day."

The King stopped toying with the noses of the Cherubim, and shoved forward his feet which were encased in red sandals of fine goatskin.

"And now, O Lord my God, I said to Yahveh, you have made your servant king instead of David my father; and I am but a little child; I know not how to go out or come in. And your servant is in the midst of your people which you have chosen, a great people that cannot be numbered nor counted for multitude."

The King straightened, and the light from the window glistened on the gold-embroidered cap he wore on his dark, thinning hair.

"Therefore, O Lord my God, I said to Yahveh, give to your servant an understanding heart to judge your people, that I may discern between good and bad; for who is able to judge so great a people as yours? And Lord Yahveh said unto me, Because you have asked this thing, and not for yourself long life, nor riches, nor the perdition of your enemies, behold, I have given you a wise and understanding heart, so there was none like you before you, neither after you shall any arise like you."

And the King rose and quickly scanned the faces of his ministers, and he saw their devout seriousness. Satisfied, he concluded, "And I shall also give you that which you have not asked, Lord Yahveh told me, to wit, both riches and honour, so that there shall not be any among the kings like you all your days. And if you will walk in my ways, to keep my statutes and my commandments, as your father David did walk, then I will lengthen your days."

Whereupon Zadok the priest and Nathan the prophet delightedly clapped their hands, while Elihoreph and Ahiah, the scribes, cast up their eyes in admiration. And Jehoshaphat ben Ahilud, the recorder, exclaimed that never in his day had he heard of a dream more pithy, or more apt to impress the hearts and minds of the people. But Benaiah ben Jehoiada stayed silent, moving his efficient-looking jaw as though he were chewing bitter cud. And King Solomon stepped down from his throne and approached me and laid his short-fingered hand upon my shoulder and said, "Eh?"

I said that I considered the royal dream a jewel of its kind, of extraordinary beauty, powerful in wording and imagination, and proof of a deep, personal feeling on the part of the King for our Lord Yahveh and for Yahveh's unfathomable intent and purposes.

"That's as a poet," said the King. "But as a historian? I understand from my district officer in Ezrah that you are working on a History of the People of Israel."

"A dream, O Wisest of Kings," I bowed, "can be as much of a historical force as a flood or a host of men or a curse of God—especially a dream as well told and documented as yours."

King Solomon gazed at me again, less certain than before; then his mouth broadened into a grin, and he said, "I have seen men swallowing knives and others eating fire, but never have I seen a more agile dance on the edge of a sword. What is your opinion, Benaiah ben Jehoiada?"

"Words," grunted Benaiah. "How many words have I heard mouthed in the days of your father, King David: and where are those from whose lips they spouted?"

The face of the King darkened; perhaps he was recalling the fate of his brother Amnon, or of his brother Absalom, or that of his mother's first husband, Captain Uriah, or of men in whose demise Benaiah had taken a hand.

But Jehoshaphat ben Ahilud, the recorder, mentioned that I had been brought into the illustrious presence of King Solomon precisely because it was said that I was well versed in the use of the word; and Nathan the prophet reminded Benaiah that some lived by the sword and some by the word, just as our Lord Yahveh, in his infinite wisdom, had created animals of more than one kind, fish as well as fowl, the beasts

7

of the wilderness and the gentle sheep, but had set above them the lion who was both powerful and wise. And he bowed to the King while Zadok the priest added that nevertheless it was the snake who started Man on the road to hell; therefore beware of the smooth tongue and the gilded word. From all of which I gathered that some differences of mind prevailed among the mighty men surrounding King Solomon and that a person thrust upon them from the outside had better move warily.

King Solomon retraced his steps to the throne and sat down gingerly between the Cherubim. Toying with their noses, he addressed me as follows, "It is of course known to you, Ethan ben Hoshaiah, that my father King David, in his own person, chose me, his beloved son, to succeed him upon the throne, and that he caused me to ride upon the royal mule to Gihon, there to be anointed king, and that he bowed before me on his sickbed and prayed our Lord Yahveh to make my throne even greater than had been his own."

I assured the King that I knew those facts and was convinced that Lord Yahveh would fulfil the last prayer of King David his father.

"You observe, Ethan," the King went on, "that I was triply chosen. First Lord Yahveh chose the people of Israel above all other people; then he chose King David my father to be ruler over the people thus chosen; and then my father chose me to rule in his place."

I assured the King that I thought his logic was unassailable and that both Lord Yahveh and King David could not have made a better choice.

"Doubtless," replied the King, casting one of his heavy glances at me. "But you will agree, Ethan, that the validity of the third choice depends on the establishment beyond question of the second."

"A man who rose from a Bethlehem sheepcote to rule in Jerusholayim," said Benaiah ben Jehoiada fiercely, "who smote all his enemies and trod underfoot their cities, who bent to his will not only the kings of Moab and of the Philistines but also the tribes of Israel in their obstinacy: such a man needs neither priest nor prophet nor scribe to prove his having been chosen by the Lord."

"But that man is dead," said King Solomon, a surge of

8

anger deepening the yellow of his face, "and Israel abounds with stories about him, most of them useless, some even harmful. Just as I will build a temple for our Lord Yahveh to put an end to this praying and sacrificing on every hilltop behind every village, and to force under one roof what passes between a man and his God, so we must have one authoritative report, to the exclusion of all others, on the life and great works and heroic battles of my father, King David, who chose me to sit upon his throne."

Although Benaiah had been a key figure in the choice of Solomon to sit upon the throne of his father, he recoiled slightly at the royal vehemence. But the King called upon Jehoshaphat ben Ahilud, the recorder.

And Jehoshaphat stepped forth and drew a clay tablet from his sleeve and read out, "Members of the Royal Commission on the Preparation of *The One and Only True and Authoritative, Historically Correct and Officially Approved Report on the Amazing Rise, God-fearing Life, Heroic Deeds, and Wonderful Achievements of David the Son of Jesse, King of Judah for Seven Years and of Both Judah and Israel for Thirty-three, Chosen of God, and Father of King Solomon*: Jehoshaphat the son of Ahilud, recorder; Zadok, priest; Nathan, prophet; Elihoreph and Ahiah, the sons of Shisha, scribes; Benaiah the son of Jehoiada, who is over the host. Redactor, but without vote: Ethan, son of Hoshaiah, of the town of Ezrah, author and historian. *The Report on the Amazing Rise* and so forth to have the working title *The King David Report*; and to be composed by careful selection from and judicious use of all materials extant on the Amazing Rise and so forth of the late King David, such as royal records, correspondence, and annals, as well as available testimony, further legends and lore, songs, psalms, proverbs and prophecies, especially those referring to the great love and preference shown by King David to his beloved son and successor, King Solomon; said Report to establish for this and all time to come *One Truth*, thus ending *All Contradiction and Controversy*, eliminating *All Disbelief* of the *Choice by our Lord Yahveh of David ben Jesse*, and allaying *All Doubt* of the *Glorious Promises* made to him by our Lord Yahveh in regard to *his Seed and Progeny*."

Jehoshaphat bowed. King Solomon looked exceedingly

9

pleased. He beckoned me near and said, "Naturally I will help you, Ethan, whenever you should falter or be undecided as to where lies error and where truth. When can you begin?"

But I prostrated myself before King Solomon, thanking him for the great confidence with which he had honoured me. I was the most surprised man from Dan even unto Beersheba, I said, and if the Angel of the Lord had appeared to me in a dream and predicted such an appointment, I should have laughed at him as did Sarah the wife of Abraham. And I was too insignificant a person entirely, I said further, for so huge and responsible an undertaking; if it was a psalm or two, I should be glad to oblige, or a short history of any of the minor tribes, or a new version of Moishe our Leader being found in the bulrushes when an infant; that was about my size as an author; you do not ask the lowly ant to build a pyramid, or the frightened rabbit to roar like a lion.

At this King Solomon laughed heartily and said to those present, "He is truly a wise man who, seeing the pitfalls in the road, prefers to stay at home." But to me the King said, "I can take your sons and appoint them to myself, for my chariots and to be my horsemen, or to run before my chariots. And I can take your daughters to be confectionaries, and to be cooks, and to be bakers. Or I can take your field and your vineyard, and your oliveyard. Or I can take you to be a cleaner in my stables or a mover of my fans. But I prefer taking you as a historian, under the guidance of my Commission, for everyone has his place under God, the shepherd with his flock and the scribe with his tablets."

So I prostrated myself more deeply and pointed out that I was a sick man, with a weak heart and an irregular stomach, and that I might be laid to rest with my fathers at Ezrah before the King David Report was half finished, and that I could recommend several younger men of stouter health and of a more flexible mind, just what was needed for the writing of books that contained *One Truth* and ended *All Contradiction and Controversy*.

To this the King replied, "You look well to me, Ethan ben Hoshaiah. Your skin has a healthy tan and your muscle shows none of the slack of age, you have a full head of hair and a full complement of teeth in your gums, and your eyes sparkle from

10

the enjoyment of wine and of women. Further, I have the best doctors in all of Israel and the kingdoms surrounding it, even unto Sidon and Tyre, and I have contracted with the Queen of Sheba for a specialist on the cutting out of stones that lodge in the kidney. Also you will occasionally eat at my table and partake of some of the finest cooking this side of the Negev, and you will be paid the wage of a minor prophet, which will enable you to bring your two wives and your young concubine to Jerusholayim and live with them in a good brick house with a solid roof and a shady backyard."

I saw that Solomon had thought of practically everything, and that there was no escaping his favour. I also saw that I might end, as some writers did, with my head cut off and my body nailed to the city wall, but that, on the other hand, I might wax fat and prosperous if I guarded my tongue and used my stylus wisely. With some luck and the aid of our Lord Yahveh, I might even insert in the King David Report a word here and a line there by which later generations would perceive what really came to pass in these years and what manner of man David ben Jesse was: who served as a whore simultaneously to a king and the king's son and the king's daughter, who fought as a hired soldier against his own blood, who had his own son and his most loyal servants assassinated while loudly bewailing their death, and who forged a people out of a motley of miserable peasants and recalcitrant nomads.

So I rose and said to King Solomon that in his boundless wisdom he had persuaded me to accept the position, though with great trepidation; and that, considering the time it would take for the necessary prayers and sacrifices and for moving my archives and two wives and a young concubine with their luggage from Ezrah to Jerusholayim, I would be ready to begin work the second day following Passover. However, I said, deciding to strike while the iron was hot, there was the matter of the education of my two young sons to which I had been attending and for which I would now lack the time and the opportunity.

"Zadok!" said the King.

Zadok bowed.

"See that the young sons of Ethan ben Hoshaiah are placed

in a good Levite school." And as Zadok raised his brow, the King added with a large gesture, "Tuition and board to be paid out of the royal treasury."

For King Solomon was truly generous with the tithes of the people.

2

THOUGHTS OF ETHAN BEN HOSHAIAH, ONE NIGHT AFTER HIS
RETURN FROM JERUSHOLAYIM, AS HE LAY UPON THE ROOF OF
HIS HOUSE IN EZRAH, WITH LILITH HIS CONCUBINE READY TO
MINISTER TO HIM

No story begins where it seems to begin; the roots of the
tree are hidden from the eye, but they reach down to the
waters.

Other peoples had kings who claimed they were gods, but
the people of Israel had God for their king: an invisible king,
for Yahveh is an invisible god. Nor are there images of him,
graven or molten; he forbade the making of them. Invisible,
King Yahveh sat enthroned between the Cherubim upon his
royal seat, which is the ark of God, and had himself carried
from place to place; even as the people moved, so did he,
living under a tent and a tabernacle as they did. On hilltops
or under an old sycamore tree he accepted sacrifices: a field
stone would suffice as his altar. He spoke, when he chose to
speak, through the thunder of the clouds or the whisperings
of the wind, through the ravings of a prophet or the dream
of a child, through the mouth of an angel or the rattle of
the oracle of Urim and Tummim. He proclaimed laws but
often was unjust; he was short-tempered at times and long-
suffering at others; he played favourites, he contradicted
himself: he resembled one of those tribal elders you still can
meet in the back hills.

"Lilith my love, bring me the flagon of wine you will find in the cool of the cellar, red wine from the King's vineyard at Baal-hamon, a gift from him. Lilith my love, whose breasts are like two young roes that are twins, we shall move to Jerusholayim, and I shall buy you a garment of divers colours like that of a princess, and sweet-smelling essences, and I shall lose you. Bring me the wine..."

Why, then, was King Yahveh replaced by Saul the son of Kish?

A visible king, however impressive in his prime, waxes feeble; Lord Yahveh, King of Israel, remained forever arrayed in the glory of man's imagination. But his will could assert itself only through interpretation, and those who interpreted him were human and prone to error. They might read their own desires into the heavenly portents; and some of the holy men were known to have tailored their messages to interests quite worldly.

Certainly Samuel the priest, seer and judge was not one of these. Having studied the book he left us, I am convinced that he was a man of integrity and principle. Who but a person of utter probity could step before an assembly of people as he did at Mizpeh, saying, Behold, here I am; witness against me before the Lord, and before his anointed: whose ox have I taken? or whose ass have I taken? or whom have I defrauded? whom have I oppressed? or of whose hand have I received any bribe to blind my eyes therewith? ... But this kind of person can create more misery by his rigidity than any son of Belial by his wickedness.

"Drink, Ethan my friend. The night has a sweet scent. Why should you lose me? I shall not leave you, unless you cast me from you. I will sing to you as you taught me.

> *I am the rose of Sharon, and the lily*
> *of the valleys.*
> *As the lily among thorns, so is my love*
> *among the daughters.*
> *As the apple tree among the trees of the wood,*
> *so is my beloved among the sons...*

14

But you are not listening to me..."

The priests at Ramah, whose fathers served under him, and the itinerant prophets hailing from his school, agree in their description of Samuel: a tall man, emaciated; his grey, stringy mane and the sparse beard never touched by the barber's knife; zealot's eyes; the mouth without grace—a man who saw an opponent in anyone not willing instantly to bow to his superior will and to the power of God, for God was king in Israel and Samuel his deputy before the people.

Samuel reasoned with the people when they demanded a king who would answer in his own voice and smite you with his own sword. In harsh words he delineated the nature of those kings-to-be, and he foretold what unchecked power does to the character of a ruler. But the people of Israel turned a deaf ear.

I don't believe that Samuel ever understood the people's insistence on a supreme lord of flesh and blood, and why he, Samuel, not the least among the long line of judges in Israel, was compelled to resign his office and anoint a mortal to be king.

"Lilith my love, taste of the King's wine. And stroke my temples, for my head is heavy. From where and whither blow the winds of change, and what causes them? One day a man might arise who charts their course; this man will be adjudged wiser even than the Wisest of Kings, Solomon..."

And Samuel reasoned with Lord Yahveh; and in the book that he wrote he quotes the words which God spoke to him: Hearken unto the voice of the people in all that they say unto you; for they have not rejected you, but they have rejected me, that I should not reign over them.

Coming from One who divided the light from darkness and the waters from the waters, the note of resignation is unusual.

Possibly Yahveh spoke in this manner so as to console Samuel; but by all reports Samuel possessed sufficient grit to survive without the divine pat on the shoulder. It seems, rather that here the interpreter of the words of the Lord speaks his own sentiments: it is Samuel who feels rejected and who transfers his wounded feelings unto God.

Still an answer is contained in the words which Samuel perceived. Listen to their tone feeling: is it not as though you heard the voice of an old man? He is the head of a smallish tribe; he has his weaknesses as well as his good qualities; he has tried to dispense justice according to his lights, he has tried to help his people: but now a new time has come...

A new time.

"Your voice, Lilith my love, is as the murmur of the brook in springtime; the words which I taught you sound well from your lips:

> *Lo, the winter is past, the rain*
> *is over and gone;*
> *The flowers appear on the earth; the time*
> *of the singing of birds is come,*
> *and the voice of the turtle is heard*
> *in our land..."*

But when did it begin, this new time with its new complexities which demanded a new lord and arbiter in Israel? When the last wandering family of the last wandering tribe was assigned its piece of land? When iron replaced brass? When on the marketplace one man's wool no longer was bartered for another man's wheat but sold for pieces of silver? When the honest shepherd changed into the hawker of wares, the tradesman, the moneylender?

The new time came upon Samuel, and though he was a seer he failed to see it. He made his appointed rounds, from year to year in circuit to Beth-el, and Gilgal, and Mizpeh, and judged Israel in all those places, and returned to Ramah, for there was his house, and there he judged the rest of the year, and there he built an altar unto the Lord and believed that things would continue in this manner to the end of his days. But it came to pass that the voice of the people could no longer be ignored, and also God spoke to Samuel, and Samuel arose and chose Saul ben Kish, from the tribe of Benjamin, who from his shoulders on upward was higher than any of the people, and who went out to seek his father's asses and found a kingdom.

Or so it is told us in Samuel's book, and his message is clear: Saul is King of Israel by the grace of Samuel the chief priest and judge and prophet, Samuel's creature, beholden to Samuel.

But there is another story on the investiture of Saul. Much of it is obscure. Those who witnessed the events are dead, the documents destroyed by the hand of David: a man who has his predecessor's last surviving male issue hanged must obliterate his memory as well.

The tellers of tales who sit in the marketplace or in the gates of the cities tell us that Saul came after the herd out of the field, and heard the outcry of the people: Nahash, the Lord of Ammon, was laying siege to the town of Jabesh in Gilead and threatening to thrust out the right eye of everyone in Jabesh, for a reproach on all Israel. It is said that at this moment the spirit of God came upon Saul. He took a yoke of oxen and hewed them in pieces and sent these throughout Israel. At all events, enough men joined him to be grouped in three companies; with them he moved on Jabesh in Gilead and attacked the Ammonites in the morning watch; by the heat of the day he had beaten the enemy and relieved Jabesh.

Here was another leader in Israel risen at Yahveh's command: like Gideon, like Jephtah, like the long-haired Samson. But now the people needed a king. And they went with Saul to the shrine of Gilgal, and there, after due sacrifices, Saul was anointed.

By the people, not by Samuel.

"You are shivering, Ethan my friend."
"The winds of change blow cold."

"My thighs are filled with warmth for you, Ethan; I will open myself to my beloved."

"Honey and milk are under your tongue, Lilith my love, and the smell of your garments is like the smell of Lebanon. How fair is your love, how much better than wine..."

3

FROM THE DAYS OF ABRAHAM our forefather, who journeyed
from Ur of the Chaldees to the land of Canaan, ours has been
a wandering people. Experience has taught us to travel
lightly and trust in the Lord.

But my archives and notes consisted of numerous tablets
of clay, and of rolls of kidskin, none of which I could leave
behind. In view of the row of donkeys burdened with cases
containing my archives, how was I to deny to Esther my wife
the carting along of her coffers and rugs, to Huldah the
mother of my sons, of her treasured earthenware, and to
Lilith my concubine, of her little jars and potions and
powders? And luggage breeds luggage, for a third donkey
carrying provisions for beast and drover must be added to
each two that carry a payload. I cursed my neglect, for I had
failed to obtain a commitment on travelling expenses from
King Solomon.

The days passed. Whenever I turned back and saw the
caravan strung along the sandy road—forty donkeys and their
drovers, and the family—I thought of the long march through
Sinai. Admittedly the children of Israel carried less per man
out of Egypt than we did out of Ezrah; but did not
Jerusholayim hold as many uncertainties for us as the
promised land at the end of their wanderings had held for
them?

Esther sat astride her donkey, swaying under the merciless
sun, dark rings under her eyes; she supported herself of
Shem and Sheleph my sons out of Huldah, who walked beside

her. My heart went out to Esther, and I called a halt in the shade of a rock which was topped by a terebinth tree.

But Esther said, "I know how eager you are to be in Jerusholayim, Ethan."

I saw her wasted face and heard her breath coming in gasps, and I recalled her as she had been: strong-willed and vital, high-spirited and witty, and of a great inner beauty. And I said, "I should like to arrive there with you, Esther my dear."

She answered, "I shall live if the Lord wills it. But if he wills it not, then an angel will come of the Lord and lay his hands about my heart, so that it stops beating."

And Yahveh caused her to fall asleep in the shade until the evening wind sprang up and time came to move on. The road grew long on us, and our progress was slow, for we rested whenever Esther waxed faint. But on the seventh day we reached the crest above the brook Kidron from where you discern Jerusholayim: its walls and its gates and the towers above the gates; its roofs sparkling; the tabernacle housing the ark a dash of purple among the white of palace and fortress.

I prostrated myself before the Lord and thanked him for leading me and all that pertained to me into the sight of Jerusholayim, and I pledged the sacrifice of a fat lamb and a tender young goat on the altar built by King David upon the threshing place of Ornan the Jebusite, the lamb in token of my gratitude for the journey completed, and the goat as an aid to my prayer for divine protection in the city of David and at the court of King Solomon.

But there were men stationed on the ramparts and the towers, who observed us from afar, and who kept their eyes on us as we came near the big gate. The Cherethite mounting guard stopped us, and when I produced my credentials he called for his captain.

"Historian?" The captain of the gate could read after a fashion. "We need stonemasons, bricklayers, hodcarriers in Jerusholayim; even a shoemaker will do; but behold, unto us comes a historian."

I pointed at the royal seal.

"These people need a history," the captain went on, "as I need a boil in my secret places. These people are born dumb and die dumb, they go in unto their mothers and unto their sheep, and you want to give them a history. Is not their life sufficiently miserable without a history to vex them?" And placing his thick, dirty finger on one of the cases, "What is therein?"

"Part of my archives," I said.

"Open up."

"But the tablets will fall out. Everything will become disordered."

"I said, open up."

The knot refused to give. I tugged at the thongs. All at once, the case came open and my precious tablets tumbled into the dirt. The rabble at the gate snickered. The blood rose to my face; I wanted to inveigh against the captain; but I saw the crowd. It was a strange crowd, quite unlike any to be found in a small town like Ezrah. These were thieves, idlers, vagrants, runaway slaves; cut-throats all, and all clad in tatters; and cripples displaying their putrid stumps, their matted hair, their diseased eyes. This was the muck on which the new Jerusholayim was being erected, this was the reverse of the splendour that was Solomon's: cast-offs of the new time, too slow-witted, too indolent, or simply too weak to catch its spirit and its ways. And they raised their voices against me, because of the forty donkeys loaded with my belongings, or because I was a historian; and they were waiting for the captain's nod so they might fall upon us like hyenas on a piece of carrion.

But the captain ripped a whip from his belt and let its tails fly over their heads. Shem and Sheleph hastily gathered up the tablets. I stuffed them into the case and tied it roughly.

Thus we entered the city.

Ah, that summer! That summer in Jerusholayim!

The glare of one day fades into the glare of the next. Esther suffers. Huldah dozes, sweat running down her puffed-up face. Even Lilith seems to droop.

I should have thought of the heat here, the flies, the stench of the city before committing myself to be available

21

for work on the second day following Passover.

Everybody who can has fled the city. The King and the court, including the harem, have moved to the royal summer houses at Lake Kinnereth, there to enjoy the refreshing waters; only the ten concubines of David who were publicly gone into by Absalom, and who were left to lie fallow ever since, these have remained behind, poor wretches. I am fortunate in that Jehoshaphat ben Ahilud, the recorder, is being detained in Jerusholayim on official business; thus I can send word to him. He refers me to the keeper of the royal estates. This worthy, impatient to get away as well, receives me briefly and assigns to me the only living quarters he says he has available, No. 54, Queen-of-Sheba Lane, a three-room house in a development for government officials and Levites of the second and third order. Though the workmen have barely finished, the plaster is cracking, straw is sticking through the ceiling, the roof sags badly. Moreover, the house is too small; I want to have a wing added to serve as my study. On the strength of my position as redactor of the King David Report a moneylender is willing to advance the necessary sum, at exorbitant interest; but where to get masons and carpenters in Jerusholayim? All the city's construction workers are toiling from sunrise to sunset, sabbath excepted, on the temple project, on the extension of the royal palace, on the stables and chariot houses for the King's new horse-drawn war chariots, on barracks for the Cherethites and Pelethites, and on buildings for the ever-expanding officialdom. Shem and Sheleph, whose school is closed for the summer, roam the streets like stray curs; they report that in Jerusholayim you can obtain everything, provided you know the right people and grease the right hands. I am not above using connections and dropping a few shekels of silver; but I am a stranger in the city, my position is too new and uncertain, the general situation too murky; I cannot risk making a false move.

Thus I am forced to abandon my modest building plans. Furthermore, my own funds are dwindling fast. The few officials condemned to hold out in the Royal Treasury, south of the building site of the temple, contrive to avoid their offices most of the day; after hours of waiting I succeed in rousing one Penuel ben Mushi, administrator third grade, who listens to me sympathetically. Then, having dug through dusty piles of potsherds and scraps of leather, he tells me that no order to pay has been received, no draft, no voucher, and none may be expected to arrive before the Feast of the Tabernacles when King Solomon and his mighty men will return to Jerusholayim.

I break into wails and enquire if there is no one in Jerusholayim who has the authority to sign a provisional voucher and might be persuaded to do so?

Thereupon Penuel, shooing the flies off his thin, puckered face: even if there were such a person in Jerusholayim, would his signature be sufficient? A man might sign today and be gone tomorrow, his signature a worthless scrawl. Who knew what names were on the list which King David handed to Solomon his son as he lay on his deathbed? Therefore a countersignature and the royal seal were indispensable to any voucher.

Thereupon I, sensing tidings of value: I had heard of that list, but had anyone ever seen it? Perhaps it was just another rumour spread to justify certain measures?

Thereupon Penuel, fearing that the talk might be taking a dangerous turn: if it were not now time for a bite to eat, the sun being high up and noon approaching?

Thereupon I, in disregard of my meagre purse: if he would not join me in a modest repast; perhaps he knew of a quiet nook outside the walls of the city where we might find shade, and a wine not watered, and a piece of succulent lamb's tail?

For the study of history is not all tablets of burnt clay.

STORY OF THE FACTIONS IN ISRAEL AT THE TIME OF THE ACCESSION TO THE THRONE OF SOLOMON THE SON OF DAVID, INCLUDING DETAILS SUPPLIED BY PENUEL BEN MUSHI, ADMIN- ISTRATOR THIRD GRADE IN THE ROYAL TREASURY, AFTER HE WAS MADE LOQUACIOUS BY THE ROAST AND THE WINE, WITH SOME OF HIS THOUGHTS QUOTED IN FULL AND SET IN BRACKETS

Now King David was old and stricken in years, and he got no heat, although Abishag of Shunam, a fair damsel and well-built, did minister to him with all her might. And he knew that his days were numbered; but if he had any preference for Adonijah, or for Solomon, or for another among his sons to succeed him, he kept it to himself.

(There he lay, and stared at the ceiling, and felt the power slip from his hands. He saw quite well how they were watching him, waiting for a word from him which they might use in the struggle for his succession: that word was all that was left him of the sway he had held over Israel.)

But Adonijah the son of David out of Haggith was a very goodly man; and his father had begot him after Absalom. And Adonijah exalted himself, saying, I will be king: and he prepared him chariots and horsemen, and fifty men to run before him and call, Move, you bastards! Make way for the Heir Apparent, the Chosen of the King! And even when the King heard the noise, he stayed silent and did not question Adonijah.

(They no longer paid heed to him. All he could do was to wait for Lord Yahveh to tip the scales this way or that. He had only his word, the word of a dying man; and if, God forbid, he spoke out for the loser, what would remain of him? For judgment lies with those who come after us; and a father's fame is fashioned by his son.)

And Adonijah conferred with Joab ben Zeruiah, who was David's captain of the host, to enlist the support of the army, and with Abiathar the priest, who was backed by the country clergy that strove to maintain the small shrines and hilltop altars and their living therefrom: and both men aided Adonijah. Then Adonijah slew sheep and oxen and fat cattle by the stone of Zoheleth, which is by En-rogel, and called all his brothers the King's sons, and all the men of Judah the King's servants. But Solomon his brother he called not.

(The Little One, his second-born out of Bath-sheba, so the dying King would muse: the Little One, famed despite his young years for his clever sayings, God had visibly favoured Solomon; but no one ever knew what was in Solomon's heart. Adonijah had the army supporting him; however the host had to be assembled before it could strike; and the village priests following Abiathar were scattered over the countryside and notoriously slow but in gorging themselves and guzzling and lying with women. In the end, this issue would be decided by Benaiah, whom he had set over the Cherethites and Pelethites, the King's Own, the only force instantly ready for action.)

But Nathan the prophet and Zadok the priest, who favoured one big temple from which to direct all priests and Levites, these did not belong to Adonijah's faction and were sore afraid. Therefore Nathan spoke unto Bath-sheba, warning her to save her own life and the life of her son Solomon. Nathan advised her to go and get her unto King David and say to him, Didn't you, O lord my King, swear unto your handmaid, saying that assuredly Solomon shall reign after you, and he shall sit upon your throne? Why then does Adonijah reign? And Nathan vowed to Bath-sheba that he would come in unto the King after her and confirm her words. So Bath-sheba spoke to the King as Nathan had prompted her, and she added, My lord, O King, the eyes of all Israel are upon you, that you should tell them who shall sit on the throne after you; otherwise it shall come to pass, when my lord the King shall sleep with his fathers, that I and my son shall be counted offenders.

(There he lay on his bed with the damsel Abishag ministering to him, and this woman kept talking at him. Had he really made those promises to her? A man's last passion is his strongest: he had killed for it, and Solomon was the child of atonement. But Adonijah was in line for the throne after Amnon was gored and Absalom hung by his hair from that oak tree. He was tired of the old woman who went on speaking for her son and the young one trying to quicken his blood: we are all of us sojourners on this earth, and he was nearing the end of his journey.)

And lo, while she yet talked with the King, Nathan the prophet also came and said, My lord O King, have you said, Adonijah shall reign after me, and he shall sit upon my throne? For he has called all the King's sons, and Joab and the captains of the host, and Abiathar the priest; and they eat and drink before him, and they call, God Save King Adonijah. But your son Solomon he has not called, nor me, your servant, nor Zadok, nor Benaiah ben Jehoiada. But the King slowly turned to Abishag, and gazed at her, saying, So fair and so well-built, and so little response from this withered flesh. And to Nathan, Did I hear you correctly: he did not call Benaiah? And Nathan said, It is as I told you. Then David raised himself and spoke unto Bath-sheba, Even as I swore to you by the Lord God of Israel, so I will certainly do this day. And he said, Call me Zadok the priest and Benaiah ben Jehoiada. As they came before the King, he said to them, Take with you the Cherethites and Pelethites, the King's Own, and cause Solomon my son to ride upon my own mule, and bring him down to Gihon; and let Zadok and Nathan anoint him there king over Israel: and blow you with the trumpet and call, God save King Solomon. And Benaiah ben Jehoiada said, Amen, and may the Lord, the God of my lord the King, say Amen, too.

(He sank back into his pillows. Lord Yahveh had visibly tipped the scales, and the word of the Lord had come to him. But it had been a strain, and he must stay alive until the Little One returned from Gihon: he had to hand him the list, so that those might yet be cut down whom he had failed to fell. Many had tried to search for that list, in his chambers and in the chamber of secret records. Fools, the dying king would muse. There was no list that anyone could find. The names were in his head. All of them.)

And Nathan and Zadok and Benaiah did as King David had commanded them, and they anointed Solomon and blew the trumpet. And all the people said, God save the King; and they marched back unto Jerusholayim, and piped with pipes, and rejoiced with great joy, so that the earth rent with the sound of them. Adonijah and all the guests that were with him heard the noise. And Joab enquired, Wherefore is the noise of the city being in an uproar? While he yet spoke, behold, messengers came and reported the latest developments. And all those about Adonijah saw that Joab, who was over the host, had brought none of his host with him, and the captains of hundreds and the captains of thousands had brought none of their hundreds and thousands with them; but Benaiah ben Jehoiada had with him the Cherethites and Pelethites, the King's Own. Therefore the guests were afraid, and without so much as wiping their mouths they rose up and went every man his way. But Adonijah fled to the tabernacle of the Lord, and caught hold on the horns of the altar. Now Solomon was not yet sure of his new power; so he said, If Adonijah will show himself a worthy man, there shall not an hair of him fall to the earth; but if wickedness shall be found in him, he shall die. Thereupon Adonijah came and bowed himself to King Solomon; and Solomon said unto him, Go to your house. And Jehoshaphat ben Ahilud, the recorder, who during the entire confusion had lain ill in his country house near Mount Lebanon, returned to Jerusholayim and bowed himself to Solomon and was received in the King's favour. And Benaiah ben Jehoiada was set over the host in place of Joab. But if any be dissatisfied in Israel, or feel oppressed, these lift their eyes towards Adonijah and wait for Joab to blow the trumpet; and King Solomon has commanded Benaiah to have a thousand ears; and the voice of Israel has become as a whisper in the fields.

By the end of his report, Penuel ben Mushi my informant was somewhat sodden with wine. He embraced me and confided that one king was much like another, Adonijah or Solomon; bloodsuckers, insatiable; and that the whole house of Jesse was accursed by Yahveh for the blood that was on David's hands and for what he had done to the people.

But as the two of us re-entered the gate, towards evening, behold, there was a clatter of hooves and a rattle of wheels, and the shouting of runners, calling, "Move, you bastards! Make way for Benaiah ben Jehoiada who is over the host, and over the Cherethites and Pelethites, the King's Own!" And my newly found friend faded away as though he were swallowed by Sheol, and I stood alone and bemused.

And a voice from above me said, "Whoa, there!"

The wheels screeched and sparks flew from under the hooves of the horses, and the voice said, "God do unto me so and so, and more also, if it isn't the son of Hoshaiah and redactor of the *Report on the Amazing Rise* and so forth."

I would have prostrated myself in the dirt of the street but

27

for the hand that imperiously summoned me on to the chariot.

"I will drive you home, Ethan, if that is where you are bound," said Benaiah. "I heard you were in Jerusholayim. Why did you not pay me a visit?"

I climbed up on the chariot, saying, "I was under the impression that my lord was gone to the royal country houses, or to the shore of the sea, or to the slopes of Mount Lebanon where the eternal snow feeds the murmuring cedars."

"Murmuring cedars." The chariot was off with a jolt; I had to hang on to the handrail. "Who will guard the straying lamb against the bear and the angry lion, and also against the jackal, if I leave Jerusholayim?"

I saw the smooth flanks of the fleet horses and the white staves of the numerous runners, and I heard the noise and the shouting about Benaiah ben Jehoiada. And the spirit of the Lord moved me, so that I perceived what pleasurable sensation is afforded a man by having power.

But the hand of Benaiah that held the reins was broad and hard-veined; and he laughed deep from his chest, saying, "My father was a bondsman in Israel and he dug in the mountain for copper, and he coughed out his lungs and died. But I, Benaiah his son, have learned to read, and your tablets hold no secrets before me. I will protect you, Ethan, if you write what is good in my eyes and in the eyes of the King; but if you harbour wicked thoughts or put them on any of your tablets, I will have your head displayed on a high stake and your body nailed to the wall of this city."

Whereupon I assured Benaiah that nothing was farther from my mind than the harbouring of wicked thoughts; also that I was a family man with a positive outlook on the state and its institutions, be they military, administrative, or religious.

The chariot halted.

"You shall have to walk now, Ethan." Benaiah pointed at the narrowing street which barely permitted two donkeys to pass one another. "This town was not built for chariots."

I jumped off, thanking him and wishing him that Yahveh might grant him both health and riches; but he seemed not to have heard. He backed the horses and managed to turn the chariot; there was the din of the runners and the clatter of hooves and the rattle of wheels. In the silence that followed, it suddenly occurred to me that I had forgotten to ask him for money. *His* signature at least should have been valid.

4

THE HEAT BROKE.

The Feast of the Tabernacles began, and the city was drunk with the new wine and the smell of the offerings being roasted on the altars.

In the vineyards of the King at Baal-hamon, in the leafy booths erected to commemorate the exodus from Egypt, men lay with women, or with men, whispering lewdly. It was as though the gods of Canaan, the Baalim and Ashtaroth, were celebrating their resurrection. Seated on a garlanded stool, wine leaves about his brow, Amenhoteph the royal chief eunuch seemed to have taken the place of Zadok the priest. With his elegant Egyptian hands he directed the full-breasted young women, the small-hipped young men to this bower or that, sending servants after them with fresh skins of wine and dishes of sweets.

I approached him.

"Ethan ben Hoshaiah?" he queried in the guttural accent of the Nile people; and to my affirmative nod, "You did not bring any of your women?"

Amenhoteph, I had been told, was a recent gift from the Pharaoh to King Solomon: an expert with women, he was much liked in the royal harem for his refined, foreign ways which contrasted agreeably with the crude manners of the old overseers.

"I was most honoured by the King's command," I replied, "and quite surprised, and therefore not sure if the invitation included any but me."

"It is indeed a very special invitation. A most distinguished person wishes to meet you."

He smiled thinly, gesturing towards a torch, his profile to the light. He was that rarity among his kind, a lean eunuch; a mere tinge of flabbiness about his jaws and an occasional treble to his voice betrayed the operation that had been performed on him.

I followed the torchbearer he had summoned. The night was alive with voices, and there was a smell of ripe grapes about. Someone sang badly but with much feeling to the accompaniment of a pipe; another laughed, then stopped laughing.

I stumbled and nearly fell into the bower. On low cushions a woman half reclined, slender, the dark robe closed at her throat. The torchbearer had vanished, but an oil lamp spread some light and the moon shed shafts of silver through the leaves of the roof. The woman turned her face to me, an aged face, deeply lined, with a large pointed mouth and large painted eyes.

I threw myself to the ground. "Princess Michal!"

I had never seen her; but I had heard of her, as who had not: Saul's daughter, who lived to see all of her family slain but that cripple, Mephibosheth; twice David's wife, who laughed at him, and was left barren.

"Who is your servant but a dog grovelling at your feet, O Light, O Sun." The words came easily from my lips; this old woman had something that made you want to humble yourself before her. "Why is it you asked for me, at this time, and here?"

She raised herself, supporting herself on her elbow. She was even older than the stories about her had led me to believe; her hands were skin and bone, her teeth, or what was left of them, long and yellowish.

"You will write the story of David?"

Her voice had stayed young.

"At best, madam, I shall compile what other men will hand me; and even that is subject to the approval of the Wisest of Kings, Solomon."

A peremptory move of her hand. "What do you know about David?"

"But for the present incumbent of the throne, Solomon,

David was the greatest man in Judah and Israel, the Chosen of the Lord God who made a covenant with David and beat down his foes and plagued those that hated him and swore that his seed should endure forever."

"In other words," again the hand, "you know nothing."

I was silent.

"How, then, can you presume to write about him, or even compile that which is given you by others?"

"A man is his legend."

She frowned.

"You wish to destroy the legend, madam?"

"I want that someone knows about him, after I am gone."

I waited.

"He was of handsome build," she said, "delicate when compared with my father's or Jonathan's. And there was the reddish hair above the tan of his face. And he came to us with his music and his poetry..."

DEPOSITION OF THE PRINCESS MICHAL UNDER QUESTIONING BY ETHAN BEN HOSHAIAH, IN THE BOWER IN THE VINEYARDS OF THE KING AT BAAL-HAMON

Question: ... he came. Just like that? Surely the court of your father, King Saul, was not the elaborate and splendid institution we have today. Still: here comes the son of a certain Jesse in Bethlehem. Even assuming that Jesse was a man of substance...

Answer: ... which he was not. Later on, it was said for appearance's sake that Jesse had many herds, and a great house, that his voice was prominent in the councils of Judah, and that his ancestry might be traced back to the founders of the tribe. In truth, Jesse was an obscure, poverty-stricken peasant with more sons than he could feed. Three of them joined the army; and David would have gone on tending his father's few miserable sheep if one of the Bethlehem priests had not discovered the charms of his body and the qualities of his voice.

Question: The priests taught him?

Answer: When he came to us, he moved gracefully. He no longer spoke like a shepherd. He played the lute. He knew the traditional songs, and he made up new ones. And he knew how to handle my father King Saul.

Question: Does my lady recall who it was that recommended him, chose him, invited him?

Answer: David never told me. He could be very evasive.

Question: Didn't others speak of it, at the time?

Answer: I do not remember. I was but thirteen, and in love with my brother Jonathan; the court gossip passed me by.

Question: Pray tell your servant what you do remember.

Answer: A bad illness from the Lord befell my father King Saul. We called in the doctors, and the men of God, and the conjurers. We tried herbs, bleeding, sacrifices, witchcraft. Then someone suggested music.

Question: Were there no musicians at court?

Answer: Scores. And they strummed, they piped, they twanged, they blared, they brayed away until my father King Saul sent them off with a curse and a kick. David's music was different. His tunes, his words, his voice dissolved all pain and filled the heart with calm. Peace would return to the eyes of my father King Saul and spread over the countenance; his hands would relax; and after days of frenzy he would find sleep.

Question: What really was your father's ailment?

Answer: The spirit of the Lord departed from him, and an evil spirit from the Lord troubled him.

Question: Could you describe the effect of the evil spirit?

Answer: It was terrifying. After all those years, it still haunts me. This huge man, who stood in battle like a tower, would cower in the corner of the tent, babbling in fear and biting his knuckles, or brood for hours, listening to voices which only he could hear, or tremble and rave and foam at the mouth.

Question: Did you discern a pattern? Did the evil spirit make itself felt on more or less regular occasions?

Answer: The phases of the moon and the rounds of the stars were vainly probed by the stargazers for any connection with the ailment. At first, months passed between visitations; later the spirit pounced with increasing frequency, and my father King Saul had only a few days' respite.

Question: Do you recall the first time that the evil spirit troubled him?

Answer: I believe it was after the victory over Amalek. Yahveh commanded through Samuel the prophet that my father King Saul slay both man and woman, infant and suckling, ox and sheep, camel and ass in Amalek. My father slew the people; but he spared the cattle. He was a peasant, the senseless slaughter of cattle appalled him; also his men demanded their share of the spoil, and he was *their* king.

Question: He also spared Agag the King of Amalek.

Answer: You can show power through death, and you can show it through mercy.

Question: But that power was Yahveh's.

Answer: Yahveh was no longer king. My father was.

Question: Yahveh was God.

Answer: And Samuel was his voice. Samuel came to my father King Saul at Gilgal, and he reproached him, saying that rebellion against God was as the sin of witchcraft, and stubbornness as idolatry. Samuel said, You have rejected the word of the Lord, and the Lord has rejected you from being king over Israel. As Samuel turned to leave, my father laid hold upon the skirt of his mantle, and it rent. And Samuel said to him, The Lord has rent the kingdom of Israel from you this day, and has given it to a neighbour of yours who is better than you.

Question: And your father believed that?

Answer: He went down on his knee before Samuel and begged him to turn again with him, before the elders of the people and before Israel, so he might worship the Lord God. Then said Samuel, Bring you to me Agag the King of the Amalekites. Agag came to my father—I saw it with these eyes —he came delicately unto him and said, Surely the bitterness of death is past. But my father stood by and watched Samuel the prophet hew Agag in pieces before the Lord in Gilgal.

Question: And after that the evil spirit began troubling him?

Answer: Yes.

The Princess leaned back. A vein pulsed bluish at her

temple. I felt weighted down by the inexorability of the events which she had described.

"Thirsty, Ethan?"

She clapped her hands. And to a servant, "Wine. Fruit. Cakes." And back to me, "I know I am an old woman, my memory crammed with a thousand images which more often than not become jumbled. But the image of the young David has remained clear in my mind.

"It is told that he behaved wisely in all his ways. I would say that he had a natural grace. He won a person by a few words, a glance, a motion of his hand. He seemed so warm, so without guile. If all this was studied, he was the best dissimulator since the serpent who talked Eve into eating the fruit of the tree of the knowledge of good and evil.

"Of all of us, I resisted him the longest. It was known that he shared the bed of my father King Saul the very night his music drove the evil spirit from him. And there were those like Abner ben Ner, the captain of the host, who said that it was less David's music than his buttocks which relieved the King. But I know how gentle David could be, and that his nearness was soothing like rain on the parched field."

The Princess toyed with a bunch of grapes.

"And then Jonathan. You surely know the dirge which David wrote upon his death:

> *I am distressed for thee, my brother Jonathan.*
> *Very pleasant hast thou been unto me:*
> *Thy love to me was wonderful,*
> *Passing the love of women ...*

Jonathan had a wife and children, he had concubines; but through David he seemed to have discovered a new meaning to his life. He stripped himself of his bow, his sword, his swordbelt, even of his robe, and clothed David with them; he would have given him half the kingdom, had it been his to give. David took it all with that grace of his; he smiled, and spoke his poetry, and played his lute. He let my father King Saul make love to him when that was my father's need; he lay with my brother Jonathan, letting him kiss his feet, his thighs, his wrists, his throat; and in the night in which I lost my restraint and spoke to him in anger, he came to me, later, and took me."

The Princess pushed aside the grapes. I refilled her cup.

"I thought, then, that he was an incarnation of the god Baal, lust of the flesh personified, and yet with that indifference only the gods possess. In my anguish I called out to Yahveh. Yahveh answered not; but David, as though he had heard my outcry, told me a day or two later quite casually that he was the Chosen of Yahveh, acting upon Yahveh's will in everything he said and did. I had never seen one chosen by Yahveh but Samuel; and Samuel was gaunt, almost skeleton-like, with perpetual sores on his pate and pus in the corners of his eyes and a ratty beard that was usually matted with dirt. But why should not Yahveh for once pour his spirit into a vessel that was agreeable to the senses? And further events seemed to confirm the magic.

"Who ever was heard to escape the javelin of my father King Saul? My father's javelin was deadly, nailing its victim to the wall, its shaft trembling from the force of the throw. Yet David escaped it three times. It was as though he had eyes in the back of his head. And he needed them. Was it that Jonathan shamelessly flaunted his feelings for David, or that Rizpah my father's concubine whispered to his ear, or that Abner ben Ner, who was over the host, enclosed in his monthly report the Levites' new chant from the hilltops, *There shall be no whore of the daughters of Israel, nor a sodomite of the sons of Israel*: the evil spirit was back upon my father King Saul, more powerful than ever, and directed his mind and his hand.

"Sometimes I suspected David of actually taunting it. But David always denied that. When the brooding came over my father, David would seat himself at his feet, not quite touching him but close enough to make him feel his presence. Then he would play a few chords on his lute, and lean back his head and start singing: tunes which made you think of the caravan moving towards the setting sun, or of the sadness that overcomes you in the hour after the hour of love. And then, suddenly, my father roaring at him. And the javelin quivering in the wall. And David saying, What have I done? what is my iniquity? what is my sin before you that you seek my life?"

She nodded to herself: this was just one of the horrors she had seen in her life; but she was the daughter of one king and twice the wife of another, and she had learned to curb her feelings.

"At a later time I asked him, David my love, aren't you ever afraid? He looked at me, and he said, My heart is filled with fear. I am a poet; I have enough imagination to be able to see myself gored by that javelin."

She ate a few of the grapes.

"So my father King Saul made him captain over a thousand and sent him against the Philistines. I said to my brother Jonathan, This will be the end of David; and Jonathan was sore afraid for David's life, saying, I gave him my bow, and my sword, and my swordbelt, why can I not give him my eye, and the strength of my fist. But by the new year David returned, the tan of his face deeper than ever and his beard toughened, and he had won many victories, and brought much spoil, and slain scores of Philistines. I heard some of his men talk: they had had their misgivings in the first days of the campaign; but when they saw David in battle their mind changed; in battle that pretty boy became as a man intoxicated by blood. And he was shrewd in his planning, with an eye for the weakness of the enemy. And word got among the people, for when the women came out of the cities of Israel, singing and dancing, to meet King Saul with tabrets, with joy, and with instruments of music, they answered one another as they played, and sang, *Saul has slain his thousands, and David his ten thousands.* Unsound though that count was, it caused the mood of my father to darken further. He recalled the sinister prophecy of Samuel the seer, and he asked himself, Could this be the neighbour who is better than I? And he said, They have ascribed to David ten thousands, and to me they have ascribed but thousands: and what can he have more but the kingdom?"

She stared as though she were trying to fathom the will of the Lord, by which the sweet musician invited to exorcise the evil spirit was calling it down upon the King.

"My brother Jonathan, hearing the women's antiphony, loved David the more; and I who was starved for him while he was in the war abandoned myself to his skills. But my father King Saul again sought to rid himself of David. Unfortunately he was more of a soldier than a plotter, and Lord Yahveh was not with him, and nothing would occur to him but a repetition of his old ruse, with a reward added. *I* was to be the reward. How will I pay the dowry? asked David, mentioning that he was a poor man and lightly esteemed. To which the royal matchmaker replied that the King, Saul, would accept a hundred Philistine foreskins in place of a dowry.

"So David arose and went, he and his men, and slew of the Philistines two hundred, and returned unto Gibeah to my father King Saul. And David was riding a light grey mule, holding before him a covered basket. He carried the basket unto my father, in the presence of the whole court. I still see him removing the cover and tumbling a pile of blood-encrusted penises on the table, and I can hear him counting up to the full two hundred.

"And that night he came to me holding a whip, and I lay before him and he punished me, and I suffered it."

A rosy dawn was rising over the vineyard of the King at Baal-hamon, outlining the pattern of the leaves of the bower. The face of the Princess appeared ashen.

"A man is his legend." Her eyes had dulled. "Isn't that what you said, Ethan ben Hoshaiah?"

I bowed. "That was the poor wisdom of your servant, madam."

"You may leave," she said.

5

BLESSED BE THE NAME of the Lord our God, whose truth is like a field arrayed with flowers of many colours, for each man to pick the one striking his fancy.

I, Ethan ben Hoshaiah, from the town of Ezrah but now living at No. 54, Queen-of-Sheba Lane, the King's Own Houses, Jerusholayim, was summoned this second day after the Feast of the Tabernacles to Government House, there to attend the first regular session of the Royal Commission on the Preparation of *The One and Only True and Authoritative, Historically Correct and Officially Approved Report on the Amazing Rise, God-fearing Life, Heroic Deeds, and Wonderful Achievements of David the Son of Jesse, King of Judah for Seven Years and of both Judah and Israel for Thirty-three, Chosen of God, and Father of King Solomon,* for short called *The King David Report.* And I was led by a servant into an anteroom in which I was accosted by three bearded individuals, none too clean, such as you might find on the marketplace or in the gates of the cities; they said they were Jorai, Jachan, and Meshullam, licensed tellers of tales and legends, and were commanded to appear by royal warrant; they did not know for what purpose, they had always paid their tenths and tithes, and they were sore afraid. They enquired if I was a teller of tales and legends, too; and as I said that I was, after a fashion, they complained that business was falling off, but that I seemed to be doing well, by the sleek looks of me, and did I specialise in ancient lore, migration stories, Judges, or recent events?

I was relieved of the three minstrels by the servant, who escorted me into a large, well appointed chamber. And there were seated on comfortable cushions all the members of the Commission; and in their midst stood a platter of fruit and a pitcher of scented water and a dish of aromatic chewing gum which is made of mastic. Jehoshaphat ben Ahilud, the recorder, bade me to squat near a low table which was to serve as my writing aid; and he clapped his hands and called the meeting to order and expressed his pleasure that the members of the Commission had returned to Jerusholayim in good health and apparently much refreshed. He said that the members had doubtless read, or had heard read, a great many books on a great many subjects and knew that there were various ways of telling a story: forwards or backwards, or starting in the middle and working in either direction, or mixing up everything, which was called tohubohu and was quite the fashion among the more modern authors. However, he went on to say, for the purposes of the *Report on the Amazing Rise* and so forth he felt that it was best to begin at the beginning, that is, with the anointment of young David by Samuel the prophet and with the Goliath story. Were the members agreed?

The members did not object.

Had I, Ethan ben Hoshaiah, in my capacity as redactor, any other suggestion?

I said I had not.

On the anointment, Jehoshaphat resumed, he had a written report from the files of Samuel's own temple at Ramah, through the courtesy of Zadok the priest. He pointed at a stack of clay tablets to his left. I asked to see a tablet, and on being handed one, perceived by the style of lettering and the treatment of the clay that it was of a late date and certainly not from the vicinity of Ramah. Zadok seemed to have noticed my misgivings and said that the Ramah tablets contained substantially the same story as that told by Samuel in his own book. Of course there were those who maintained that the anointment of young David by Samuel the prophet was a legend spread so as to sweeten the sound of David's name and to support his claim to the throne of Saul; such people were obvious enemies of King Solomon, of established religion, and of lawful government in general; but it was my task as redactor of the King David Report to rewrite the material in such a manner that no one could find fault with it.

"If my lords will permit their servant to say a few words on the subject," I rebutted. "I have studied Samuel's book, and I know the oral tradition as well; so I believe I can say that we have here one of the most charming and poetic narratives current about the youth of a man destined for greatness. Just visualise the old seer arriving in Bethlehem, his mind filled with the word of the Lord God who told him, I will send you to Jesse the Bethlehemite, for I have provided me a king among his sons. See the shepherds crowding about him, the young girls, the toothless old hags; hear them ask his blessing or an inexpensive little prophecy; but Samuel, tall, thin, dour, pushes on towards Jesse's hut. Behold the villagers craning their necks: what seeks the great prophet under the lowly roof? And the big prophet inside the hut letting Jesse's sons pass in review, six lumps of brawn, while Yahveh whispers to him, Look not on their countenance, or on the height of their stature, for the Lord God sees not as man sees, man looks on the outward appearance, but the Lord God looks on the heart. And Samuel saying unto Jesse, Are here *all* your children? And young David being fetched from the sheep, making his way through the gaping crowd, entering into Samuel's presence: ruddy, and withal of a beautiful countenance, and goodly to look at—I am sure my lords are familiar with the description. And then the Lord God commanding Samuel: Arise, anoint him, for this is he."

Benaiah ben Jehoiada drummed on his knee, and Jehoshaphat ben Ahilud swallowed as though some sticky matter were stuck in his gullet; only Zadok the priest oozed satisfaction all over his oily face.

"Well," Nathan the prophet said uncertainly, "what is wrong with the account, then?"

I waited for someone else to point out its improbabilities. Finally I said, "Suppose Samuel came to Bethlehem and behaved in the manner described—don't you think it would have made David the most famous boy in the locality, and everybody in Bethlehem and surroundings would have gossiped about it for months, and Jesse and his six older sons would have journeyed to all their out-of-town uncles and

41

cousins and in-laws to inform them of their new prominence? In no time the whole tribe of Judah would have known and gone around bragging that one of their bright youths was to be King of Israel. How long, do you presume, would it have taken King Saul to learn of the affair and to have young David seized and tried for assumption of office, or for conspiracy? Yet, as David makes his first appearance at the royal court, no one raises his voice, saying, Look, my lord, is not that pretty young man with his lute and his poetry the same David the son of Jesse who was anointed by Samuel to be king in your place?— Not a one!'"

I caught the dirty look Zadok gave me. "I am glad Ethan ben Hoshaiah brought up the question," he said, his voice strained, "because this is a matter of principle which we might as well decide now. There are, it seems, two kinds of truth: the one which our friend Ethan wishes to establish, and another which is based on the word of Lord Yahveh as interpreted by his prophets and his priests."

"On dogma," said Benaiah, popping a piece of chewing gum into his mouth.

"On dogma, yes!" Zadok puffed his cheeks. "And where the two kinds of truth fail to agree, I must insist on dogma being followed. Where would we arrive if everybody doubted everything and went on his own search for the truth? Why, the great and resplendent temple we are building would collapse before its construction was finished; the throne which King David erected and on which his son Solomon sits would topple!"

Jehoshaphat ben Ahilud raised his hands soothingly. "My lord Zadok is justified in his demand that religious traditions which over the years have become sanctified and part of our lore be heeded even where they appear to contradict reality. On the other hand, Ethan ben Hoshaiah must warn us of the pitfalls hidden in our material; this is part of his duties. But contradictions are there to be smoothed over, Ethan, not to be stressed. Contradictions puzzle and embitter the heart; but the Wisest of Kings, Solomon, wishes all of us, and especially the writers of books, to accentuate the more edifying aspects of life. We are to strike a happy medium between what is and what we want people to believe, and to reflect the greatness of our epoch."

42

Elihoreph ben Shisha, the one scribe, moved that the anointment story be included in the *Report of the Amazing Rise* and so forth, and his brother Ahiah seconded him. The motion was carried unanimously, with the proviso that I was to edit the temple document with a view towards making it read plausibly. Whereupon Jehoshaphat ben Ahilud suggested a recess during which a small meal was to be served, consisting of cubes of lamb done on the spit. And after the meal, of which I was permitted to partake, Nathan the prophet proposed a period of rest under the shady trees of the palace garden, until the heat of noon and the stuffed feeling they all had were gone.

And after they had snoozed for a while, or strolled through the garden, the members reassembled in the session room, and Jehoshaphat ben Ahilud, the recorder, announced that the second point on the agenda was the Goliath story, and as this was primarily a matter of war, he wished that Benaiah ben Jehoiada would give his view first.

Benaiah looked up. The Goliath story, he said, while no doubt the concern of the army, could not be entirely its responsibility; other elements, some personal, some dynastic, were woven into the tale and could not be separated from its military aspects—such as use of light weapons against armoured troops, or the effect of pre-battle boasting on the spirit of the men. At the request of his friend Jehoshaphat he had had a search made of the records of Abner ben Ner, who was captain of the host in the time of King Saul and in command against the Philistines at Ephes-dammim; but despite the most thorough search, which left no tablet unturned and no scroll unopened, not a word was found of David having killed an enemy giant named Goliath, either before, during, or after the battle. This did not mean that no giant by that name was killed at Ephes-dammim, or that David might not have killed him; a battle consisted of a thousand-and-one individual actions, and you could not have a scribe attached to every soldier who bashed in his opponent's skull. Still, it seemed strange that a wily man like Abner, who was compelled to be cautious because of his affair with Rizpah the concubine of his supreme commander King Saul, should have

43

failed to record a duel which was alleged to have decided the outcome of one of his campaigns.

Was there no written record elsewhere, enquired Nathan the prophet, perhaps in the annals of King Saul?

Elihoreph ben Shisha, the scribe, shook his head, and his brother Ahiah confirmed that nothing to that effect was contained in King Saul's annals.

"But there were giants among the Philistines, I hope!" called out Zadok the priest.

Benaiah appeared bored. "Several dozens of them."

"And some of these giants were killed by the children of Israel?"

"We know that at Gezer a giant named Sippai was slain by Sibbechai the Hushathite," said Benaiah, "and in another engagement Elhanan ben Jair slew the giant Lahmi, and at Gath a giant whose name we could not ascertain but who had twenty-four fingers and toes, six on each hand and six on each foot, was killed by Shimeon ben Shimea; and if you will forgive my mentioning it, I myself slew two lion-like men of Moab, and a goodly Egyptian who had a spear in his hand; I went at him only with a staff, and plucked the spear out of the Egyptian's hand, and slew him with his own spear."

"Then why should not David have killed Goliath with a stone from a brook?" said Zadok. "Or does my lord wish to deny that achievement?"

"The armed forces," retorted Benaiah, "especially the Cherethites and Pelethites, have the greatest interest in inculcating the children of Israel with the spirit which induced young David to his valiant deed, and in demonstrating that the father of King Solomon, aside from being a great poet and musician, philosopher and theologian, administrator and organiser, strategist and diplomatist, never shrank from tackling an opponent, were he twice or three times his size or, if you will, four times. But the armed forces cannot furnish you the documents. We haven't got them, and we can't fabricate them. This is what I wanted to bring to your attention."

He folded his mighty hands. For all his bluster and self importance, I thought, Benaiah was the shrewdest of them all: if one day someone proved to the world and to King Solomon that the Goliath story could never have happened and that the Royal Commission, God bless them, had fallen for a myth and thus jeopardised the credibility of the entire King David Report, *he* would be free of blame.

Thereupon Jehoshaphat ben Ahilud, the recorder, declared that in view of the lack of written records the Commission would have to rely on oral tradition. He sent out the servant, and the servant brought unto the Commission Jorai, Jachan, and Meshullam, licensed tellers of tales and legends, who prostrated themselves, and beat their foreheads to the ground, and in the name of the Lord God cried for mercy. Jehoshaphat commanded them to rise and explained to them that they were to tell to these mighty lords the story of David and Goliath, each one in his own words and exactly as he learned it from his teacher. And Jorai, Jachan, and Meshullam vowed that this they would do, and they blinked their inflamed lids and stroked their scraggly beards and glanced with longing towards the platter of fruit and the pitcher of scented water and the dish of aromatic chewing gum which is made of mastic; but these were not for the likes of them, and I recalled the old proverb: that a hungry bird trills the prettiest.

Of the three minstrels, Jorai was chosen to begin. And Jorai plucked the strings of his harp, which was much bruised and lacerated, as though it had been in several street fights, and he twanged away and raised his voice.

But I, Ethan ben Hoshaiah, wrote down the salient points of his epic and numbered these according to sequence.

THE GREAT FIGHT OF DAVID VERSUS GOLIATH, AS TOLD BY JORAI, LICENSED TELLER OF TALES AND LEGENDS, IN OUTLINE

(1) Tactical placement of Israel and Philistine armies at Ephes-dammim. Each army occupying the hill area on opposite sides of the valley of Elah, the valley between them with the brook forming no man's land.

(2) Goliath, a champion of the Philistines. His height (six cubits and a span); his armour: brass helmet, brass coat of mail weighing five thousand shekels; brass greaves for protection of shins, brass target between shoulders; his

45

weapons: sword (length unspecified), spear (like weaver's beam), iron-tipped (tip weighing six hundred shekels), shield (carried by special bearer).

(3) Goliath challenges Israelites from no man's land; customary pre-battle boasting repeated twice daily for several successive days.

(4) David arrives in Israel camp, bringing bread and tidbits for three elder brothers serving with the host, and ten cheeses for buttering up the captain of their thousand.

(5) David hears the noise made by Goliath; sees that no one volunteers to tackle the giant. His questions elicit the acute embarrassment of the army command, and reward offered by Saul to successful challenger of Goliath: riches, king's daughter, tax-free house.

(6) Oldest brother Eliab reproached David for his pride and naughtiness of heart. (Note: Eliab seems to have forgotten the deference due to his little brother in the latter's capacity as the Anointed of the Lord—viz, the Ramah temple tablets.)

(7) Upon learning that a young man in camp might be willing to take on Goliath, Saul sends for David. Saul doubts that the skinny youth will measure up to the giant, but David assures him that he single-handedly killed a lion and a bear, and that the Lord will also deliver him out of the hand of this Philistine. (Note: Neither before nor during this conversation does Saul enquire the name or antecedents of the young man, nor does David introduce himself.)

(8) Saul feels obliged to lend David his own sword and armour; David, unable to move with that much metal on him, returns the equipment with thanks.

(9) David's armament: shepherd's staff, five smooth stones out of brook, sling.

(10) In no man's land: Goliath notices David coming at him. He disdains him, and vows to give David's tender young flesh to the fowls of the air and the beasts of the field.

(11) David proves just as good as Goliath at shouting invective; vows he will smite Goliath and take his head from him, for the battle is the Lord's. (Note: This sounds like the real David, who frequently boasts of his private affiliation with Yahveh.)

46

(12) Goliath lumbers forward; David nimbly dodges him, slings stone at him, hits Philistine in the forehead, the stone penetrating the skull.

(13) Goliath falls face forward; David jumps on him, grabs the giant's sword, severs his head. Their champion defeated, the Philistines flee and are pursued by the Israel army.

(14) Carrying Goliath's head, David returns from the slaughter of the Philistine. Abner happens to see him and takes David and his trophy to Saul. Now, finally, Saul enquires, Whose son are you, young man? Whereupon David: I am the son of your servant Jesse the Bethlehemite.

(15) Saul decides to keep the deserving youth at court.

And Jorai bowed and stowed away his harp; and Jachan stepped forth with a lute as disreputable as Jorai's harp, to tell his story of the great fight of David versus Goliath; and after him came Meshullam, who had two small drums on which he drummed with his fingers, gently sometimes and sometimes more forcefully, and thunderously when Goliath fell on his nose. And all three having done, and their stories having been compared, behold, these agreed to a tittle, from the first word to the last, although Jorai had told his with much passion, throwing about his arms and grimacing, while Jachan had spoken in low tones, much like a conjurer, and Meshullam had howled and rolled his eyes like a priest of Baal, the god of the Canaanites. And Nathan the prophet exclaimed at the wonder of the likeness of the stories, forgetting that the audience of these minstrels on the marketplace and in the gates of the cities were like children who would not tolerate any deviations from the text of their favourite fairy tales. Truly, said Nathan, the Lord God has spoken through the tongue of these men, and this weighs more heavily than any number of tablets of clay. And it was plain that the members of the Commission felt quite relieved; for miracles preclude argument.

"Now when is all this supposed to have taken place?" I enquired meekly. "Before David was called in to soothe by his music the evil spirit that bothered King Saul, or after?"

The faces of my lords fell: in their joy over the miracle of the three-fold Goliath story the members of the Commission had lost sight of that other story in which young David is invited to court so as to assuage the evil spirit. But in both these stories David and Saul encounter one another for the first time: thus David the giant-slayer and David the musical healer were mutually exclusive; that was the trouble.

"Before! After!" Zadok the priest was annoyed. "What, pray, is the difference? Yahveh intended David to encounter King Saul, and Yahveh made doubly sure."

"Quite," said Jehoshaphat ben Ahilud, the recorder. "Yahveh is supreme, but even Yahveh does things in sequence, in the beginning creating heaven and earth, and then dividing light from darkness, and the waters under the firmament from those above it, and so forth, down through the week, until he created male and female in his image."

"Why not let our friend Ethan decide the sequence?" suggested Benaiah ben Jehoiada. "He is the expert."

"If my lord Benaiah will forgive his servant," I said sweetly, "in my capacity as redactor I can adulterate history a little, touching it up here or there, but my competency does not extend to changing it."

Then Elihoreph ben Shisha, scribe, scratched his scalp and said, "So let us assume, for argument's sake, that David killed Goliath before he appeared at court to sing to Saul. How would that do?"

"Most awkwardly," I told him. "Why should a search have to be made throughout Israel for a musician with the necessary qualifications, why should messengers be despatched to old Jesse in Bethlehem telling him to send David his son who is with the sheep, when that celebrity, having killed Goliath, was sitting at the royal supper table? Or view it from David's angle: upon learning of the need for effective therapy against the evil spirit, wouldn't he have risen immediately to proclaim, Save the expense for the messenger; I am here and at your service; as soon as my lord the King has finished his meal, we will try some of my music. Wouldn't he?"

And there was deep silence among the members of the Commission. Finally Ahiah ben Shisha, the other scribe, said uncertainly, "And if we assume that David first comes to court

48

to sing to Saul, and only then goes out to kill Goliath? Would that help?"

"Hardly," I replied. "If David is at court, singing to King Saul and exorcising the evil spirit of the Lord, how do we get him back to Bethlehem to pick up that bread and those tidbits for his big brothers, who serve with the army, and the ten cheeses for their captain? And should not then King Saul have noticed that the valiant challenger of Goliath and the young fellow of the lute and the pretty voice were one and the same? We know from Jorai, Jachan, and Meshullam that Saul hung his own armour on David and lent him his own sword: enough opportunity to recognise him. And after the battle, when David again is brought to Saul with the head of Goliath, and upon the King's query tells him his patronymic —does the King wake up? Not at all. He blithely invites David to come and live at the court where the freshly baked hero, as the King's musical healer, already has his berth and meals. Now, King Saul suffered from an evil spirit of the Lord, but nowhere is it said that he was feeble-minded."

Another silence, longer than the previous one. And in the end Elihoreph and Ahiah both threw up their arms and said, "It seems we'll just have to leave out one of the stories."

"But which one?" said I.

A babel ensued in the Commission, one member arguing this way, another that, and they failed to understand one another, as though the Lord God had confounded their language. Finally Jehoshaphat clapped his hands, and said, "We cannot omit either story." And at their querying him, he explained, "Because the one story happens to be true; and there are people still alive who have seen young David at the court of King Saul. And the other is legend; and an established legend is as valid as the truth, indeed more so, for people believe a legend more readily than the facts."

"If my lords will forgive their servant..." I began.

But Benaiah ben Jehoiada frowned at me, and he rose, saying, "God do unto me so and so, and more also, if I let the subtleties of this man Ethan continue to complicate a perfectly simple thing. We have to have both stories? We shall have them. We have to get David from the royal court back to Bethlehem? We shall get him back. We shall write —let me see—we shall write, *But David went and returned*

49

from Saul to feed his father's sheep at Bethlehem. And if there are any to whom these words seem insufficient, and who will split hairs and go about doubting the work of a commission named by the Wisest of Kings, Solomon, they will be dealt with accordingly."

And thus it was written in the King David Report, and both stories are contained therein.

6

Upon my coming home, Esther placed before me bread and cheese and a slice of cold mutton. And I asked her, had she had a good day, or was she plagued by her chest pains and her shortage of breath? And she smiled and replied, No matter; but was not my mind troubled, and would I want to talk with her?

Now it was so, and my mind was sorely troubled, but I had not shown it by word or manner: Esther read my face as though it were a tablet of clay. So I said, "Let there be cushions placed in the yard, and a coverlet, and a lamp filled with oil, for I want to sit with Esther under the olive-tree." And she and I went there, and I bedded her on the cushions and covered her, and we held hands.

After a while I said, "This city, Jerusholayim, is like a curse. It is built on rock, they say, but the ground sways and is slippery. And one man is the other man's wolf."

"I am worried for the time when I will be gone," said Esther.

"Esther my dear," I tried to laugh, "you will survive us all."

She tapped the back of my hand as though I were a child. I noticed the whitish rim about her irises; this was something new, and frightening. She lay quiet. Finally she said, "I do not want to go, Ethan. I am afraid of Sheol, as who is not. I shall force my heart to go on beating as long as it can . . ."

The leaves of the olive tree rustled slightly, the flame of the lamp flickered. I bent over Esther and kissed her.

"It is not the city that troubles you, Ethan my husband," she went on. "A city is made of stone and is neither good nor bad."

I then told her of the several kinds of truth, and of the opinions of the members of the Commission, and of the decisions passed. "There are parties, and parties within parties, and the Commission itself is split, so that I am like a bird during a flood, not knowing where to alight."

Esther looked at me. These many years, she said, Lord Yahveh had blessed us with peace and a moderate, steadily rising income accruing from a fair literary success and a wise investment in landed property; in all this we had held to the law of the Lord; but the Lord our God was a righteous God and would not cast from him those who walked in his ways.

"The Lord our God," I said, "caused Benaiah ben Jehoiada to approach me after the session. Benaiah put his arm about me as though I were his best friend, saying he was in possession of some notes of Abner ben Ner, who was over the host in the time of King Saul; the notes had come to light when he had the army's files searched for evidence on the great fight of David versus Goliath; he would send them to me, and would I let him know what I thought of them."

"Might it not be that Benaiah esteems your knowledge and learned opinion?" suggested Esther.

Benaiah's esteem of a person's knowledge and learned opinion was restricted to the use he could make of these for his own purposes; but before I could inform Esther accordingly, a great noise sounded at the gate. I arose to go there; Shem and Sheleph, however, had preceded me and were returning with a captain of the Cherethites and with soldiers who carried in a pouch filled with tablets of clay.

AND THIS IS WHAT WAS WRITTEN IN THE TABLETS SENT ME BY BENAIAH BEN JEHOIADA:

To King Saul, the Foremost in Battle, the Anointed of God, from Abner ben Ner.

May Yahveh cause my lord to see this season in excellent health. In the matter of David ben Jesse the Bethlehemite I have done as you commanded. I have undertaken an investigation, and have placed in charge of it Doeg the Edomite, and I have further employed two of my best men, Shuppim and Huppim, both of them Levites friendly with priests of Samuel's temple at Ramah and of the temple at Nob. Doeg has journeyed to Bethlehem to enquire from the people, and he reports that David was with his father's sheep up to his eleventh year, and then was not seen in the village until he came home in his sixteenth year and once more tended the sheep. Some say that he was taken by strangers to Egypt, as was Joseph who was given a coat of many colours by his father Jacob, but others will tell you that he stayed with the priests at Nob. David himself never was heard to speak about this; he had his lute and he sang songs, and when a lamb strayed from the flock he went and fetched it, and served his father Jesse the Bethlehemite, and waited.

To King Saul, the Pride of Israel, the Chosen Ruler over the Twelve Tribes, from Abner ben Ner.

May Yahveh cause the evil spirit to depart from my lord, never to return. I had had word from Shuppim the Levite, who has gone to Ramah with a crowd of people, there to sacrifice and hear Samuel judge, for though he no longer travels the circuit, Samuel takes cases that are brought to him, and judges at a small fee. Shuppim spoke to the assistant priests, even the novices, and to some of the people assembled; and they said that Samuel was filled with venom against my lord the King, because my lord the King refused to do as Samuel bade him. Also Shuppim brought a fat lamb to Samuel, saying this would be his last offering, as the King, Saul, was taking all. And Samuel rose and stretched his arms to the heavens, and before the people he said to Shuppim, Just as you see this cloud vanish in thin air, so will Saul vanish; I have made him and I will blow him away, thus speaks the Lord. For Saul has not kept the commandment of the Lord our God, and now his kingdom shall not continue, the Lord our God has sought him a man after his own heart. Thus Samuel is cutting the ground from under the feet of my lord the King.

To King Saul, the Great Liberator, the Shield of the People, from Abner ben Ner.

May Yahveh grant peace unto my lord, and riches and health. Today I have heard from Huppim the Levite, who was sent to the temple at Nob. But Huppim has made himself close to Ahimelech the chief priest at Nob, and told him he wanted a temple student to teach his sons the word of the Lord God and also the aleph-beth-gimmel, and thereupon was permitted to see the roster of students. Lo, there was listed a David ben Jesse, from Bethlehem, and it was remarked of him that he was a comely person, and most docile and talented, and of a sharp mind and winsome ways. Huppim said to Ahimelech, Can you let me have this young man David? But Ahimelech laughed, saying, You do not think we would waste that much time and effort on a boy, so as to have him tutor the children of the likes of Huppim? Nay, this youth was selected and groomed for a special purpose, and he is now with King Saul, singing to him and playing with his hand; and though I am no prophet like Samuel, I daresay you will hear more of him.

To King Saul, the Mighty among Men, the Sword of Benjamin, from Abner ben Ner.

May Yahveh cause my lord to feel joy at the successes of our investigation. Huppim and Shuppim have reported to me that the antiphony, *Saul has slain his thousands, and David his ten thousands,* was written and composed at Nob, and the word distributed by priests from Dan even unto Beer-sheba, so they might be sung by women wherever my lord the King showed himself.

To King Saul, the Victor in Wars, the Terror of the Uncircumcised, from Abner ben Ner.

May Yahveh settle peace upon the mind of my lord. I have sent Doeg the Edomite to Ahimelech the chief priest at Nob. Doeg told Ahimelech that his connections with Samuel the prophet were bared unto us, as were the plans they had concerning David ben Jesse. And that we would cut off the head of Ahimelech and nail his body to the wall of his own temple, unless he confessed fully; but if he did confess, we might show mercy unto him and turn our wrath on the true culprits. Ahimelech was sore afraid, and he confessed that the plot was Samuel's; Lord Yahveh had spoken to Samuel as he hewed King Agag in pieces, saying, Thus you shall hew in pieces the mind of King Saul; and Samuel summoned the evil spirit who plagues my lord the King; and the young man David was brought in to watch over the coming and going of the spirit while he sings to the King and plays with his hand; but that Yahveh had favoured their plan, even unto David's rising to become the King's son-in-law. And it is my sense that messengers be sent to David's house to lay hold of him, before morning.

From King Saul, in his own person, to Abner ben Ner.
Do as you will.

To King Saul, the Lord over the Host, the Dispenser of Justice, from Abner ben Ner.
May Yahveh cause my Lord to hear good tidings. I sent messengers to David's house, as you commanded. They were received by Michal your daughter, who bade them to step lightly, for David her husband was ill, and in bed, and asleep. As the chief of the messengers said that the matter would brook no delay, Michal pulled aside a curtain. And behold, there was David on the bed, lying under the cover, and not moving. So the chief messenger left four of his men, two in front of the house and two in the back, and he came to me for instructions. I commanded him to hasten back and bring David to me on his bed. But the chief messenger returned without David, saying, We entered the house from the front and the back, and we shoved aside Michal the King's daughter, and pulled the curtain, and found in David's bed a contrivance covered with cloth, a wooden image with a bolster of goat's hair. We then searched the house, even unto the roof and the yard and the walls beyond, but David had escaped. I have caused the chief messenger to receive fifty lashes, and his men, twenty-five each.

"Ethan!"

Esther's voice recalling me to the present. "You look as though you had seen an evil spirit of the Lord, Ethan."

I nodded. "Sheol opened up, and the ghosts of the past rose from the depths."

"The ghosts of the past are your business."

And I understood that it was not the ghost of David that frightened me, or that of Samuel or of Saul or any other, but Benaiah ben Jehoiada, who was very much alive and who could read, as he himself told me, and who therefore must be familiar with the contents of the reports of Abner to his lord King Saul. Why, then, had Benaiah sat through the whole session, listening to the tales being presented there and to the debate, without ever mentioning his facts? And then sent the tablets to me?

"He knows I can't use what's in them," I said after briefly telling Esther of the contents of the tablets and of my thoughts concerning them. "Not as long as Zadok the priest and Nathan the prophet are on the Commission."

"Benaiah knows you have a weakness for the truth," said Esther.

"And he has heard me wagging my tongue," I admitted. "He just might expect me to do that once again."

"I hope you will restrain yourself."

"I value my life. Or do you suppose King Solomon would feel pleased at being faced with written evidence that his father served as a male whore in the employ of the priests?"

"That is not very probable," said Esther.

"On the other hand," I argued, "the King might also look at it differently. What is the main point of Abner's reports to his lord King Saul?"

Esther smiled. "You tell me."

"The main point, obviously," I explained, "is the conspiracy of a prophet and a priest against a king. And should not this cause Solomon to take heed, of whom it is said that he is wiser even than Ethan of Ezrah."

"Possibly," said Esther.

I thought it over. There were certain undeniable, publicly known facts which fitted in with the contents of the Abner tablets. After David fled his house, he had turned to Samuel in Ramah, and then to the priests at Nob. Working from there, as a weaver inserts a new thread into his web, could

56

I not weave into the King David Report some of what Abner had written?

"Perhaps I could..."

"You will not!" Esther's thoughts were far ahead of mine. "If the King's response to the tablets were that certain, Benaiah would have sent them to him. You are to Benaiah but what the wine taster is to the King: and this wine might be poisoned. And now I am tired, Ethan, and my heart has begun to pain. Place another pillow under my head, please, and douse the light."

I did as she told me and watched by her side until she fell asleep. Then I tiptoed away, and into the house, and sat down in my study to write to Benaiah ben Jehoiada as follows:

May Yahveh shower blessings on my lord Benaiah.

Your servant has read the reports of Abner ben Ner to King Saul in reference to Samuel the prophet and to Ahimelech the chief priest at Nob and to David the father of the Wisest of Kings, Solomon. Your servant submits that the King should be apprised by my lord of the contents of the tablets; the King then should decide how much of this, if any, shall be included in the *King David Report*. In returning the tablets, your servant vows to keep their contents secret, unless the King or my lord by their own hand permit them to be told.

And no mention was ever again made of the matter, either by Benaiah ben Jehoiada or by another. But I knew from this time on whose creature the young man David was, who came from the sheepcote; and Benaiah knew that I knew.

57

7

As I RETURNED from the market, this day, with a shoulder of
lamb to be roasted and with flowers for my women, behold, a
green and gold litter with a red, tasselled roof stood before
my house, its bearers lounging in the shade of the gate. And a
great number of people were gathered, agog, also beggars
and thieves, and urchins hastening everywhither, so that I
was hard put to make my way to my own door.

But the house was filled with a sweetish scent, and voices
sounded from the inner room. Shem and Sheleph my sons
came running to greet me with much merriment and capers,
Shem swaying his hips, Sheleph tilting his hands; and they
said that Amenhoteph the royal chief eunuch was awaiting
me. Whereupon I cuffed their ears for impudently imitating
high government officials, and gave them the shoulder of
lamb to carry to the kitchen.

Amenhoteph was seated on cushions, his eyebrows painted
and his nails dyed with henna, and sipped from my wine and
ate cheese tidbits. He was recounting to my women the glories
of Egypt: the power of its gods, the grace of its men, the
luxurious life of its great ladies. And Esther said to him how
much she commiserated with him at his having to live among
such primitives as the children of Israel; and he replied that
he was compensated by his service to such goodly women as
were the wives and concubines of the Wisest of Kings,
Solomon. And I saw the way in which he disrobed Lilith
with his eyes, and my heart filled with misgivings.

But the eunuch let his hand be kissed in succession by

Esther and Huldah and Lilith; and he gazed after them as they departed, saying unto me, "I believe I know the field though I no longer till it. It is a rare female who combines the three main virtues of her sex in a satisfactory manner. You were wise, therefore, to choose one woman for your soul, one for your seed, and one for the joy of your loins. I pray that Yahveh, your god, may let you keep your blessings to the end of your days."

To his guttural sounds he tilted his hands just as my son Sheleph had enacted. But to me this was no cause for mirth; the Egyptian refinement of the gestures seemed to add a menace to the kindly words. So I said, "Surely my lord has not troubled himself to visit his servant's house, located in a smelly street of one of the smelliest quarters of Jerusholayim, so as to praise my choice of consorts?"

At which Amenhoteph took from the fold of his robe a small vial. "Want some?" he offered. "I have this sent to me directly from the perfumer's, a very good house in the city of the sun god, Ra, in Egypt."

I let him sprinkle a drop on the back of my hand. My nostrils filled with an aroma between lavender and attar. I thought of the ten plagues with which Lord Yahveh had smitten the Egyptians, and I wished one or two of them on my visitor. But Amenhoteph continued unconcerned, discoursing most cleverly on the art of making salads, boat racing on the river Nile, the ninety-nine ways of copulating, and the respective ages of Lord Yahveh and the sun god, Ra.

Then, with an extraordinary tilt of his hands, he enquired, "Ethan, why is it that the Princess Michal wishes to see you again?"

"Oh, does she?"

"I have come to invite you into her presence."

"I can only surmise," I said, wondering whom the royal chief eunuch might be working for besides King Solomon. "But I am a historian. I deal with facts, not with suppositions."

"You spent nearly an entire night conversing with the Princess, Ethan. You have more than suppositions by which to judge."

"It was a night of fables, my lord. Once a year, in Israel, we have a night such as this, with the air spiced by the fumes of the wine. Let us say that the Princess dreamed, and I

59

was privileged to listen to her dreams."

The eunuch offered me a view of his profile: slanted forehead, jutting nose. "Both you and I, Ethan, are strangers in this city. Which means that both of us are vulnerable and need the help of a friend. But as you are capable of loving and being loved, you are more vulnerable than I."

There was the threat: Lilith.

"I will give you my thought on the matter, Ethan. Your god, Yahveh, is said to have created man in his image. However, he carefully avoided making him fully as himself, for man is mortal. Yet there is in man this desire to be god-like, to live on forever; wherefore the kings in my country have themselves embalmed and shut off in the innermost chambers of the pyramids, surrounded by their servants and by all things necessary for life eternal. But you, Ethan, and all those in your trade make man immortal by your words; so that the names of the men you wrote of will be remembered thousands of years hence. Therein lies your power. That is why people bare their souls to you. That is why this old woman has you listen to her fables. But I . . ."

He broke off. He rose and stood, slender, beautifully groomed, elegant to the tip of his sandal.

"Since my testicles were crushed," he concluded, "I don't much believe in any god, Yahveh or Ra."

And left.

The royal harem was built in rings around a circular hall, in the centre of which a small fountain splashed gently. The structure was obviously planned for extension: supplementary rings of rooms could be added as King Solomon enlarged the swarm of his playmates. But in that case the air in the rotunda would be well nigh unbearable; even with the present complement, a sourish mixture of body odours and costly perfumes clogged your gullet and lung.

Amenhoteph had gone to announce me to the Princess Michal, but he seemed to be taking his time. I felt as though dozens of critical eyes were scrutinising me through the filigreed stones of the walls. I tried to appear immersed in viewing the colourful mosaics: mostly flower patterns with little about them that would inspire the senses. Then I heard a swish and a patter, and a damsel stood before me with breasts as fine as Lilith's but fuller, and with buttocks as firm and as juicy as melons from the valley of Jesreel. She moistened her red lips with the tip of the sweetest tongue; her round eyes pleaded more ably than did the hired orators on judgment day before the King Solomon; and she beckoned to me with a pretty pink finger.

But I whispered to her, "You are courting trouble, little beauty; and besides I am an author, and a family man."

Just then Amenhoteph returned. "Be gone!" he shrieked. And the damsel trembled and shrank and vanished as suddenly as she had come.

"What did she tell you?" Amenhoteph enquired hastily.

"Nothing," I answered. "She only beckoned to me with her pretty pink finger."

The eunuch breathed more easily and wanted to know if I knew who the damsel was. And as I knew her not, he said, "That, Ethan, is about the stupidest woman in Israel: Abishag of Shunam, the fair damsel picked to lie in the bosom of King David, so he might get heat when he was old and stricken in years. Now it is no secret that she was unable to pass on any of her heat, and the entire supply stayed with her and is burning her in her bowels. But no one is permitted to quench her fire because she has lain with King David, and thus whoever enters into her would thereby claim David's kingdom and the throne on which his son, Solomon, now sits. Only the damsel fails to understand this complication, and has cast an eye on Prince Adonijah, Solomon's older brother, who has trouble enough. And Adonijah has fallen for her charms; and she constantly sends him messages, through sandal-makers or pastry-bakers, through laundrymen or night-soil removers, through masseurs or manicurists, it's all the same to her; but I must catch the messages, and she knows I do catch them and the affair will have a nasty end: so why does she insist on trying?"

I said there was no fathoming a woman's mind; and he agreed sadly, and escorted me to a small sitting room which was richly appointed with cushions and low tables and soft rugs, and left me there.

*　　*　　*

Question: ... and placing the image of wood in your husband's bed was your idea, madam?

Answer: Apparently David had not expected my father, King Saul, to act. David had come to rely on Lord Yahveh to smooth the ways of his Chosen; but now that Jonathan sent word of Abner's intentions...

Question: Yes?

Answer: This man who had slain the Philistines by the hundreds and brought their foreskins to me for a dowry, seemed suddenly helpless. I held him to me like a small boy, and said to him, You must leave me, my husband, my dearest; if you do not save your life tonight, tomorrow you will be slain.

Question: He had made no preparations for escape?

Answer: His mule was stabled with the royal light horse, his sword was at a swordsmith's, and there was no bread in the house. With the King's messengers lurking near the door, I let him out of the window; and I placed the image on his bed, and covered it.

Question: Didn't you fear that you might be slain in place of your husband?

Answer: In the morning, as Abner's men dragged me before my father, I thought the moment had come. There stood Jonathan before my father, and my father called out at him, Why have you sent word to David, warning him? Jonathan answered, Wherefore shall he be slain? what has he done? And the wrath of my father, King Saul, was kindled against Jonathan, and he raged, saying, You have chosen David to your own confusion and unto the confusion of your mother's nakedness! Don't you know that as long as the son of Jesse walks upon the ground, you shall not be established nor your kingdom? And my father cast a javelin at Jonathan, and missed, and Jonathan stalked off in fierce anger. Then my father turned on me, saying, Why have you deceived me so and sent away my enemy, that he is escaped? I said that David told me he would kill me unless I aided him. But my father cried out, Behold the shame of the King! That all of you have conspired against me, and there is none that showed me that my own son has made a league with the traitor, and there is none of you that is sorry for me. There was a bitterness in my mouth over the anguish in the eyes of my father. He was moving his head from side to side like a bear with an arrow stuck in his throat, and his eye fell upon a pageboy who stood, frightened, at the door to the hall, and he waved him close and asked him, Whose son are you? And the boy said, I am Phalti the son of Laish, from Gallim, and your servant. But Phalti had a cast in his eye, and crooked teeth, and one shoulder was higher than the other. And my father, King Saul, said unto him, I hereby give you this woman, Michal my daughter, to be your wife and to serve you. And Phalti prostrated himself before me and kissed my feet. I remember the touch of his lips: they were hot, and trembled.

I must interpolate at this point what I know of the strange report of Saul among the prophets.

It is established and was confirmed to me by the Princess Michal that David, on his flight from Saul, stayed with Samuel at the temple in Ramah. But there is no certainty as to what took place at the temple, and indeed if King Saul ever went there and was seized by the Spirit of God, so that he stripped off his clothes and prophesied before Samuel and lay down naked all that day and all that night.

Hoping that Zadok the priest might have in his possession some authentic evidence, I went to see him. But Zadok enquired as to the reasons for my curiosity; we were writing the story of David, not that of Saul, were we not?

I countered that the conflict with Saul was part of the story of David. Three times Saul had sent messengers to Ramah to lay hold of David; three times they were met by a band of prophets prophesying, with Samuel standing as appointed over them; and three times the Spirit of God descended upon the messengers so that they fell into convulsions and prophesied also. Finally Saul himself journeyed to Ramah, it was said, and was also seized: from which stemmed the proverb, Has Saul, too, gone among the prophets?

Zadok smiled, saying, "Since you know that much, Ethan, why ask me?"

But I answered, "Surely my lord Zadok does not claim that a horde of unwashed fanatics who roll their eyes and twist their limbs and foam at the mouth would with their babble affect the King of Israel? That would be madness."

"But if the King had a history of madness?" Again Zadok smiled. "Was it not madness to cast a javelin at his own son? Was it not madness to drive away David, the one person able to ban the evil spirit of the Lord?"

I remembered the reports of Abner to his lord King Saul. How much did Zadok know of David's part in the play with the affliction of the King? But Zadok's eyes remained veiled.

"And would a man like Samuel," I said, "a serious prophet and priest of renown, a former chief judge in Israel and elder statesman, have placed himself at the head of an obsessed rabble?"

Zadok folded his hands across his paunch. "Was not Samuel obsessed by the Lord when he hewed King Agag in pieces?"

And I saw that there was a streak of madness in both Samuel and Saul, and a shiver went through me as I thought of the dark forces that move man.

SECOND DEPOSITION OF THE PRINCESS MICHAL, CONTINUED

Question: ... you were saying, madam, that you were given to Phalti the son of Laish.

Answer: Ah, yes, Phalti. Phalti waited on me, he washed me when I was hot and warmed me when I was cold, and in bed he lay at my feet. In his awkward way he even aided me to stay in touch with David: I was being watched, and he was inconspicuous.

Question: So you heard from David?

Answer: Just that he was alive, and in hiding.

Question: Where?

Answer: He hid with the priests, first at Ramah, then at Nob. From there he fled to the wilderness of southern Judah, into the caves.

Question: Did your father, King Saul, ever journey to Ramah in pursuit of David?

Answer: No.

Question: You are certain of that?

64

Answer: Ramah was Samuel's temple; my father would never go there. But he did use his royal prerogative of summoning the priests of the temple at Nob; and they came.

Question: You were present at the hearing?

Answer: It was public, my father the King sitting in judgment. I recall the rows of priests in their grey linen vestments; before them, clad in white, Ahimelech the chief priest. And my father the King said unto his retainers who stood about him, Hear now, will David ben Jesse give any of you fields and vineyards, and make you captains of thousands, and captains of hundreds? Is there not one among you who will speak up and testify concerning the traitor?

Question: Did they?

Answer: A little man stepped forth looking as kindly as a nurserymaid. He said he was Doeg the Edomite, and in charge of the enquiry into the matter of David ben Jesse. He had gone to Nob, he said, and had seen David come to Ahimelech the chief priest. Ahimelech, he said, had consulted the oracle for David and given him victuals and also a sword.

Question: No other witnesses?

Answer: The words of Doeg were sufficient unto my father. He turned to Ahimelech, saying, Hear now, why have you conspired against me in that you have given the son of Jesse bread and a sword, and consulted the oracle for him, so he should rise against me and lie in wait, as at this day? But Ahimelech raised his hand and swore, denying his guilt. David had told him, he said, that the King had sent him on secret business, and so great was its haste that he had brought neither his sword nor his weapons with him; therefore David demanded five loaves of bread in his hand, and a spear or sword. And I thought, said Ahimelech, who is so faithful among all the King's servants as David, and he is the King's son-in-law, and he goes at the King's bidding; therefore I did as David asked. But as for consulting the oracle for him, be it far from me: let not the King impute anything unto his servant. And all the priests raised their hands and protested their innocence, and the clamour was heard as far as the walls of the city. But I thought, praise be unto the Lord that David my husband was not laid hold of; at the same time my heart was heavy for my father the King.

Question: And then followed the execution?

Answer: My father the King rose, supporting himself on his spear, and proclaimed, You shall die, Ahimelech, and all your house. And he commanded the retainers about him, Turn, and slay this man, and slay all those priests, because their hand also is with David, and because they knew when he fled, and did not show it to me. But these people would not put forth their hand to fall upon the priests of the Lord. And my father the King said, Of what are you frightened?. They are not holy men, neither do they work. They are like the maggots in the carrion, waxing fat on what the people give unto Yahveh. And there was a whispering about, and everybody expected the evil spirit of the Lord to descend upon my father the King and twist his face to the back; but my father stood calmly, and beckoned to Doeg the Edomite. And he said to Doeg, Turn you, and fall upon the priests. And Doeg the Edomite turned, and slew on that day fourscore and five men of the cloth, and we watched it.

The wax tablets on which I had been scribbling were filled. The air in the rotunda seemed to have thickened further. But the Princess did not dismiss me. She sat on her cushion, very straight, her skeletal hands flat on her knees, and stared into the distances beyond the wall.

Suddenly, as out of a dream, she said, "How do you see David?"

An odd query to be directed at the redactor of *The One and Only True and Authoritative, Historically Correct and Officially Approved Report on the Amazing Rise* and so forth. I glanced up at the carvings in the ceiling, wondering if behind it were hidden vents that led to the ear of Amenhoteph. "Madam," I said, "he is the father of King Solomon."

She laughed contemptuously. "And King Solomon will decide how you see the man who was twice my husband and the lover of my brother Jonathan and the whore of my father King Saul?"

I bowed my head.

But she waved away my apology, saying, "I grant his many facets are a baffling thing. My brother Jonathan and I have often talked about it. We grew close to one another in those days. We would ride out from the royal residence at Gibeah to

66

where the red rocks rise, and climb up, and look over the land, as though we might see a sign of smoke on the hills. But there was nothing, only the vultures circling. And Jonathan spoke of the covenant he made with David, because he loved him as his own soul; and that David was the Chosen of the Lord; and that David had sworn unto him forever to guard and protect his seed, for the sake of their great friendship and of their covenant. But what about the kingdom, I said; won't you be king, my brother Jonathan?"

The Princess rose and slowly walked up and down. Her sandalled feet were remarkably beautiful.

"And Jonathan said unto me, To rule, you must see one purpose only: power. You must love one person only: yourself. Even your God must be your exclusive God, who justifies your every crime and covers it by his holy name."

The Princess stopped pacing and faced me.

"Mind you, Ethan: he knew all that, and yet he loved David. The vultures hung suspended in the sky. Then one plummeted down. I asked, Do you know where he is? And Jonathan answered, He is in the cave Adullam, and his brothers and all his house went down there to him, and many that are in distress, and many that are in debt, and many that are discontented, altogether four hundred men, and he has become a chieftain over them. And I saw David my husband issue forth from the cave Adullam at the head of these brigands and felons, I saw his tanned face and his supple body, and I said unto my brother Jonathan, Be he a cattle thief or a spoiler, there is a longing inside me, and I will to him. But Jonathan answered, Wait; the King's messengers are about you, the men of Abner ben Ner; you will be caught and killed. And I waited, and the rains came, and spring again, and Phalti the son of Laish held my hands; and there was no more word from David, either through Phalti or through my brother Jonathan. But when the rains came again, I heard it said that David had taken to be his wife Abigail the widow of one Nabal, a rich sheep raiser in Maon, who was struck by a stroke. And I cried out, and I sat in mourning and tore my clothes and did not eat until Phalti came and brought me wine to drink and oil to rub on my body, and he ministered to me, and I let him, but I felt nothing."

I tried not to look at her.

She laughed, gently this time, and in a changed voice said, "It all happened so very long ago."

And there was Amenhoteph the royal chief eunuch, bowing, "Supper is being served. Madam is expected in the dining room."

She left, her gait a little stiff but her carriage magnificent, considering her age. In the door she turned and nodded to me as though we were fellow conspirators, saying, "You will see him properly, I'm sure."

8

PRAISED BE THE NAME of the Lord our God, who divulges his truth by the dreams of the seers and poets, but otherwise sets before it much painstaking search and laborious investigation.

An outlaw, head of a band of thieves and cut-throats, will cover his tracks rather than leave behind him clay tablets filled with the accounts of his exploits. He will avoid encounters with the forces of the law; thus any reports about him from that source will be few and hazy at best. Perhaps a song or two, a ballad embellishing his deeds might furnish hints that can be followed; or we might find a surviving witness of his raids, either a fellow marauder or a victim.

Abigail is dead. The questions I should have asked of her remain unanswered. She died in Hebron at the time that David was King of Judah, after she bore him a son named Chileab, a poor idiot boy whose skull was deformed in birth. By all accounts of her she was quite a woman; she must have exerted considerable influence on David during his bandit period and in his years as an exile and as a small local king in Hebron.

I talked of her with one Deborah. This sprightly beldame keeps a boarding house for foreign specialists from Sidon and Tyre who are employed here for the construction of the temple. Deborah was one of the five damsels whom Abigail brought into her marriage with David. A handmaid to Abigail, she saw and heard much of what took place between her mistress and David. Also the servants of Benaiah ben Jehoiada brought to me from the gates of the city one Mibsam ben Mishma, a one-legged old beggar: his missing leg was cut off him in the time that he was with David in the wilderness, he said. Mibsam, it appears, headed the ten young men whom David sent unto Nabal the first husband of Abigail with orders to offer him peace and ask for a sizeable contribution.

And there were others to whom I spoke, and several documents, so that I was enabled to piece together a mosaic, albeit a fragmentary one.

By Madmannah ben Jerahmeel; chosen elder of the tribe of Caleb:
Assessment
of Nabal a member of this tribe, residing at Maon, his pastures being in Carmel,
Sheep—to the number of three thousand
Goats—to the number of one thousand

Mibsam ben Mishma told me as follows:
David a cattle thief? Never. He was too wise for that. Men, he used to say, if I catch one of you stealing as much as a lamb's tail, God do to me so and so, and some more, if I don't personally flail his skin off him. For what will the stealing of sheep avail us in the end? After a few raids the shepherds would flee us and hide their flocks; or they will band together and pursue us with their slings, and a good shepherd with a good sling is the equal of any warrior, you heard of the story of me and Goliath; or they might send word to King Saul, and the King would dispatch against us several thousands of his host, and then where would we be? No, men, David used to say, that is not the way to subsist in the wilderness. But the good lord Yahveh spoke to me in a dream, saying, David, follow the law which I have given your forefathers, and I will show you the right way, so that you and your men will fare well; and this way shall be called the way of sweet persuasion. Do not steal from the shepherds or attack them; nay, said the Lord, make friends with them and

70

protect them against thieves and nomads and rustlers of cattle. But when the time is nearing that the herds are driven unto their master for the shearing of his sheep, and there is feasting and drinking and merrymaking, behold, you will go there also and collect from the bounty your share for protecting sheep and shepherd. Thus spoke the Lord to me in my dream, and thus, men, we shall enjoy a steady income in coin and in kind, in meat, in parched corn, in wine and in everything that is good, and all Israel will praise us and cherish us. But if any master refuses us, saying, I do not know you, nor did I command you to protect what pertains to me, then we shall tell him, Listen, you son of Belial, God do so and more also unto us if David ben Jesse leaves of yours any that pisses against the wall.

Mibsam ben Mishma rubbed the stump of his leg, which was red and sore and itching, and there was in his constantly watering eyes a reflection of the glory that was David's. And he continued as follows:

Now this Nabal, he had thousands of sheep, all fat and of the finest wool, and goats of the best sort, also thousands; so that we were licking our chops towards the time when Nabal would shear. And David said to me, Mibsam, I know you in that you have a good head on your shoulders and a fast tongue in your head. So you pick yourself nine fellows, all of them looking mighty like you, and ride unto Nabal and wish him peace and so forth, but try to be civil, and remind him that he lives in affluence, while we are in the saddle, in the wilderness, protecting what pertains to him, and that we come to him on a good day and expect to find favour in his eyes, and he should please give you what comes to his hand for his friend David ben Jesse. But this Nabal, he was a thick man, with a paunch hanging to his knees and his cheeks drooping over his jawbones, and his anger was kindled, so that he spluttered, Who is this David ben Jesse? there may be many servants nowadays that break away every man from his master: shall I then take my bread, and my wine, and my flesh that I have killed for my shearers, and my good, hard shekels, and give all that unto men whom I know not whence they be? And I feared lest this Nabal would be struck by a stroke, for he turned a deep plum colour; but I remembered

David telling me, Always be civil, Mibsam; and thus I said calmly to Nabal, Never mind, you soul of generosity, you will surely be hearing from the son of Jesse.

Mibsam ben Mishma scratched himself under the arm, and caught what he had searched for, and bit on it, and spat. And he continued as follows:

But all the time this woman was watching us. She was goodly to look at, and dressed in fine raiment, with rings on her fingers and bracelets on her ankles. And I saw she had an eye on me, because I was broad of shoulder and small in the hips and sat well in the saddle; and when I was about to ride off, having finished with Nabal, she came up to me, saying, This David ben Jesse your captain, is he somewhat like you? And I answered, Lady, if I find favour in your eyes, your heart will go for David like a brush fire, for he is ten times the man I am; but who might you be? Whereupon she said, I am Abigail the wife of Nabal; and by the tone of her voice you knew that she had as much use for her husband as for a carbuncle on her backside. And a spirit from the Lord whispered unto me that we would be seeing some more of this wife of Nabal, and I hit my mule between the ears with my fist, so that he streaked off like an eagle. When he came back to the place appointed by David, he was waiting for us with all his men; and I told him the sayings of Nabal. Then said David, Let every man gird on his sword. David also girded on his sword, and he vowed a vow on the morrow there would not be left of Nabal's any that pisses against the wall; but to me he said, Mibsam, you and two hundred of the men, you stay with the baggage and the carts, and guard them, for I am going to do some fast riding. And there went up after David about four hundred men; and further I do not know what developed, except that on the morrow he brought back quite some victuals and looked exceeding happy, like a frog which has swallowed the fly.

Among the items left after her death by Abigail the wife of David and widow of Nabal, and kept in a storeroom of the royal harem, several potsherds were found and brought to me by a servant of Amenhoteph the royal chief eunuch. One of the potsherds contained a list written in an awkward hand, and with many errors.

The list:

> To David son Jese
> 2 hun loavs bred
> 2 skinns bestest wine
> 5 sheap reddy dressd
> 5 meshures parchd corne
> 1 hun clustrs resins
> 2 hun caikes figs
> 8 donkies for to carrie

You try this wine, sir. This is none of the stuff which I serve to those boarders of mine who would not know the difference between goat's piss and vinegar. This is better than what they grow in the King's vineyards at Baal-hamon, and it has waited in this vessel these many years. This is from the special stock of Nabal my mistress's first husband who was struck by the stroke. My mistress, the Lord have mercy on her soul, she gave it to me, saying, Deborah, you hold that wine towards the day when the man comes that sweeps you off your feet as David swept me off mine; then you open the vessel and drink with him what's therein. But there came this man and that, sir, and I never quite knew, did he now or didn't he sweep me off my feet as David did my mistress; and I kept the vessel sealed. And the men came and they went, and I waxed old and wrinkled, and sometimes I say to myself, Deborah, maybe that vessel you kept sealed is like your life: the sweetest wine untasted.

So I'll open it now, sir, in memory of Abigail my mistress. Not that she took to a man that quickly and that readily. She was no bleating lamb by the time she met the son of Jesse; she was easily six or eight years his elder; but her flesh was firm and her breasts stood out like rams. She managed the house, and ruled the servants, and did the accounts while Nabal her husband gorged himself and guzzled until he was as stuffed derma, and about as useful to a woman. They say that my mistress took unto herself a donkey driver, and a travelling potter, and a stableboy, and a teller of tales and legends, and a tax collector; but she was a virtuous woman, and she preferred the company of her five damsels, of whom I was one, and she had us pet her and dandle her, and kiss her and fondle her and stroke her and cocker her, until she moaned with delight and her eyes grew misty.

May Lord Yahveh bless this drop of liquid sunshine. Now when Abigail my mistress saw the young men that David sent unto Nabal, and heard Nabal rail at them, she said to me, Deborah my dear, if this David ben Jesse is anything like those young men of his, we shall have trouble. Therefore take this potsherd and collect all I have listed on it, and have the things loaded on asses, and make haste, and go on with the drivers before me, I will come after you. And say nothing about this to Nabal my husband, she added, for he is such a son of Belial he would misunderstand. When she caught up with us, riding on her ass, I saw that she had painted her eyes and rouged her cheeks; her lips were as the flesh of the pomegranate, and her scent like a whole garden of flowers. And as we came down by the covert of the hill, there was a big noise, and David and his men came against us; but Abigail my mistress rode ahead to meet them.

That wine is surely good; you want another cup of it, sir? If you write of my mistress, as you said you will, listen well, for now comes her encounter with David. There he was, sitting straight in the saddle, red hair over tanned face, his eyes lighting up; and Abigail sliding off her ass, and bowing herself to the ground before him. David enquired, Who is this woman bowing before me? So I thought I would enlighten him, and I said, My lord, she is my mistress, Abigail the wife of Nabal, of Maon, who has his possessions in Carmel. And David dismounted and said, for all to hear, Sorry, madam, but I have protected all that your husband had out on pasture, and he has requited me for good. But Abigail my mistress raised her face to David, so that he could see that her breasts stood out like rams. And she said, Upon me, my lord, upon me let this iniquity be. Regard not Nabal, I pray you, for folly is with him. Regard your handmaid, for her heart beats higher at your sight, because my lord fights the battles of Yahveh, and evil has not been found in you all your day. And now this blessing which your handmaid has brought unto my lord, even two hundred loaves, and two skins of wine, and five

74

sheep ready dressed, and five measures of parched corn, and one hundred clusters of raisins, and two hundred cakes of figs, let that be given unto the young men that follow my lord. And when God shall have dealt well with my lord, then remember your handmaid.

This wine, sir, it does something to a body. It brings back a vision of the days past, of Abigail my mistress, and of David ben Jesse that brigand. Behold him lifting her up from the ground and handling her tenderly. Blessed be the Lord God of Israel, he said unto her, who sent you this day to meet me. And blessed be you, who have kept me this day from coming to shed blood. For as the Lord God of Israel lives, except you had hasted and come to meet me, surely there had not been left unto Nabal by the morning light any that pisses against the wall. And David bowed before her, and the two of them walked off some way into the wilderness, and when they came back, my mistress had a tilt to her head that made her look ten years younger. But David said unto her, Go up in peace to your house; see, I have hearkened to your voice, and have accepted your person.

You have failed to empty your cup, sir. Pray, do not trouble yourself about me; more wine has run down this old gullet than would fill the skins of a thousand goats. So Abigail my mistress came back to Nabal her husband; and he was besotted and lay in his own vomit, having feasted all this while, wherefore she told him nothing until the morning light. But when he woke up, groaning, and stinking like a sty of pigs, and not knowing where his head was or his elbow, she stepped up to him, fresh as the dew on the rose, and said, Why, you fat lout, you sot, you mountain of impotence: I saved your life by hasting to meet David the son of Jesse and bringing him of your riches bread and wine and dressed meat and parched corn and raisins and figs, for surely by this time David would not have left of yours any that pisses against the wall. Nabal jumped up, faster than a flea, and raised his hands, and cried unto Yahveh, Did you hear, God, what this she-devil, this whore of Belial, has spoken? She is my perdition, she will utterly ruin me! Sheep, and parched corn, and figs! May her breasts wither and her crotch turn yellow, for you, Lord God, are a righteous God who punishes the wicked. And he called for his steward, and for his servants, and railed and ranted, until his lips turned blue and thereupon his whole face, and he fell on his back and became as a stone. The steward said that Nabal must be bled, and the servants ran to fetch the barber; but Abigail my mistress said, Pray all you want unto Yahveh, but do not tamper with your master's blood, for it was thickened by the Lord and stopped from flowing, and the will of the Lord be done. For ten days the servants prayed, and the barber waited, and my mistress sat by the side of Nabal her husband who lay as a stone; but on the tenth day the Lord smote Nabal that he died.

She was a great woman, sir, let's drink to her soul wherever it may be. Ten days of sitting there and watching your husband die and making sure that he dies truly shows character. After she buried him, she said to me, Deborah, have an ass saddled and ride unto David, and tell him, Blessed be the Lord who has pleaded the cause of your reproach from the hand of Nabal, and who has kept you from evil: for the Lord has returned the wickedness of Nabal upon his own head. And I met some of David's young men not far off in the wilderness, and they took me to the son of Jesse, and I told him as my mistress had told me. Whereupon David rewarded me richly with a silver clip and ten spans of finest linen three spans in width, and sent some of his servants with me. And when we were come to my mistress to Carmel, they spoke unto her, saying, David sent us to you, to take you to him to wife. There was about her lips a smile that was like triumph, and she quickly bowed herself on her face to the earth, and said, Behold, let your handmaid be a servant to wash the feet of the servants of my lord. Then she arose, and hasted, and rode upon an ass, with us five damsels following her; and we went after the messengers of David, and she became his wife.

SHIGGAION OF DAVID, WHICH HE SANG
UNTO THE LORD

Oh let the wickedness of the wicked come to an end; but establish the just; for the righteous God tries the hearts and reins.

My defence is of God, which saves the upright in heart.

76

*God judges the righteous, and God is angry with the
wicked every day.*

*If he turn not, he will whet his sword; he has bent his
bow, and made it ready.*

*He has also prepared for him the instruments of death; he
ordains his arrows against the persecutors.*

*Behold, he travails with iniquity, and has conceived
mischief, and brought forth falsehood.*

*He made a pit, and digged it, and is fallen into the ditch
which he made.*

*His mischief shall return upon his own head, and his
violent dealing shall come down upon his own pate.*

*I will praise the Lord according to his righteousness: and
will sing praise to the name of the Lord most high.*

By Madmannah ben Jerahmeel, chosen elder of the tribe
of Caleb:

Certificate of Transfer

of all that pertained to Nabal of Maon a member of this
tribe, him having died childless, mainly,

Sheep—to the number of three thousand

Goats—to the number of one thousand

to David ben Jesse a member of the tribe of Judah and now
husband of Abigail the widow of Nabal, in view of the ties of
blood and friendship between the tribes of Caleb and Judah,
and in consideration of payment in kind to the tribe of Caleb
of one tenth of all that pertained to Nabal.

9

REMARKS OF ETHAN BEN HOSHAIAH to the members of the Royal Commission on the Preparation of *The One and Only True and Authoritative, Historically Correct and Officially Approved Report on the Amazing Rise, Godfearing Life, Heroic Deeds, and Wonderful Achievements of David the Son of Jesse, King of Judah for Seven Years and of both Judah and Israel for Thirty-Three, Chosen of God, and Father of King Solomon*, for short, *The King David Report*, during its session on the military aspects of the conflict between the King, Saul, and David ben Jesse.

My lords!

I plead indulgence for restricting my remarks to the expedition, or expeditions, of King Saul against David ben Jesse. The subject of David's campaigns in the service of the Philistines appears to your servant too delicate to be dealt with by a mere redactor.

Further, I wish to express appreciations and thanks to my lord Jehoshaphat ben Ahilud, the recorder, for graciously placing at my disposal certain notes he took of conversations with the King, David; to my lord Benaiah ben Jehoiada, captain of the host, for letting me peruse certain records from the files of Abner ben Ner; and to my lords Elihoreph and Ahiah b'nai Shisha, scribes, for their selfless but unavailing search of the royal archives.

The documents and testimony available to us are somewhat contradictory, which makes it difficult to determine the actual number of expeditions undertaken by King Saul against David. We hear of three: one, into the wilderness of Ziph and Maon, had to be broken off when the Philistines once more invaded the land of Israel; a second, into the caves and gorges of the wilderness of En-gedi, and a third, again into Ziph, both ended with a personal, most touching encounter between Saul and David. Both times David and some of his companions managed to sneak up on Saul: at En-gedi this occurred in a cave which King Saul entered to relieve his bowels, in Ziph, while Saul lay asleep in a trench. Both times David's companions urged him to kill the King, telling him that the opportunity was too good to be missed, and didn't the Lord always say, Behold, I will deliver your enemy into your hand? Both times David refused, arguing, Who can stretch forth his hand against the Anointed of the Lord?—an attitude quite understandable on the part of a future king. But while in the cave at En-gedi David cuts a piece of fringe off the robe of the peacefully squatting Saul, at Ziph he takes the sleeping King's spear and cruse of water. At both En-gedi and Ziph David then calls Saul from a safe distance, gives his name, and shows him the exhibits that prove his generosity; whereupon the King answers, Behold, I have played the fool and have erred exceedingly, I will do you no more harm because my soul was precious in your eyes this day, and now I know well that you shall surely be king and that the kingdom of Israel shall be established in your hand.

My lords! These are prophetic words, full of noble sentiments, and coming from the lips of King Saul they are of special significance, for they furnish additional grounds for the right of David to the throne of Israel. Nor are they folk tales embellished in varying ways by their tellers; nay, but the King, David, in his own person related the incidents to my lord Jehoshaphat, who noted them down. They have only one flaw: neither in the files of Abner ben Ner, who was over the host in King Saul's time, nor in the royal archives do we find any mention of a military expedition into the wilderness of En-gedi or of a second campaign into Ziph.

Abner reports only one expedition: the one broken off when word arrived of fresh Philistine trouble. It seems that, after limiting himself for a long period to petty forays conducted from desert hide-outs, David decided to establish himself in the town of Keilah. Keilah had been plagued by Philistine raiders; he drove these off and thought that thereby he would gain the hearts of the townspeople. But now that David was out of the bush, his movements no longer hidden, word of his whereabouts reached the King. Saul exulted, God has delivered him into my hand, for he is shut in by entering a town that has gates and bars. The thought entered David's mind as well, and it troubled him; and after consulting the oracle he left Keilah and its people, who were uncertain friends, and retired into the wilderness of Ziph. But by this time Saul was marching against him with three thousand picked men of the host. David retreated from the wilderness of Ziph into the wilderness of Maon, and Saul followed him there, Saul marching on this side of the mountain and David and his men on the other. In a brilliantly executed move Saul's men encircled David, and it is doubtful that David would have escaped but for the messenger arriving at Saul's camp, saying, Haste you and come, the Philistines have invaded the land.

My lords! I have spoken to you of these points at some length not so as to cast doubts on this item or that; for who would be brazen enough to set the word of a man like Abner above that of King David. I have merely tried to throw some light on a rather murky period in the life of the son of Jesse, and to indicate the editorial problems it presents. I am mindful of the wise sayings on the relative value of truth and legend which my lords propounded at the Commission's last session. Despite the confusing evidence, I shall therefore do my best to enrich the noble image of the Chosen of the Lord, to buttress his claim to the throne, and to further the purposes for which the Wisest of Kings, Solomon, has caused the King David Report to be written.

But as to David's joining the enemy of Israel, namely the Philistines: this is, as I remarked in the beginning, too bewildering a question to be left to your servant's poor wisdom. Concerning this, I wait the pleasure of my lords.

Debate of the members of the Royal Commission on the

Preparation of the *Report on the Amazing Rise* and so forth, on the inclusion of undesirable matter in works of history and the ways of presenting same, as noted down by Ethan ben Hoshaiah.

Jehoshaphat ben Ahilud, the recorder: My lords, you have heard the remarks of Ethan our redactor. Any objections? Additions? Are my lords agreed, then, that the various stories of King Saul's expeditions be placed into the King David Report?

Ahiah ben Shisha, scribe: Agreed.

Jehoshaphat: We now come to our second point. My lord Zadok?

Zadok the priest: What about supper?

Jehoshaphat: There will be a reception tonight at the Palace, in honour of the Egyptian delegation, with drinks and lamb on the spit; was not my lord Zadok's presence requested?

Zadok: I wish my wife would cease cleaning my work table.

Jehoshaphat: In fact, the reception leaves us little time. I suppose my lords are familiar with the essentials of the case. David with his six hundred men passed over to Achish the King of Gath, which was one of the five kingdoms of the Philistines. David and his troop, and their households, dwelled in Gath until Achish shifted them to his town of Ziklag. By accepting Ziklag as his fief, David agreed to render service to the Philistines and made his allegiance to Achish a matter of public knowledge.

Zadok: In view of the intricate nature of David's move, I should like to know what he himself had to say about it.

Benaiah ben Jehoiada: David's attitude was perfectly clear. I should have perished one day by the hand of Saul, he said, so there was nothing better for me than that I should speedily escape into the land of the Philistines.

Zadok: But the man in the marketplace and in the gates of the city will say, Behold, here is a fine upright boy, a leader in Israel, an Anointed of the Lord, and what does he do?—he joins up with the uncircumcised against his own people. What do you answer to that? ... We need some excuse that will stuff the mouths of the evil-minded. Perhaps the Lord could

81

have commanded him to pass over. Did not King David ever remark on that?

Jehoshaphat: King David rarely spoke of the affair; and when he did, he sounded as though he was not much troubled by it.

Nathan the prophet: And why should he have been? As the Chosen of the Lord, he had the duty to survive; for how else would God's will be done and David become King of Israel and father of King Solomon?

Zadok: You know it and I know it, but do the people know it? ... Might it not be wise to forget the whole thing? ... How long exactly did David dwell with the Philistines?

Jehoshaphat: One year and four months.

Zadok: It is two thousand years since Noah landed on top of that mountain. What is one little year, in terms of history?

Nathan: I do not live off the sacrifices of the people, as does my friend Zadok. I deal directly with the Lord. Therefore I feel we should be consistent: once we are agreed that David is the Chosen of the Lord, then everything he does is for the good of Israel. But as knowledge of the facts may lead a person to dangerous thoughts, the facts must be presented so as to direct the mind into the proper channels.

Zadok: That has been tried since the Lord God told Adam certain facts, back in Eden. The most excellent words may be twisted by any serpent that happens along.

Benaiah: I wonder how my lord Nathan will make the following fit with the avowed good of Israel. Once in Ziklag, David and his men had only one way of supplying themselves: by robbery. But the nearest people to be raided were the people of Judah, David's own tribe. This meant killing every man, woman and child in the village, for any survivors would have gone through the land and cried out against David. Which was what Achish King of Gath counted on. Achish said, He will make his people Israel utterly abhor him, therefore he shall be my liegeman forever.

Nathan: If it were not that I heard the voice of my lord Benaiah, I would believe I was hearing a libel on David the father of King Solomon.

Benaiah: I am only being consistent, as my lord Nathan demanded. God must have known what he did when he chose

David ben Jesse to rule over Israel and establish the realm. And if that is so, then it was also God's will that the reigning King, Saul, and Saul's son Jonathan be destroyed. Then it was only right and proper of David to sell himself to Achish King of Gath and to march his men up north, ready to aid the Philistines in the battle of Aphek in which Saul and Jonathan were killed and the host of Israel routed. Now, if the road along which Yahveh led his Chosen appears to have been too circuitous, our friend Ethan can always straighten it out for the purposes of the King David Report.

Zadok: The ways that David took may have been circuitous, but they were not the ways of the wicked.

Benaiah: Ways of the wicked! I fought for David when Absalom his own son rose against him, and many another time. I have seen David act when decisions were required; David knew what it means to win power and hold it. And when it came to a clash between the word of the Lord and what David thought necessary, why, then he would have a quick talk with the Lord, and somehow God changed his word to suit the needs of David.

Jehoshaphat: I notice the silence of my lords. Well, then we might let Ethan our redactor tell us his conclusions from our debate, and how he plans to develop this section of the King David Report.

But as I was about to speak to the members of the Commission, behold, there was a noise, and the doors sprang open, and a servant announced King Solomon. And Jehoshaphat ben Ahilud, the recorder, bowed himself to the ground, and everybody prostrated himself while Solomon was being carried in on a portable throne with a pair of very artistic Cherubim.

The King bade us rise. He looked fatter than when I saw him last; and he was in a high good mood, saying, "This is truly a great day in Israel, as I find all of you busy in the labour of the Lord, and also an Egyptian delegation has arrived to offer me a daughter of Pharaoh for a wife, and there will be drinks and lamb on the spit."

Whereupon followed one of those pauses that will occur when a great man has delivered himself of a statement. Then

Jehoshaphat enquired if the King perhaps would like to know of the deliberations of the Commission; and the King said he would like to know very much indeed; and Jehoshaphat summed up briefly, ending his words by saying, "And now, oh Wisest of Kings, we were just about to hear from Ethan ben Hoshaiah our redactor."

And King Solomon clapped his hands, exclaiming, "Ah, yes, Ethan, of whom they say from Dan even unto Beer-sheba that he is one of the wisest men in Israel."

I bowed my face. "As my lord the King well knows, my poor wisdom is unto his as is the mouse unto the elephant that lives in the kingdom of Sheba."

The King toyed with the precious stones on the wings of the Cherubim, and he replied, "Let us hear, Ethan, what you have to tell us on the question of including undesirable matter in works of history and the ways of presenting same."

I began by saying that I was most grateful to the mighty lords on the Commission, because they had put the problem so neatly and spoken on it so sagaciously. On the basis of their debate, I said, I had listed the various possibilities of dealing with undesirable matter: (a) tell it all, (b) tell it with discretion, (c) don't tell it. To tell it all (possibility a) was obviously unwise; people were quick to draw the wrong conclusions from facts and to form wrong opinions of persons whom we wished to be highly regarded. Not to tell it (possibility c) was equally unwise; things had a way of being noised about and people always picked up what they were not supposed to know. This left us with possibility (b): tell it with discretion. Discretion, I said, was not the same as lying; surely the Wisest of Kings, Solomon, would never condone lying in a history of his father King David. Discretion was truth controlled by wisdom.

"If the King and my lords permit," I said, "I will try to show how we might use discretion in depicting the somewhat circuitous road which was taken by the Chosen of the Lord.

"There was some question in the Commission as to those raids which David conducted out of Ziklag. Now David himself, upon being asked by Achish King of Gath, Whither have you turned today? made the admission, Against the south of Judah. But what does that prove coming from the

84

lips of a man in David's plight? Might it not have been an artifice? But whether he spoke true to Achish or not, there are no witnesses either way as David had everyone slain in the places he pillaged. Therefore, would it not seem proper to suggest in our text that David raided among the hostile tribes in Geshur, or Gezer, or Amalek, rather than among his own people Judah?

"Then there is the question of David's role in the battle against Saul and the people of Israel, which was fought at Aphek. He surely was there in fealty to his liege-lord Achish of Gath. But did he participate in the battle? Might we not assume that there arose a dispute among the Philistine lords, who told King Achish, Is not this David of whom it was sung in the streets of Israel, *Saul has slain his thousands, and David his ten thousands*; make him return to his place which you have appointed him, lest in the battle he turn against us, because blood is thicker than water, and wherewith could he better reconcile himself with his master, King Saul, than with the heads of our men? ... For one thing is certain: in the final hours of the battle, while the host of Israel scattered over Mount Gilboa and the bodies of Saul and of Jonathan were being nailed to the walls of the town of Beth-shan, David and his men were returning in forced marches to Ziklag, which had been raided by spoilers from Amalek. They caught the spoilers and rescued their wives, among them Abigail; and they made so much booty that David could afford to send of it unto the elders of Judah, saying, Behold a present for you of the spoil of the enemies of the Lord."

King Solomon looked at me from his beady eyes, and he laughed without mirth, and said, "You know how to use words with great cunning, Ethan, and to direct thereby the thinking of people: so that it seems to me I have chosen wisely in making you redactor of the report about my father King David."

But I thought, If his father, King David, was a great murderer, then this one is a petty cut-throat. And I said, "What is your servant in the presence of the Wisest of Kings but a flyspeck, a wisp of chaff, an insignificant flatulence."

At which the King poked his short, fat finger at me, replying, "To each according to his deserts. I should be pleased if you attended tonight's reception."

And nodding graciously he beckoned to his bearers and was carried off.

I returned to No. 54, Queen-of-Sheba Lane, to have my feet washed by Lilith and my beard trimmed by Huldah, and to tell Esther of the honour which had fallen to my share. "Guard your step, Ethan," she said; and when I put on my new green-striped robe and turned to go, she raised her hand as though to bless me.

The reception was enlivened by scores of musicians with cymbals and pipes, and with psalteries and tabrets, and with harps; by dancers who circled and jumped and bent every which way; and by singers of varying talents who sang songs in praise of the Lord, of Solomon the Wisest of Kings, and of Pharaoh from whose loins had sprung the Princess Helankamen, her eyes like dark jewels and her thighs like the columns of the temple of Ammon-Ra. The face of Amenhoteph the royal chief eunuch was aglow with satisfaction, and as he had had a drop of the wine from the King's vineyards at Baal-hamon, he said to me, "Well, done, eh? And the Princess will be given to Solomon, provided he grants free passage through Israel to Egyptian goods."

So I drank to Amenhoteph's years, and said to him, "I wonder, my lord, if you are more of a matchmaker or an expert on trade between countries."

"Why, Ethan," he replied, "I am many things to many people, but to you I am a friend, because you are a stranger here as I am, and because you have a discerning mind." And jabbing his elbow into my ribs, "Do you know who the fellow is over there, the one struggling with the piece of fattail?"

I saw a man of dark countenance and with bristly hair grown white at the temples, a man goodly to look at but for his chin which was weak and receding.

"That is Prince Adonijah who nearly was king," Amenhoteph told me. "They say that from the nose up he is the image of King David his father, but that the mouth and the jaw are from a captain of the archers whom Haggith his mother preferred."

Prince Adonijah, meat in one hand and a cup of wine in the other, discovered Amenhoteph and hurriedly directed his

86

steps towards him. "How is that most ravishing of damsels," he said, "the lady Abishag of Shunam? Has she not given you a message for me?"

Amenhoteph bowed. "The lady Abishag is as well as any of the ladies in the royal harem."

"Will you convey my adoration to her," said the Prince. "Tell her that her servant longingly awaits word from her, or a token of her feelings, even a lock of hair, or the bundle of myrrh she wears betwixt her delightful breasts."

I recalled with interest that since coming to Jerusholayim Lilith had taken to wearing a bundle of myrrh betwixt *her* delightful breasts. But just then I saw Adonijah stiffen, and Amenhoteph bowed to the waist, and a murmuring and whispering was about, for King Solomon was coming towards us with his entourage, which included Jehoshaphat ben Ahilud, the recorder, and Nathan the prophet, and Zadok the priest, and Benaiah the son of Jehoiada, the captain of the host.

The King was resplendent in gold and in silver, and rings sparkled on his fingers, and he said unto Adonijah his brother, "I see my lord is conversing with Ethan ben Hoshaiah, whose wisdom is excelled only by mine, and who is the redactor of the *Report on the Amazing Rise* and so forth of King David our father."

Adonijah, who up to that moment had taken no notice of me, looked me over, his large grey eyes shining with some of the radiance which the eyes of David his father were said to have had. Then he wiped his greasy lips with the sleeve of his robe, and said, "I am curious how he will deal with the succession question."

Whereupon King Solomon started angrily; but I bowed my face and said to Adonijah, "Your servant is in a position to assure my lord that the Wisest of Kings, Solomon your brother, wishes to see nothing contained in the book but the Lord's truth."

"Then your *Report on the Amazing Rise* and so forth will truly be one of the world's most remarkable titles," said Adonijah.

"Quite," said the King. And turning to me, "I hear from your friend Amenhoteph that Lilith your concubine is most pleasing to behold, and possesses exceeding charm, and is

87

wise in the ways of love. His description is correct, I presume?"

I felt fear in my bowels, and I replied, "Your servant is unto you like a worm, and anything he possesses is unto your splendour like a grain of sand, not worth the attention of my lord."

"A modest man is agreeable in the sight of the Lord," said the King. "But I wish to honour you for the deep thought you have devoted to writing the history of David my father, and I was wondering if it might not be an idea to bestow distinction upon you by taking your Lilith to be handmaid to Princess Hel-ankamen my wife-to-be if I grant free passage through Israel to Egyptian goods."

I glanced at the eunuch who was tilting his hands in the elegant Egyptian manner, and I thought, if his testicles were not crushed I would crush them with my own fingers; and I bowed to the King and said that this new honour was entirely too much for me, and that I was still struggling with the previous honour he had heaped on me by making me redactor of the *Report on the Amazing Rise* and so forth. But the King raised his pudgy hand, and said, "We shall see," and turned and left with his entourage.

And Prince Adonijah the brother of the King graciously offered me a share of his piece of fattail; but I declined, thanking him.

IO

ONE NIGHT, as I slept beside Lilith, an angel of the Lord appeared in my dream who had two heads. The one head was of a benign countenance, while the other was terrible to behold, and snakes curled from its brow. The two heads fell to arguing, the kindly one saying, Let him be; haven't you clawed at him enough. But the other replied, Nay, I have done but little, and I must whip him on so that he digs to the root of things. At this the first head smiled mildly and asked, Are then the roots of things to be reached by man? Surely not, said the head that was terrible to behold, and added, Yet he must try. Whereupon both heads faded into each other and became like one, its face indifferent as only the faces of angels are. And this one head spoke unto me, Go you to Endor, Ethan ben Hoshaiah, and seek out the woman that has a familiar spirit, and enquire of her as to the end of King Saul.

I woke up stained with sweat. Lilith stirred and said sleepily, "I heard you talk there, Ethan my friend, but I failed to understand your words."

"I don't know that they were my words," I answered.

She sat up and stared at me.

I calmed her, saying, "Probably they were mine. For what are dreams but ourselves gone astray?"

Lilith dried my forehead. "My mother, may God rest her soul, told me that in our dreams live the gods that no longer are because Lord Yahveh drove them to Sheol and bound them with heavy chains: the god of thunder and the god of the forest, the god of the raging sea and the god of the desert wind that scorches your lungs; and the goddess of fertility, she of the giant womb, and the goddess of the well that springs gurgling from the rock; and all the sprites and wraiths and spooks that haunt the night; and Belial himself the whoreson of Fire and the Darkness of the Deep—all them Lord Yahveh drove out, but they come back to live in our dreams."

But I thought of the two-headed angel of the Lord, and of the woman of En-dor that people spoke of in awe, and of King Saul who asked the woman to bring up the spirit of Samuel the prophet; and from the fear in my bowels grew a thirst for life and a lust of the flesh so that I became big with love and went in unto Lilith my concubine.

There was much wonder and raising of brows among the members of the Royal Commission on the Preparation of *The One and Only True and Authoritative, Historically Correct and Officially Approved Report on the Amazing Rise* and so forth about my wanting to travel to En-dor to enquire further into the circumstances of the end of King Saul. Zadok the priest was heard to mutter that little good would come of it; Nathan the prophet stated that he is a wise man that lets sleeping dogs lie; Jehoshaphat ben Ahilud, the recorder, said that he had no appropriation for witchcraft, and would have to deduct my travel expenses from my allowance; but Benaiah ben Jehoiada offered to have me escorted by fast horsemen. I thanked Benaiah, saying that soldiers were likely to frighten people and that a frightened man was a bad source of information. Benaiah chewed thoughtfully on his lip and said, "In this kingdom, Ethan, the eyes of the law will be upon you whatever your mode of journeying."

And so, on the morrow, Shem and Sheleph helped me to saddle the little grey donkey I had hired; and after prayers, and after kissing Esther and Huldah and Lilith, I set out through the north gate towards Shiloh which is in Ephraim.

Nothing is as calming to the spirit as a leisurely donkey ride over the roads of Israel. Behind you are left the clang and the clamour of Jerusholayim. The hills move by in slow procession, covered in this month of spring with lilies and with cyclamen; the lambs peep out from under the teats of their mothers; the women of the villages stride by lithely, baskets on their heads or pitchers of oil. Here merchants transport their goods, cursing the drovers and urging them on; there pilgrims carry their poor offerings to the nearest shrine; or a hundred of the host come straggling by, the captain astride his dappled horse barking orders at them. By the wayside the beggars crouch, stretching out their hands and whining of their miseries; tellers of tales keep braying for listeners; peasants sell parched corn and soured goat's milk to the weary traveller. Ah, and the inns crowded with folk, sweating, stinking, belching their garlic and cheese. A room? A bedstead? Where do you think you are, man: in the palace of the Wisest of Kings, Solomon, where every farting son of Belial has his own suite of chambers appointed with rugs, and with cushions, and with heathenish luxuries? Why, come in and convince yourself, they're lying on the floor like fish in the basket, not a span's worth of space between them. May Lord Yahveh do to me so and so and much more of it if I can squeeze you in, man. Night is falling? And the road ahead unsafe? Why, that road has been unsafe since Abraham our forefather journeyed over it from Ur in the Chaldees, and night has been following upon day since God divided the light from the darkness, this cannot be news to you, you look wise in the ways of the world. Huh? Oh. May Lord Yahveh shed blessings on you and your wives and your children born and unborn, may your days be increased. Why did you not mention that purse in your belt? You appeared like one who has to struggle for his piece of bread and who fails to get it two days out of three. I shall kick a few of those bastards, so as to have them make room for you; there is a nice cosy place; the little black specks on the wall mean nothing, the beasts have been hit on the head and will not bite you. And later in the evening there shall be in this house a multitude of Moabite dancing girls with breasts which you cannot cup in your two hands and with buttocks that are round and firm and resilient; and all this quivers as they dance, so that men who would kill an ox with a blow of their fist have been known to faint for lust and fall to the ground. But after the dancing any of the girls you choose will join you and drink with you, and she will let you touch her so that you may see for yourself that her charms are just as Lord Yahveh created

91

them, smooth and solid. Put the little grey donkey in the rear of the stable. The price of the hay is included; you pay now, sir.

By the will of the Lord God I rode into En-dor the fifth day of my journey, having passed Shechem in Manasseh and paid homage at Joseph's tomb, and having passed En-gannin in Issachar, and gone through the Valley of Jezreel, leaving Mount Gilboa to my right, towards the rising sun, and having spent the last night in Shunam from where hails Abishag the fair damsel that ministered to King David when he was old and stricken in years and got no heat. It was a bright day, with hardly a cloud in the sky, and larks rising from the fields and turtles cooing in the thickets. And the women of En-dor stood gossiping at the cistern, the water asparkle on the bucket.

One of the women, who was buxom and dimpled, turned to me, saying, "What are you staring at, stranger? Are you a merchant trying to sell us perfume or the juice of the lice which dyes everything purple? Or are you a lecher who waits for us to bend over the rim of the cistern so he may take delight in the view?"

"Neither, kind woman," I said. "I am a poor wayfarer seeking advice and enlightenment."

"That's what they all say," commented another. "But they seek for it under your skirt."

"Looking at you," I countered, "I surely would not know what's so enlightening there. But I wish to find a wise woman who has a familiar spirit and who must be very old, if she's still alive."

"Didn't I tell you," a third said to the one that was buxom and dimpled, "a customer."

And the buxom one said, "I am the wise woman who has a familiar spirit; I inherited the trade from my mother and my mother's mother."

"Frankly, my dear," I said, "you lack the shrunken skin and yellowed teeth and wispy hair, also the warts on the nose and wens on the scalp that go with a wise woman."

"If the spirits don't care," she threw back her head saucily, "why should you?" At which she pulled the bucket towards her and filled the pitcher of clay she had with her, and walked off; but the women giggled, and gestured at me, so that I felt like a fool and asked myself if I might have misunderstood the two-headed angel of the Lord and if my journey to En-dor would prove a chase after nothing.

And as I sat on my little grey donkey, not knowing whither to turn it, behold, an old man came unto me who leaned on a staff. He said he was Shupham ben Hupham an elder of En-dor, and who was I and what was my purpose? And I told him my name and the name of my father, and that an angel of the Lord had appeared to me in my dream and had said unto me, Go you to En-dor and seek out the woman that has a familiar spirit and enquire of her; but the purpose of my enquiry I did not reveal, nor the angel's having two heads. Shupham ben Hupham clicked his tongue regretfully. There had not been such a woman in En-dor, he said, since King Saul put a ban on wizardry and on those that had a familiar spirit. To which I replied that I knew of the royal decree of King Saul and of further decrees that were decreed by King David; but that there was a long way from the royal council chamber to the huts of the poor, and that the commands of the mighty were among the people as a handful of water which is spilled onto the sand; and had not King Saul in his own person come to a wise woman at En-dor and begged her to divine unto him by her familiar spirit, because Lord Yahveh had not answered his enquiries, neither by dreams nor by the oracle of the bones, which is called Urim and Tummim, nor by prophets?

Shupham ben Hupham thought for a while; but finally he winked at me, saying, "I see from your answer, Ethan ben Hoshaiah, that you are a man of exceeding wisdom; how is it, then, that you fail to see our houses crumbling, our fields untilled, and the spindly shanks of the cattle? Don't you know that the Wisest of Kings, Solomon, has called all men that are able-bodied to serve in his host and in his construction gangs, and yet the King's governor collects the King's tithes? Therefore the elders of En-dor took counsel together and we said, The Lord our God will help those that help themselves; so why not cause strangers to journey here and spend their shekels; and what will draw strangers more surely than a woman that has a familiar spirit? Let her hours be from the

93

rise of the moon until the cock crows, and her rates two shekels a query, and no bargaining."

Thus I became the guest of Shupham ben Hupham in his house and partook of his bread and his sour wine, but by nightfall he reached for his staff and limped ahead of me to the mud hovel in which the wise woman of En-dor plied her trade. And within it I saw my buxom friend with the dimples, and she smiled at me, displaying a fine set of teeth, and saying, "So you did come; sit down on that cushion, I'll attend to you presently." But Shupham ben Hupham crouched in the corner, his staff by his side, and was silent.

And the woman put more sheep dung onto the fire. Smoke whirled up, biting the eye; but she stirred the gummy mass in her cauldron and added herbs and powders, causing bubbles to rise which burst with a slight plop; and she muttered what sounded like words but which was abracadabra, and sometimes she cried out to the spirit. I thought, may God do unto me so and so and more also: this will awe the peasants, but surely King Saul was too wise to fall for such folly. And the woman kept stirring and smiling at me, and I smiled back at her, because for a witch and a daughter of Belial her build was uncommonly handsome.

But it came to pass that the flames nearly died down, and there was only a flicker that threw immense shadows. The woman dipped a spoon into the cauldron and put some of the mass on a dish and brought it to me, saying, "Chew it well."

And I said, "What is it?"

"It's a stew," she said. "My mother stewed it, and my mother's mother before her, and it is called hasheesh."

"And it will bring on the spirits?"

"It will bring on anything you like," she said, shifting her weight so that the curve of her haunch showed against the last glow of the fire. "Take it and chew; don't let me wait here forever."

I took some of the matter from the dish and tasted it; it had a strange taste, somewhat like nuts, but with a burn to it; and it smelled spicy. And I began chewing the stuff, and its juices were rich and intoxicating, and I swallowed them.

"Take all that's on the dish," the woman said.

I followed her urging, and I felt the burden of the world

slide from my shoulders, and I knew there was no limit to my strength and that I, too, might command the spirits of the deep to rise from Sheol. And I said to the woman, "You are the angel of my dream; so why don't you get your second head?"

Though her laughter was the laughter of a daughter of Belial, it sounded agreeable to my ear; and she looked mockingly at me, saying, "Whom shall I bring up unto you?"

I said, "Bring me up King Saul."

Her face paled, and she said, "I had rather not; he is too terrible even among the shadows."

This time I laughed at her, and said, "Are you then frightened of your own trade? For I have no fear; I conjure the shadows from Sheol every day but on the sabbath, and I do it without your hasheesh."

Thereupon she faced towards the fire; and the flames rose as she raised her hands, and her robe fell off her so that she stood naked in the yellow glow, and she cried out with a loud voice.

I enquired, "What did you see?"

"I saw gods ascending out of the earth," she said, her body twisting as in pain.

"But did you see King Saul?" I queried. "What form is he of?"

"He is tall," she said hoarsely, "taller than any man, his blood-covered trunk driven through with spikes, and he carries his head in the crook of his elbow."

And it was to me as though I saw taking shape among the shadows the huge hulk of the murdered King, whose head was severed from him by the Philistines and sent into their land round about, to publish it in the house of their idols, while his body was fastened to the wall of Beth-shan. I thought of King Saul coming to this hut before his last battle, disguised and in other raiment, and saying unto the woman, Bring me up Samuel; and the ghost of Samuel rising, a gaunt old man covered with a mantle, and asking Saul, Why have you disquieted me, to bring me up; and Saul saying, I am sore distressed, for the Philistines make war against me, and God is departed from me and answers me no more, neither by prophets nor by dreams; and Samuel's hollow-voiced prophecy, The Lord will do to you as he spoke by me: the Lord will rend the kingdom out of your hand and give it to your neighbour, even to David, and tomorrow shall you and your sons be with me, and the Lord also shall deliver the host of Israel into the hand of the Philistines.

And I called out to the woman, "Bring me up Samuel."

From somewhere I heard Shupham ben Hupham saying, "This will cost you double." And the flames rose again, and the woman's face contorted with suffering and her body twitched and quivered, and the darkness beyond the flames seemed to part, and a voice quavered, "Why have you disquieted me, to bring me up?"

"Are you then the spirit of Samuel?" I said, trying to discern among the swaying shadows the apparition of the prophet.

But something seemed to have gone awry, for the face of the woman showed utter fear, and she fled towards me and crawled into my arms. And I felt yet another presence in the room, and I knew it was David the son of Jesse risen from the dead, and the ghost of David said unto the ghost of Samuel. "Have I finally found you, my fatherly friend? Why do you flee me? For I have searched the seven depths of Sheol and passed through its seven times seven hells, and was told in every one that you were just departed."

And the ghost of Samuel crossed his hands before his face as though to fend off a vision of horror, and said, "Oh son of Jesse, behold King Saul, his blood-covered trunk driven through with spikes, and carrying his head in the crook of his elbow."

"Even as I see you," the ghost of David replied, "so I see him."

"And wasn't he the Anointed of the Lord?" said the ghost of Samuel. "Yet you sent out a young man from Amalek to take his life."

"You forget, my fatherly friend," replied the ghost of David, "that I, too, came to the woman of En-dor, before that battle, and bade her to bring you up from Sheol; and you came up and answered me even as you answered Saul. I merely made sure, my fatherly friend, that your prophecy would come true."

The ghost of Samuel called out, "Was not the word of the Lord sufficient unto you, that you went out and hired an assassin and brought the blood of the Anointed of the Lord upon my head and yours?"

"You are a fine one for morals, my fatherly friend," said the ghost of David. "If the Lord willed that the kingdom be rent from Saul's hand and given to me, then the assassin I hired was a tool of the Lord, and my hiring him was in fulfilment of the Lord's will. But as to the end of King Saul, you might ask him, for he is present, his trunk driven through with spikes, and carrying his head in the crook of his elbow."

But the ghost of King Saul pointed mutely at the position of its head, as though it were trying to explain that a head could not very well speak while severed from its body. And the ghost of Samuel bowed its face and moaned pitifully, while the ghost of David kept laughing soundlessly as at a huge, secret joke, and the woman in my arms trembled and shook; and then the cock crowed.

I woke up to a pale light that fell through a narrow window and through the gaps in the thatched roof. The woman of En-dor, naked, was huddled in my arms. Shupham ben Hupham rose laboriously from his corner and limped over to me and said, palm up, "Including personal services, this will be thirty-four shekels."

97

I I

BUT THE MYSTERY of the end of King Saul and of the part played in it by David grew on me.

Esther said unto me, "What perturbs you, Ethan? Since your return from En-dor your words to me are as by rote, and you have no patience with Huldah, and Lilith goes about red-eyed."

I hesitated. But I had more wild thoughts than could forever be contained in one skull, so that I finally told Esther what I had learned from the woman that had a familiar spirit. And I said, "It looks as though I will find no peace until I have answered the questions that haunt me: is it true that David sent out this young man from Amalek to kill King Saul, and to kill Jonathan with whom he had made a covenant? And is it true that the assassin did as David bade him; and must we add to all the other blood in David's shoes the blood of Saul, and also the blood of Jonathan upon whose death David wrote:

> *I am distressed for thee, my brother Jonathan.*
> *Very pleasant hast thou been unto me:*
> *Thy love to me was wonderful,*
> *Passing the love of women . . ."*

"And what would it help if you had the answers?" said Esther. "Could you write them into the King David Report or into any other book?"

"Not very well. But *I* must know. I must know about

the man David. Was he as an animal that strikes indifferently? Or was there within him a vision which he pursued, whatever the cost? Or is all our effort but vanity, and are even the greatest among us as grains of sand, buffeted about by the winds of time?"

"Poor man," said Esther.

"David?" I enquired.

"No, you." And she kissed my eyes.

I went to the house of Jehoshaphat ben Ahilud, the recorder, which was in the upper town near the site of the construction of the temple, and asked to be heard.

A servant took me into the presence of Jehoshaphat, who said he was glad to see me looking so well, and had my journey to En-dor been fruitful?

"My lord," I said, "it is with the search into history as with the march of the children of Israel through the desert: you climb one dune of sand to discover another looming before you."

"But the march did end, and standing on top of Mount Nebo Moishe our Leader did see lying before him the promised land with its rivers and fields and vineyards and villages."

"The words of my lord are as balm to your servant. Yet I often feel as though we were stumbling in circles."

The face of Jehoshaphat clouded. "Perhaps you stumble in circles, Ethan, because you stray in too many directions?"

"If I do stray, my lord, it is because lips that could advise me are sealed. Also King David was a man of many facets requiring research in many directions."

"King David was of a single mind," stated Jehoshaphat. "In all the years that I knew him he strove to please the Lord by building this realm."

I bowed, saying that this was what should be stressed in the King David Report; but that there were certain doubts and confusions which might mar the great picture, and which should be untangled so as to avert later misunderstandings.

"Doubts and confusions?" Jehoshaphat peered at me from narrowed eyes. "As to what?"

99

"As to the end of King Saul and the part played in it by David."

I recalled men who for saying less than this had ended with their heads cut off and their bodies nailed to the city wall, and I thought of my loved ones who would be left without their provider.

Jehoshaphat smiled. "And what is doubtful about the end of King Saul?"

"To my lord, possibly nothing. My lord has seen with his own eyes and heard with his own ears, and does not depend on the words of other people."

"You forget, Ethan, that I joined the councils of King David long after Saul was dead."

"And are there no witnesses," I enquired, "who might be commanded to appear before the Royal Commission on the Preparation of *The One and Only True and Authoritative, Historically Correct and Officially Approved Report on the Amazing Rise* and so forth, as Jorai, Jachan, and Meshullam were called, the licensed tellers of tales and legends?"

"There is a witness," admitted Jehoshaphat, "Joab the son of David's sister Zeruiah, who was David's captain of the host; I suspect, however, we shall learn but little from him, for a deathly fear is shaking him all his day, and he has turned into a gibbering idiot."

"And if I went to Joab and spoke with him in the privacy of his four walls?"

"I should not recommend it." Jehoshaphat spread his hands. "You do not want to tangle with Benaiah ben Jehoiada, whose eyes are on Joab. Perhaps you may find enlightenment at less risk in the files of Seraiah the scribe of King David, which are kept in the royal archives."

So I thanked Jehoshaphat ben Ahilud, the recorder, for his good advice and his patience. I was but an undeserving dog, I said, who had basked in the favour of my lord and who was now slinking off.

On the morrow I betook myself to the royal archives, which were kept in a stable built for the horses of King Solomon. There I found Elihoreph and Ahiah the scribes, who sat at a table, throwing dice. Ahiah had before him a heap of shekels, and several rings, and a bracelet, and a pair of fine sandals of Egyptian leather, and a robe of linen of byssus; but Elihoreph sat in his shirt.

And Elihoreph spoke unto the dice, "Ah, you first cousins of Urim and Tummim the oracle, you bones of bliss and happiness, why have you forsaken me? Look at Ahiah, my angels, look at the riches amassed by him who is but a sore on the face of mankind, an idler wasting the King's time! Why do you not fall in a manner pleasing to Yahveh; why do you follow a pattern chosen by Belial the lord of evil? Come now, you darlings, do not fail me. Do not slay me as Cain slew Abel, but show yourselves in your true noble nature: the aid of the poor and the stave of the downtrodden. I shall prove my trust in you, my sweet ones: I shall wager my shirt which is the last thing I own. Do not cause me to walk the streets of Jerusholayim in my nakedness, a laughing-stock to the maidens of Israel and an annoyance to its beldames. Shed your luck over me; give me a three, or a seven, or a twelve!"

And Elihoreph ben Shisha cupped his hands about the dice and shook them, while his eyes swept up unto Lord Yahveh the creator of the world and all which is contained therein. Then he threw the dice. They showed a two and a four. Elihoreph hammered his head. He cursed the sun that shone upon him, and his father who begot him, and the mangy ram from whose horn the dice were cut; Ahiah his brother however, who had not moved as much as a muscle on his face, stretched out his hand and said, "Your shirt."

But I took pity on Elihoreph. I told Ahiah that I was come at the suggestion of Jehoshaphat ben Ahilud, the recorder, to find certain files and records, and I would need his help and that of his brother, who could not very well go searching in the nude.

Ahiah tossed shirt and sandals to his brother. Then he shook his head, saying he was amazed at Jehoshaphat. Didn't the recorder know that the archives were in the state of tohubohu, so that no one could find anything? And he pointed to stalls in which piles of tablets of clay were stacked up every which way, and to other stalls in which countless rolls of leather lay in disarray. "And this is nothing," he added, "you should have seen the royal archives when they were kept in a barn, with the sand blowing and the rain raining on the scriptures."

I began to wonder if Jehoshaphat had not sent me on a fool's errand, and I enquired of Ahiah and Elihoreph if they knew of any files of Seraiah the scribe of King David, and where they might be located.

Both said they had heard of such files; and Elihoreph said he thought they were in the third stall of the first row, on the left side; but Ahiah said he thought they were in the sixteenth stall of the third row, on the right side; and the two fell to quarrelling.

I said, "Is there not a listing of books and of files that are kept in the archives?"

Both agreed that such a listing was desirable; and Ahiah said he had heard that one was to be compiled when the archives were housed permanently in the upper storey of the great temple which the Wisest of Kings, Solomon, was erecting; but Elihoreph said that man proposes, while the Lord disposes, and wait till that new batch of horses was brought for the King from Egypt and was stabled in these stables; and the two fell to quarrelling.

But I suggested that we begin searching for the files of Seraiah the scribe of King David; and Elihoreph and Ahiah bestirred themselves and followed me, Elihoreph selecting the first row of stalls, on the left side, and Ahiah the third row, on the right side, and I chose the second row, which was in the middle. And we dug among the tablets of clay and among the rolls of leather; and it came to pass that a pillar of dust rose and went before us as did the pillar of cloud that went before the children of Israel on their long march out of Egypt and through the wilderness. But while the children of Israel, after much shifting and turning, did reach the land which the Lord had promised them, neither Elihoreph and Ahiah nor I succeeded in finding the files of Seraiah. And as our knees trembled and our arms ached, and we were covered with sweat and with dirt and cobwebs, we ceased searching, and Elihoreph coughed greatly and said, "May God do so to me and more also if I will ever again touch one tablet of clay in these archives," and Ahiah added, "Amen."

"If my lords will forgive the words of your servant," I replied, "I am as tired and bedraggled as either of you, and have two wives to tend to and a concubine that wants satisfying. But in the service of the Wisest of Kings, Solomon, and of history, I know neither fatigue nor weariness, and with my lords' permission I shall return another day, even with two slaves that are skilled in the use of the aleph-beth-gimmel and in deciphering various scripts."

Ahiah said, "He whom the devil itches will rub off his skin." And Elihoreph appended gloomily, "You had better search soon, Ethan; for else you might find us encamped in the fields, the royal archives a prey to birds and mice and to the vicious red ants."

But I returned to No. 54, Queen-of-Sheba Lane, to have myself bathed and massaged by Lilith and to eat a piece of bread with olives and onions in the company of Esther.

"You plan to go out again?" she asked.

"I must," I answered. "I must see Joab ben Zeruiah, who was over the host in David's time, to enquire from him about the end of King Saul, and if David also had Jonathan murdered with whom he had made a covenant."

Esther pressed her hand to her heart. "There is a temptress you will always follow: her name is Truth the daughter of Fate."

"Is that ache in your chest very bad," I said miserably, "and can I do nothing to relieve it?"

She shook her head.

And I arose and went, passing through the south gate and through the gardens beyond the gate, until I came to a house that was built of bricks of various colours. A Pelethite stood guard at its door, and he lowered his spear at me, saying, "You aren't a peddlar trying to sell his wares, for you carry no tray, nor are you a peasant that brings vegetables, or eggs, or sweet grapes. So you had better explain yourself credibly, since the eyes of Benaiah ben Jehoiada, the captain of the host, are on this house."

"Blessings on you, young man," I replied, "for your sharp mind has discerned that I am neither a peddlar trying to sell his wares nor a peasant bringing his produce; yet I wager five shekels against your one that you will never guess who I am."

"Agreed," said the Pelethite, and grinned at me. "You are

Ethan ben Hoshaiah, and redactor, whatever that is, of *The One and Only True and Authoritative, Historically Correct and Officially Approved Report on the Amazing Rise* and so forth, and my lord Benaiah has commanded me to let you in, if you insist, but not to let you out."

I paid my five shekels to the Pelethite, and I would have turned and run but for the voice speaking within me, saying, You have put your head in the noose, Ethan; you might as well be hanged for the whole thing.

Wherefore I entered the house and found a rheumy-eyed, weak-kneed old man who stooped in the half-light of a corner, his hands atremble, his beard awry, his scalp scurfy. "Is that you, Joab," I called, "who was over the host?"

The man stirred slightly and said, "I am he."

I stared at him, not wanting to believe that this was the hero who stormed impregnable Jerusholayim, which could be defended by the lame and the blind; who smote Syria, and Moab, and Ammon, and Amalek, and the Kings of the Philistines, and Hadadezer King of Zobah; and who slew Abner who was over the host under King Saul and also Absalom the son of David.

Joab said, "Have you come from Benaiah so as to torture me further?" And he shrank into himself, whimpering like a sick child.

"I am Ethan ben Hoshaiah," I answered, "an author and historian; and I have come on my own to enquire from you concerning certain points that are unclear to me."

"How will I know," said Joab, "that you have not come from Benaiah, and that my words will not be turned against me, so that my head may be impaled on a stake and my body fastened to the wall of Jerusholayim, which I took from the Jebusites and handed to King David?"

"You once were among the mighty of the kingdom," I replied, "and among those who decided if a man was to be put to death or allowed to live out his days in peace. But I decide how a man lives on after he is dead, in the eyes of the generations to come, and if a thousand years hence he is viewed as a frightened dotard, spittle running into his beard, or as a soldier facing his fate with dignity and with courage."

Joab's hands ceased trembling. He rose and came towards me, enwrapped in his stench, and said, "I always was a soldier, and have done what I was commanded. But then I learned that King David cursed me on his deathbed and said unto Solomon, Do therefore unto Joab according to your wisdom, and let not his hoar head go down to the grave in peace. Imagine the man damning me for the murder of Absalom his son, and of Abner ben Ner, and of others, all of whom I killed on his behalf. Oh, he never killed; there is no blood upon the girdle that was about his loins and in the shoes that were on his feet. He killed by proxy."

"Did David also have King Saul assassinated," I asked, "and Jonathan, with whom he had made a covenant?"

Joab scratched his filthy beard. "You draw your own conclusions. I can only tell you what I saw and heard. On the third day after David returned to Ziklag, this young man came with his clothes rent, and earth upon his head; and he cried that the host of Israel were fled from the battle and many of them fallen and dead, and Saul and Jonathan were dead also. David was standing among his followers, and he said unto him, Did you see with your own eyes that Saul and Jonathan be dead? And the young man answered, My lord knows that I am your loyal servant and beholden to you, and that I speak the truth. As I happened to come on Mount Gilboa, I espied Saul leaning on his spear, and the chariots and horsemen followed hard after him. He noticed me, and he called unto me, Who are you? I answered, I am an Amalekite. He said unto me, Slay me, I pray you, for anguish is come upon me, because my life is yet whole in me. So I slew him; and I took the crown that was on his head, and the bracelet that was on his arm, and have brought them hither unto my lord; and may my lord reward me according to my deserts."

"And what did David do?" I said.

"He took the crown and the bracelet," said Joab, "and did some lamenting about Saul, and about Jonathan, and then he turned upon the young man from Amalek, saying, How were you not afraid to stretch forth your hand to destroy the Lord's Anointed? And as the young man paled and stammered disjointed words, David told him, Your blood be on your head, for your own mouth has testified against you. And he commanded one of his companions to fall upon the young man from Amalek and smite him."

And a shudder befell me as I saw that the familiar spirit of the woman of En-dor had spoken the truth about the death of King Saul and David's share therein, and I said to Joab, "So it would seem that the blood of King Saul is in the shoes of David?"

But before Joab could reply to me, voices sounded, and heavy steps. Immediately Joab recoiled; his hands shook and his mouth began to slaver. And Benaiah ben Jehoiada came striding into the room and spoke to Joab, "Up to your old wiles, eh?" And turning to me, "Has he been telling you that hoary tale about the young man from Amalek?"

At this Joab prostrated himself before Benaiah and slobbered over his feet. But Benaiah booted him in the arse, so that Joab came to lie sprawling in the corner. "Behold," said Benaiah, "this man once held in his hands the power of the kingdom. And you, Ethan, with your fine mind and your words which have more than one meaning, what did you enquire from this pile of putrescence?"

I bowed my face and stayed silent.

"Don't be stubborn," said Benaiah, "or shall I obtain the answer from Joab?"

"I enquired from him as to the end of King Saul," I said, "and of Jonathan with whom David had made a covenant."

"Joab," said Benaiah, "come here."

Joab came crawling.

"Tell us as to the end of King Saul," said Benaiah, "and who it was that slew him and Jonathan."

"The Philistines slew Jonathan, and Abinadab, and Melchi-shua, Saul's sons," said Joab meekly, "and the battle went sore against Saul, and the archers hit him. Then said Saul unto his armourbearer, Draw your sword and thrust me through therewith, lest these uncircumcised come upon me and thrust me through and abuse me. But his armourbearer would not; so Saul took his own sword and fell upon it. And when his armourbearer saw that Saul was dead, he fell likewise upon his sword, and died with him."

"And how do you know that this was so?" asked Benaiah.

"A captain of Philistine archers," said Joab, "whom I later took prisoner and questioned, he swore unto me by all his gods that he saw it happen, and he also saw a young man spring forth from the brush and snatch the crown of King

Saul and his bracelet and scurry off with them before the Philistine archers could descend unto the dead king."

"So it would seem," said Benaiah, "that neither the blood of King Saul nor that of Jonathan is in the shoes of David."

"And isn't that a joke," said Joab.

At this, Benaiah raised his fist and smashed it across Joab's face so that he bled from the mouth and fell to the ground. But I bowed myself and thanked Benaiah for the great help he had given me in obtaining the truth about the end of the King Saul and of Jonathan with whom David had made a covenant. Benaiah looked at me with eyes that were as lead, and I prayed unto the Lord that he might make this moment pass. And the Lord heard me, for Benaiah began to chuckle, and his elbow hit my ribs, causing me to gasp, and he said, "If you know as much as I think you know, Ethan, I think you know too much."

12

Praised be the name of the Lord our God who blesses the seekers after his truth and who provides the blind chicken with a grain of corn also.

On the sixth day of our search through the stables of the King, in which were kept the royal archives, the two slaves that were skilled in the use of the aleph-beth-gimmel and in deciphering the various scripts cried out unto me jubilantly. And as I hurried to their side I saw under a heap of rubbish a cracked earthen jar, and about it lay a mess of potsherds and of tablets that were partially broken or nicked. Most of the tablets were written in the manner of the scribes of the house of Judah, at the time when David was King in Hebron; but the potsherds and a few tablets were written in various hands: some in the manner of the scribes of Ephraim, and some, of those of Benjamin.

At first I dared not believe that I might have before me the files of Seraiah the scribe of King David for seven years in Hebron and for twenty-three in Jerusholayim. Therefore I called out loud for Elihoreph and his brother Ahiah, and they came running, and I enquired from them whither the old jar.

Elihoreph picked up a potsherd and gazed at it emptily, and Ahiah said he had never before seen this jar, and he suspected that it got there by magic. At which Elihoreph dropped the potsherd in his hand as though it were burning him, and exclaimed, "God do to me so and so if I will have the jar and all that pertains to it even one more night in these stables."

It being the sixth day, and the eve of sabbath approaching, the two slaves and I scooped potsherds and tablets into several bags; these we carted to No. 54, Queen-of-Sheba Lane, arriving just as the sun sank beyond the western wall of the city.

And Esther blessed the light in the lamp, and the house in which the lamp stood, and all who dwelled in the house; and she looked young to me and beautiful as I gazed on her with love; but I also was impatient for the sabbath to pass, so that I might open the bags and sort out my find.

Now I, Ethan ben Hoshaiah, have selected such documents from the files of Seraiah as pertain to the history and the spirit of the man, David. Where a tablet, or potsherd, was damaged and the missing part or parts could not be restored despite the most diligent effort, I have left the text in its fragmentary form. Any annotations, queries and so forth are mine.

The files at hand cover the period from David's moving on Hebron, there to become King of Judah, up to and including his conspiring with Abner ben Ner, and with others, to overthrow the one remaining son of Saul, Ish-bosheth, who was King of Israel at Mahanaim. Later events were doubtless recorded with equal care by Seraiah, and correspondence relative to them collected; but the containers holding these scriptures are either stored elsewhere, to await their discoverer, or they are lost, which God may prevent.

DAVID SPEAKS UNTO SERAIAH

David spoke unto me, "Seraiah, behold these men that have come to Ziklag for no ostensible purpose, and who look about what each of us may be doing, and if a spear be sharpened or a sword hammered. Surely they are spies from Achish the King of Gath my liege-lord, or from the other kings of the Philistines, who distrust me. And well they may, for matters are unsettled among the children of Israel and fraught with possibilities. On the one side is Abner ben Ner with the remnants of the host that fled from the mountains of Gilboa; Abner has gathered these about Mahanaim, east of the river Jordan, among the tribe Gad, and he has made Ish-bosheth King of Israel, Saul's last surviving son. And on the other am I, David ben Jesse, still sitting in Ziklag with nearly a thousand well-armed men. But between me and Abner, in the mountains west of Jordan, even up to Dan, there are no armed forces and no authorities, so that he who first moves into these lands may pluck a kingdom into his hand."

"God willing," I said, "and all things being favourable."

Thereupon David said, "Go, and have a male of the sheep brought to me that is without blemish, and call Abiathar the priest, and tell him to wash his filthy hands, for I want him to sacrifice unto the Lord."

I did as I was commanded, and returned to David, who was washing himself, and oiling his skin, and putting on fresh raiment. And he followed Abiathar the priest to the tabernacle, and Abiathar slit the sheep's throat. As the steam of the blood rose unto Lord Yahveh, David spoke to God, saying, "Oh Lord, you took me from the sheepcote; you ...

(Here the tablet breaks off. Thus we are deprived of the main part of Seraiah's account of David's parley with God. And David marched on Hebron, and there the elders of Judah anointed him King.

But why did the victorious Philistine princes fail to restrain David from establishing his rule in Hebron? The answer seems to be that by splitting Judah from Israel David played into their hands. And when Judah and Israel fell to warring upon one another, the Philistines could well afford to hold aloof.

The consistency with which David pursued this war evidences itself in his dispute with Joab, as noted down by Seraiah. The dispute must have occurred some time after the well-known bloodbath at the pool of Gibeon, where the men of Ish-bosheth, led by Abner ben Ner, encountered a troop of David's men that were headed by Joab, and each named twelve champions, who caught every one his fellow by the head and thrust his sword in his fellow's side; whereupon there was sore battle that day, and the men of Ish-bosheth were beaten by the men of David and fled; but Asahel Joab's brother pursued after Abner, and Abner with the hinder end of his spear smote Asahel under the fifth rib, so that the spear came out behind him and he fell down there and died; by nightfall however, when Abner called out to Joab with words of sweet reason, Joab blew a trumpet, and all his people stood still and pursued after the men of Ish-bosheth no more.)

ON UNITY AND DISUNITY

...so you concluded a truce with Abner. By what right? by whose authority? was there an angel of the Lord that commanded you? There you had Abner; you only needed to close the ring about him, and he and Ish-bosheth the son of Saul would have been finished; but you had to go and blow your cursed trumpet.

May it please my lord and brother of Zeruiah my mother: as I saw them stand on the hill of Ammah, I heard a voice calling me, saying, Behold, Joab, the flesh of your flesh and blood of your blood; are not they children of Israel quite as you are and your men?

Was that before Abner called you or after?

Before, my lord, before.

Then it surely was the voice of Belial, which you did not recognise because your brain is the size of a bird's.

But are not the children of Israel of one seed? is not unity better than disunity, is not the tree stronger than its branches?

You think as a man of yesterday, Joab. Before there can be unity, there must be disunity; before a new tree can grow, the old must be felled and its roots burned out. Did not Samuel the seer anoint me? Did not Yahveh choose me to be King over Israel, over all of Israel?

My lord the King speaks right. I shall avenge the blood of my brother Asahel, whom Abner smote with the hinder end of his spear.

Again you look at things emotionally, Joab. Thus you fail to see that our time is a time of vast changes, in which all that exists is turned upside-down and great kingdoms arise, so that people will no longer live as they please and go wherever their fancy tells them, but will work under firm rule, and under a new law. And you either will think in this way, Joab, and conduct yourself accordingly, or you will be cast out onto the rubbish heap of history.

As the Lord lives, and as my soul lives, I do not wish to be cast onto the rubbish heap of history. I am a soldier and...

(All search for the part of the tablet containing the conclusion of the dispute between David King of Judah in Hebron and Joab the captain of his host proved in vain. I doubt, though, that Joab fully understood the mind of his mother's youngest brother.)

AN INTERMEDIARY REPORT

...now there was long war between the house of Saul and the house of David: but David waxed stronger and stronger, and the house of Saul waxed weaker and weaker...

HOW TO WIN FRIENDS AND INFLUENCE PEOPLE

...came unto Hebron two strangers of sinister mien, and of uncertain business, and were apprehended by the messengers of Joab, and brought before King David. And David said, Who are you? They answered, We be Baanah and Rechab the sons of Rimmon a Beerothite, and captains of bands in the service of Ish-bosheth the son of Saul, at Mahanaim. And David said, Why have you come to Hebron, if not for mischief? But Baanah and Rechab prostrated themselves before David and cried, May God do unto us so and so if we have not come for the noblest reasons and for purposes pleasing to the eye of the Lord, even to offer our lives and the strength of our swords to David ben Jesse who was anointed to be King over Israel.

Whereupon David bade Baanah and Rechab to rise, and asked, How do you propose to employ your lives and the strength of your swords in my service? And Baanah said there was nothing they would not do, and Rechab added, At a reasonable fee. David enquired, was not King Ish-bosheth paying them reasonably well? So Baanah spat, and said, Can you press oil from a stone, or perfume from a goat's droppings? And Rechab added, Why, my lord, this son of Saul has hardly wherewith to cover the feebleness of his privates; he has mortgaged his soul to the lenders of money, and all that pertains to him would fit on a donkey's back.

But David said, Return you unto Mahanaim, and stay there with your bands, and follow for the present the commands of Ish-bosheth and of Abner ben Ner; but report to me all that is worth knowing, and all that concerns Michal my wife who was given by King Saul to Phalti the son of Laish. And you shall be rewarded according to your deserts.

And David ordered Baanah and Rechab b'nai Rimmon to be escorted beyond the gates of Hebron and to be set loose...

(Some of the following was written with brush and ink on potsherds. By the haphazard manner in which these invaluable documents were stored much of the writing was damaged.)

SCANDAL IN MAHANAIM

To David ben Jesse, the Anointed of the Lord, the Lion of Judah, from Baanah and Rechab b'nai Rimmon.

May Yahveh cause your seed to be as numerous and brilliant as the stars over Hebron. This is the latest, and from usually trustworthy sources...

...Abner has made himself strong for the house of Saul...

...and he goes in unto Rizpah, who was Saul's concubine and has borne him two sons. But Ish-bosheth is much wrought-up, for who goes in unto a king's woman claims the King's place. Ish-bosheth drank of sweet wine spiced with cinnamon, and chewed of the weed that is called hasheesh, so that his head swelled with courage; and he spoke unto Abner, Wherefore have you gone in unto my father's concubine? are there not women enough among the daughters of Ephraim or Manasseh or Benjamin for you? or is this your way of preparing yourself to be King in Israel?...

...was Abner very wroth for the words of Ish-bosheth, and he said, Am I a flea-bitten dog that you charge me today with a fault concerning this woman? I could have delivered you into the hands of David, but I have shown kindness to you up to this day...

...I have made one king, I can make two as well...

...so do God to me, and more also, if I do not do as the Lord has sworn to David, and translate the kingdom from the house of Saul, and set up the throne of David over Israel and over Judah, from Dan even to Beer-sheba...

...and Ish-bosheth could not answer Abner a word again, because he was as a skin drained of the wine within, limp and unshapely, and he feared Abner...

TRANSCRIPT

From Beraiah scribe to King David, to Baanah and Rechab b'nai Rimmon, loyal servants of King Ish-bosheth.

May Yahveh provide you with strength for the good work. My lord, the King, has received your report, and he wishes you to continue in this useful manner. But have you no word about Michal the daughter of Saul who was espoused to my lord, the King, for a hundred foreskins of the Philistines? Also you have been credited by the royal treasury at Hebron with a hundred head of cattle each: twenty milk kine, and forty sheep, and goats to the number of forty. For which you will...

(The remainder of the writing on this potsherd was washed out. We may presume, however, that David would not pay a total of two hundred head of cattle for any trifling service.)

THE MAKING OF A LEAGUE

To King David, the Slayer of Goliath and Beloved of the Lord, from Abner ben Ner, Captain of the Host.

May Yahveh multiply the seed of your loin, may your days bring you success and your nights be the source of joy. Now this is my proposal...

...for is not unity better than disunity, and the tree stronger than its branches? And has not the Lord caused you to wax strong, and me to wax strong, so that his word may be fulfilled? There should be one king over both Israel and Judah, and one captain over their combined host...

...make your league with me and I will translate the

kingdom from the house of Saul unto you...

...my lord agreeing, I shall ride unto Hebron with
twenty armed horsemen, and I shall blow my trumpet
before your gate as a signal of peace, three times, and after
your answering trumpet, three times again...

MICHAL PINING AWAY

To David ben Jesse, King in Judah, the Wisest among
men, the Kindliest of lords, the Most Generous of princes,
from Baanah and Rechab b'nai Rimmon.

May Yahveh cause the ranks of your enemies to dwindle
and the host of your friends to increase like fish in the sea.
Michal is weeping from sunrise to sundown and pining
away for you. But Phalti is hopping about like a young
he-goat, and fondling her, and cockdandling her, so that
the poor woman does not know where to turn and succumbs
to him with tears and with moans and with sighing. Also she
has taken unto herself the five sons of her sister Merab,
who are counted as sons of Saul in the next generation:
for Merab has died and they are motherless.

Now concerning the credit our lord has graciously
established for us with the treasury at Hebron: who would
not labour freely to the end that Yahveh's words be fulfilled? But we are without riches, and we must feed and
clothe our young men and keep them well armed; so that
two hundred head of cattle, or their equivalent in shekels
of silver, are as a mouthful of sand to a man dying of thirst.
But King David has waxed strong, and even a thousand
head of cattle or two thousand mean little to him...

TRANSCRIPT

From King David to Abner ben Ner, Captain of the
Host.

I will make a league with you: but one thing I require
of you, that is, You shall not see my face except you first
bring Michal Saul's daughter, when you come to see my
face.

TRANSCRIPT

To Ish-bosheth, King of Israel at Mahanaim, my beloved
brother-in-law, from David ben Jesse.

May Yahveh shed his blessing over you and grant you
health, and riches, and issue to your loins. Deliver me my
wife Michal, which I espoused to me for a hundred foreskins of the Philistines, but which Saul your father gave
unto...

(It is noteworthy that by this time David felt sufficiently
powerful to issue orders to Ish-bosheth his fellow king. And
Ish-bosheth's situation, whether he knew it or not, was indeed
desperate: without resources of his own, his tribal support
uncertain, his house infiltrated by spies, his own captain
of the host bargaining with David, he faced a resolute
opponent who seemed to be visibly favoured by the hand of
the Lord.)

THE DEALINGS OF ABNER BEN NER

To King David ben Jesse, the Star of Judah which is
rising to the summit of the sky, the Chosen of Yahveh,
from Baanah and Rechab b'nai Rimmon.

May Yahveh cause all your plans to come to fruition.
Ish-bosheth has sent, and he has taken Michal his sister
from Phalti. And Abner had secret communication with
the elders of Israel, and he also spoke in the ears of the tribe
of Benjamin, saying, You sought for David in times past to
be king over you: now then do it; for the Lord has spoken
of David and has said, *By the hand of my servant David
I will save my people Israel out of the hand of the
Philistines, and out of the hand of all their enemies...*

(Here the tablet breaks off. On another tablet, written
in the same script, the message of Baanah and Rechab is
continued in part.)

...but Abner went to King Ish-bosheth and told him,
Behold, we are sore afflicted, and our men starving and
marauding in the land; and many have gone back to their
huts and their families. Therefore we must make a truce,
and a covenant, with David the King in Hebron, so that
we may fight him another day. I will go to him with twenty
horsemen, and with a trumpet that shall blow three
times...

...and deal with David...

...but Ish-bosheth had us called unto his house where he sits between two Cherubim made of wood and painted yellow, for he has no gold. And Ish-bosheth said to us, I know that you and your bands are loyal servants of the house of my father Saul, and that you will do what is pleasing in the eye of the Lord. Now Abner will go to Hebron with twenty horsemen and with Michal my sister whom I took from Phalti; and he will make a truce with David, and a covenant, so that we may fight him another day. But God do unto me so and more also, if Abner be not planning to betray me to the son of Jesse; for we had ill words over his going in unto Rizpah my father's concubine, and he threatened to set up the throne of David over Israel and over Judah, from Dan even to Beer-sheba; he thinks I forgot; but I remember all that is said, for I am as wise as Abner any day of the week. Therefore, now, Baanah and Rechab, I charge you to ride after Abner with your bands, and to fall upon him, and smite him under the fifth rib, and bring me his head; after which I shall make you captain of the host and assign to you the tithes of the tribe of Ephraim; but Michal my sister you will return to me unharmed. Furthermore...

(There is in the files of Seraiah one last potsherd of importance to us. Both script and contents show that it was sent by Baanah and Rechab.)

...as to crediting us at the royal treasury in Hebron with three hundred and fifty head of cattle each: ninety milk kine, ten bullocks, a hundred and twenty-five sheep and a hundred and twenty-five goats, or their equivalent in shekels, we accept; and our hearts bleed at the penury of the son of Jesse which keeps him from rewarding us according to our full deserts.

It is not part of my duties to label people as good or bad. I collect, I order, I organise, a minor servant in the house of knowledge; I interpret, trying to outline the shape of things and to chart their drift. But words have their own life: you cannot trap them or hold them or rein them in, they are of many hues, they both conceal and reveal, and behind each line that is written lurks danger.

Lord, our God, why of all your sons have you chosen me to awaken the dead King from his grave! He grows on me as I learn about him; he is unto me like an excrescence, a canker which I should burn out but cannot.

13

JOAB WOULD HAVE TO know what occurred when Abner ben Ner came to see the face of David. But the lips of Joab, I fear, will not open to me a second time; nor dare I visit his house without the consent of Benaiah, to whom I am suspect.

Thus, again, I am left with the Princess Michal. She journeyed with Abner from Mahanaim to Hebron; she should have some recollection of that which followed there. But Michal has not sent for me, as she was wont to do, and who am I to request to see the face of the daughter of one king and twice the wife of another?

Finally I wrote to Amenhoteph, wishing him long life and riches, and asking for a few moments of his valuable time. And Amenhoteph sent back, saying that on the third day, at the hour of noon, he would have a piece of bread and a drop of wine at a certain place which was administered by the royal overseer of guest houses for such men as were working in the fields of art, even for singers and tellers of tales and legends, and for those who pluck away on the psalteries and who blow the horn, and for builders of tabernacles and layers of mosaics, and for writers of discourses on how to sing and tell tales and play the psaltery and blow the horn and build tabernacles and lay mosaics.

As I came there on the third day, at the hour of noon, I was led into a fairly large hall in which milled about a great number of people, all trying to reach the spit on which a greasy cook turned an ancient ram; and those who succeeded in tearing a morsel of flesh from the carcass were hustled by those that were empty handed, and there were curses and outcries. But in the thick of the struggle I saw Jorai, Jachan, and Meshullam, the tellers of the story of the Great Fight of David Versus Goliath. They were each wielding a bone with a few scraps of tendon on it, indiscriminately battering all skulls within reach; but upon their seeing me, they came rushing unto me, calling out loud, "Pray, sir, bear witness for us unto these gluttonous sons of Belial that we were summoned as specialists before the Royal Commission on the Preparation of *The One and Only True and Authoritative, Historically Correct and Officially Approved Report on the Amazing Rise* and so forth, and that we are therefore entitled to partake in the bounty of the Lord which is being turned on the spit; for certain persons in this tavern who are of high brow but of low and envious character deny us artistic recognition, so that we were given but these old bones which are leftovers from yesterday."

I confirmed that Jorai, Jachan, and Meshullam had indeed been summoned before the Royal Commission, and there had recited the story of the Great Fight of David Versus Goliath, their text agreeing to the word, so that my lord Nathan the prophet had called it a miracle.

Whereupon Jorai, Jachan, and Meshullam proclaimed, "Oh, you learned men with your gentle voices and your fine manners, who wish to refuse to the simple singers of folk tales even a morsel from the bounty of the Lord, behold, we are workers of miracles! And the time will come when Yahveh casts you out from the fleshpots, and when the shekels of the King will flow into our purses: for your elaborate words, your fancy images, your studied art avail but little unless you know how to agree on your text and to please such mighty men as Nathan the prophet."

At which the awed crowd gave way, and Jorai, Jachan, and Meshullam proceeded towards the spit. They tore from the ram its fattail and a hunk of loin, and returned unto me with their booty, to squat at my feet and chew and smack and swallow.

But it came to pass that two runners arrived, crying, "Move, you bastards! Make room there, you worthless scum, you intellectual timeservers, for the mighty and noble Amen-

120

hoteph the royal chief eunuch, who is over the wives of the King and over his concubines and over the widows of the King's father!"

And everybody bowed their faces to the ground, and some prostrated themselves in the dust among the bones and the offal. Amenhoteph entered in splendour. He was greeted by the chief servant, and he crossed the hall and passed by the spit, raising the delicate hem of his coloured robe and shaking his stiffly coiffed head at the vulgar customs of the children of Israel and at the stench that wafted from the mangled corpse of the ram; but to me he waved graciously and invited me to follow him. Thus we were seated in a separate chamber with a view on a shady garden, before us a table laden with dishes that were filled with all kinds of delight, even pickled young onions, and fresh leeks, and tender anchovies, and mushrooms preserved in vinegar, and also the chef's special: lamb's eyes staring up from a semi-transparent jelly which the Egyptians call aspic. At the chief servant's clapping his hands, several young maidservants entered. These were naked to the waist, their breasts bobbing most prettily as they came unto us and placed before us a soup which was made of the flesh of the turtle, and a very fine white wine from the vineyards of the King at Baal-hamon, and squabs basted with oil and baked in vine leaves, and melons cooled in the depths of the cistern, and apple with cheeses, and a small cup of sweet brown wine that is obtained from dried grapes.

Amenhoteph the royal chief eunuch wiped his lips with a piece of linen of byssus, and said unto me, "That was a good meal, wasn't it, Ethan?"

I agreed, saying that I enjoyed it greatly, and that I never expected to find such service and excellent cooking in an establishment administered by the royal overseer of guest houses.

But Amenhoteph, waxing philosophical, replied, "This goes to prove, Ethan, that not everything which is done by the servants of the government need be shoddy, and of low quality, and witless. If you know the chief servant, and grease his hand with the necessary shekels, you will partake of the finest, and you will be treated in a manner pleasing to the eye of Yahveh your god. But if you rely on the people's love to the King or on their eagerness for the good cause, you will

121

be served late if ever, and you will find grit in your soup and hairs in your sausage."

"Your words fill me with sadness," I said, sipping of the sweet brown wine that was made from dried grapes, "for is there not the law, and the word of the Lord, and the teachings of the wise men and of the judges and prophets which people must follow?"

But Amenhoteph gazed at me from between painted eyelids and said, "Truly, Ethan, you amaze me. Being a student of events past and present, have you not noticed that the mind of man is strangely split in two, as is his tongue? We seem to be living in two worlds: one that is described in the teachings of the wise men and judges and prophets, and another which nobody speaks of but which is real; one that is fenced in by law and by the word of your god Yahveh, and another whose laws are written nowhere but followed by everybody. And praised be that split of the mind, because it enables a person to do what is necessary by the laws of the real world and yet believe in the teachings of the wise men and judges and prophets; and only those will end in despair who, seeing the cleavage, take it upon themselves to make reality fit the doctrine. For there is no way back to the garden of Eden, of which I have read in your books, and you cannot make undone the sin of your forefather who ate of the fruit of the tree of knowledge of good and evil; but people have learned to live with the knowledge."

"Your servant is awed by the power of your reasoning," I said. "Also you have touched on the heart of the matter concerning my work on the King David Report: I, too, am constantly of a split mind, knowing one thing and saying another, or trying to say what I know, or saying what I do not think, or thinking what I do not say, or wanting to say what I know I must not think, or wanting to know what I think I will never say: thus I turn in circles like a dog trying to catch the flea that is biting its tail."

I had confided more than I should have, and I suddenly felt frightened. He, however, said patronisingly, "You had better castrate your thinking, Ethan. Castration hurts only once, and you will feel the better for it: calm, almost happy. And remember the vast number of men who never had a virile thought."

I laughed uncertainly, and fearing further embarrassment, I directly put forth my request: I once more needed to see the Princess Michal, so as to enquire from her as to certain facts and events; and since he was over the wives of the King and over his concubines and over the widows of the King's father, I hoped I could count on his help.

The painted eyelids narrowed. "Now you know, Ethan, that I am a friend to you. But it was noted that the Princess Michal spoke with you twice, and without witnesses. The Wisest of Kings, Solomon, asked me why you had not informed him of what passed between you and the Princess. I answered him that all which passed between you and the Princess would surely be written in the King David Report; he replied that he who trusts to the rule is bound for a fall, and that his father before him was vexed by Michal."

And I stared at my empty cup, wondering what really had transpired between king and eunuch.

Amenhoteph beckoned to one of the maidservants to refill my cup, and I drank more of the sweet brown wine and listened to the Egyptian's guttural sounds. "Now, Ethan," Amenhoteph was saying, "cast the shadows from your soul, for an angel of Yahveh your god might yet change the mind of the Wisest of Kings, Solomon, or the Princess Michal might be seized by a desire to impart to you some more of her memories. But in the meantime I may compensate you by a surprise, a sweet tidbit such as the wise host offers his favoured guest after a fine meal, to be held on the tongue and savoured for its taste." He tilted his hands in the most exquisite manner and smiled mysteriously, adding, "You have always dealt with things past, Ethan, brushing the dust off ancient tables and gathering yesteryear's echoes. But I will lead you to a place from where you will view history in the making."

. . . is it the wine the flowers the heat or the scent of that gelded son of an Egyptian bitch my head spins what strength in his elegant hand crushing my wrist history in the making history as seen through a gap in the foliage a pair about to copulate how many beside us I wonder sweat trickling eyes smarting are watching this tryst the man there by God Adonijah from the nose up David his father but his mouth and jaw from a captain of archers whom Haggith his mother preferred groaning Abishag A—bi—shag longingly stretching his arms as towards an angel of the Lord but she is all flesh ripe bursting with juices and oh so dumb eyes dumb mouth dumb the stupidest woman in Israel to come here and meet with the King's brother but Adonijah is equally stupid what manner of king would he have been with his thought on nothing but that young woman howbeit like father like son was not David also that breed heedless under the urge of his loins David would kill for a woman but he would never jeopardise his life over her as does Adonijah his fool son groaning Abishag A—bi—shag tearing veil after veil from her and she slowly grinding her haunches that wretched eunuch crushing my wrist what can he feel it is purely his mind a perverse pleasure at what this will lead to this ageing spark struggling to shed his raiments O Lord God is that your image do we all of us look so absurd a flat-chested round-bellied spindle-shanked son of Israel groaning A—bi—shag is it the wine the flowers the heat I fear I shall vomit on history in the making but I had better keep down the soup made of the flesh of the turtle on the squabs basted in oil and baked in vine leaves the melon the apple with cheeses my wrist praise be unto the Lord my wrist is free look at this stinking turd of a dog whose stinking forefather survived by mistake when Yahveh slew the first-born in Egypt look at him soundlessly chuckling at Abishag seashell-pink skin orange-tipped full breasts Abishag chosen among the daughters of Israel to minister to King David when he was stricken in years and got no heat Abishag kneeling down and ministering to Adonijah and he raising his eyes unto the Lord groans and prays and prayer of thanks and vows offering unto the Lord two he-goats and also a young bullock and groans again and falls down beside her and spreads her before him and goes in unto her a flat-chested round-bellied spindle-shanked son of Israel doing unto a woman as is befitting her and she writhing and clawing him and whimpering may God do to me so and so and some more and some more and some more ...

But when Adonijah the son of David and Abishag the fair

damsel of Shunam had tearfully parted and gone their separate ways, Amenhoteph the royal chief eunuch turned unto me, saying, "I wish to correct myself, Ethan. I told you that this was one of the stupidest women in Israel; behold, no woman is ever entirely stupid, for when her brain fails her she can think with her womb."

I answered, "It is as my lord says; but I fear the issue of the thought of the womb."

And Amenhoteph tilted his hands as though saying that this was beyond his province.

14

"MADAM," I SAID, "at your call your servant has come flying to you as on the wings of Cherubim, and my eyes turn to you in gratitude."

The Princess twisted her lips into a mocking smile. "I would suggest that you direct your gratitude at your Egyptian friend by whose plea you were permitted to see my face; in return for which the King has charged him to note all that is noteworthy in what I may tell you."

Amenhoteph bowed. "I am sure that madam will be saying only what is agreeable to the ear of the Wisest of Kings, Solomon."

As I saw the Princess's anger being kindled I quickly explained that whatever passed between the lady Michal and myself concerned times long gone and could not possibly ruffle present-day sensitivities.

"Times long gone," the eunuch repeated. "And you are convinced that certain contemporary personages might not see themselves lampooned in the mask of the ancients? Is it not said among the people of Israel, Who fears to see himself in the mirror cries out at a puddle?"

The Princess gestured impatiently. "I am an old woman whom death has spared for reasons of his own."

"You, madam, are beyond reach." Amenhoteph tilted his hands. "But is my friend Ethan?"

THIRD DEPOSITION OF THE PRINCESS MICHAL UNDER QUESTION-

Question: To save ourselves time, madam, I should like
briefly to summarise what I know from other sources.
Would you tell me where I am wrong?

Answer: I am listening.

Question: While David your husband was being pursued
by your father King Saul, and while he dwelled with
his men at Ziklag, serving the Philistines, you remained in
the house of your father with the young man Phalti, to
whom you had been given.

Answer: It is as you say.

Question: And after the death of your father and of
your brother Jonathan, you followed the remains of the
host across Jordan and joined your brother Ish-bosheth of
Mahanaim and dwelled there with Phalti and took care of
the five small sons of your sister Merab who had died.

Answer: It is as you say.

Question: And in all that time, while David waxed ever
stronger and became King in Judah, he never sent for you
nor had you word from him?

Answer: Never.

Question: Nor did you send word to him?

Answer: I did not.

Question: Had you no longer any feelings for him?

Answer: The feelings of a woman are not considered
important.

Question: But you felt happy when your brother Ish-
bosheth informed you that David had sent to him, saying,
Deliver me my wife Michal whom I espoused to me for a
hundred foreskins of the Philistines.

Answer: I felt exultant! ... And bitter. And full of
fears. And there was poor Phalti.

Question: Your brother Ish-bosheth immediately
acceded to your husband's wish?

Answer: Ish-bosheth probably thought that by delivering me unto David he could buy himself a few months'
reprieve.

Question: Did David ever tell you what moved him to
call you unto him from Mahanaim?

Answer: He did not.

Question: What did you think were his reasons?

Answer: That would be conjecture.

Question: But as you, madam, are one of the few people alive who knew the David of that period intimately, your conjecture weighs greatly.

Answer: I had enough occasion to conjecture on that journey from Mahanaim. I sat on my donkey in the broiling sun, before me the clang of weapons where Abner rode with his men, behind me the laboured breath of Phalti who trotted at the donkey's tail. I thought of David and of the hundred foreskins he paid; no, two hundred, to be precise; and I thought he wants what he paid for and has waxed strong enough to collect. And then I thought, maybe he wants me: wants the woman I was when he came to me and took me. But why, then, his long silence? Because of this Abigail or of any other of his women, or because of the young men he favoured when the mood moved him? And I remembered what always had dominated his thought: that he was the Chosen of the Lord. That was why he wanted me back after all those years. I was part of his design: through the daughter of Saul he had a claim to the throne of Saul.

(Here Amenhoteph interrupted to say, "May your servant remind you, madam, that you are speaking of the father of the Wisest of Kings, Solomon, and of the throne upon which he sits." To which the Princess Michal replied, "I am speaking of my husband.")

Question: Perhaps we might return to the events of the journey. You spoke of Phalti trotting at the donkey's tail.

Answer: Ah, poor Phalti. But it was comforting to know that hanging on to the tail of my donkey was the one human being who felt affection for me. Whenever I turned, I saw him looking at me with love. In the nights, when my tent was pitched, he came crawling unto me and bedded his head at my shoulder, and the tears rolled down his cheek into his sparse beard. Abner and his men took no notice of Phalti, nor did they feed him from the stores they carried; he ate my leavings. But when we reached Bahurim, where the lands of Benjamin are divided from Judah, Abner turned on his horse and said to Phalti, Come here. And Phalti went to him, and stood as he always did, one shoulder higher than the other, and said, Here I am, my lord. And Abner said to him, It is time you turned back. And Phalti turned back, and I never saw him again.

(The Princess drank of the scented water which stood on a tray by her side and leaned back, closing her whitish lids.)

Question: Shall I continue, madam?

Answer: You may.

Question: The five small sons of your sister Merab, your wards, remained in Mahanaim?

Answer: It was felt by my brother Ish-bosheth and by myself that any male descendant of my father King Saul was safer away from David.

(At which Amenhoteph tilted his hands most alarmingly, so that I felt compelled to change the subject.)

Question: What happened, madam, when you arrived at Hebron?

Answer: Upon entering the new kingdom of my husband, David, I had expected to be welcomed as befits a wife of the King, with an escort of runners to run before me, and a chair borne by bearers, and with gifts. But though we were being watched from the time we crossed into Judah at Bahurim, I rode unto Hebron sitting on my tired donkey that had been rubbed raw by the saddle. In sight of Hebron, Abner ben Ner blew his trumpet three times, and from the gate sounded an answering trumpet, three times again, and twenty horsemen with a captain of horse galloped out of the gate. They rode up to Abner, and the captain of horse exchanged salutes with Abner, after which all of them cantered into the city, leaving me and my donkey on the field among the beggars that had gathered. And these stretched forth their hands, feeling my robe, and my sandals, and the rings on my fingers, saying, Who are you, lady, that you were left behind on the field among the beggars? And I said, I am Michal the daughter of King Saul. But they laughed, and capered, and turned hand-springs and somersaults, and some that were crippled and had sores on their heads limped alongside me as I turned my donkey towards the gate, and they called out, Behold the daughter of the King among the beggars; ah, what

great times have come over Judah that a spoiler and way-
layer turns into the Chosen of the Lord, and a whore into
the daughter of the King.

(Thereupon Amenhoteph clapped his hands in anger and
said at his most guttural, "Strike this from your notes,
Ethan.")

Question: No doubt, madam, you were finally met by a
servant of King David and taken to see the face of your
husband?

Answer: Oh, yes. It was explained to me that a mistake
was made, and please to accept the regrets of the King.
And I was brought into the house of David, and was bathed
and rubbed down with ointments and sprayed with essence
of attar and myrrh and given fine raiment. I felt life return
to my limbs, and joy to my heart, and I lay waiting for
David my lover who had espoused me to him for two
hundred foreskins of the Philistines. When night fell he
came. He stepped into the light of the lamp. It was
he: the grey eyes with the radiance in them, the lips
whose touch I remembered; yet he was a stranger unto me.
He sat down by the side of the bed, and looked me over,
and said, The daughter of Saul, no denying it. I said, My
father King Saul is dead. And he said, You will be the wife
of the King of Israel. I said, Ish-bosheth my brother is
King of Israel. David moved his hand as though he were
brushing a spider off his robe, and he replied—

(Just then Amenhoteph rose, saying, "Madam, you must
try one of these pomegranates. I receive them from my special
dealer, who scours the gardens about Jerusholayim, and the
orchards, on my behalf." He deftly opened the fruit for her,
and the Princess took of the sweet flesh of the fruit and ate it.)

Question: What did your husband, David, reply?

Answer: He said, I have lately written some very
interesting verses. You might want to hear them. I do not
myself do much singing, these days; I have a choir master,
and singers of various voices, high and low, who sing to the
accompaniment of psalteries, or harps, or lutes; I may send
a few of them to you. So I thanked him, saying that his
offer was most gracious, and that he was my favourite writer
of verse.

Question: And then?

Answer: Then he placed four fingers of his hand on my forehead and said, May Lord Yahveh bless your coming into this house; good night. And left.

two assassinations closely upon one another by which Abner removed and also Ish-bosheth the only two men still obstructing David's grasp for power over all Israel

query: by hand of God or hand of David

common traits

both slayings profiting David, who publicly laments both victims (thereby pleasing people)

in both cases slayers certain of gaining great favour with David but he condemning them with strong and in places poetic words

differences

Joab slaying Abner possible vengeance for Asahel Joab's brother whom Abner slew with hinder end of his spear (cf. bloodbath at pool of Gibeon)

Baanah and Rechab b'nai Rimmon slaying Ish-bosheth premeditated murder for lucre's sake and to benefit of presumable master mind

David dealing differently with slayers

has Baanah and Rechab struck down on the spot (cf. young man from Amalek who confessed to killing Saul)

David to Baanah and Rechab upon receiving bloodied head of Ish-bosheth: *I took hold of him who told me, Behold, Saul is dead, thinking to have brought good tidings and that I would reward him, and had him done away. How much more, when wicked men have slain a righteous man in his own house upon his bed? Shall I not therefore now require his blood of your hand, and take you away from the earth?*

Joab merely being cursed extensively

David *Let there not fail from the house of Joab one that has a putrid discharge, or that is a leper, or that leans on a staff, or that falls on the sword, or that lacks bread!*

curse remaining without influence upon Joab's further

progress (he commands in all but one of David's campaigns)

but deathbed plea of David to Solomon (cf. statements by Penuel ben Mushi and others): *Do therefore unto Joab according to your wisdom, and let not his hoar head go down to the grave in peace.*

on Abner's arrival Hebron Joab absent on minor foray

talks between David King of Judah and Abner Captain of Israel held in private

warm send-off by David at gate embraces kisses permitting conclusion that new covenant satisfactory to both parties

Joab upon returning with rich spoil and learning of Abner visit greatly upset

Joab to David: *What have you done? I hear Abner came unto you; why is it that you let him go away? You know Abner: he came to deceive you, and to spy on your going out and your coming in, and to know all that you do.*

David unlikely to have taken fright thereby but possibly changing his mind after Abner's departure to the effect that throne of Israel more cheaply had by ridding himself of Abner Joab taking measures

query: with David's knowing or without

David: *I and my kingdom are guiltless before the Lord of the blood of Abner ben Ner; let it rest on the head of Joab.*

by letter of law David guiltless as actual deed Joab's

Joab's messengers overtaking Abner at well of Sirah with request he return Hebron

Joab meeting Abner Hebron gate taking him aside as for confidential talk smiting him under fifth rib Joab's favourite target also Abner's but Joab first to draw

David as usual decreeing state funeral public mourning throughout Judah all David's mighty men including Joab to rend their clothes and gird themselves with sackcloth

David following bier to one of finest Hebron gravesites situated on hill with good view and cypresses

lifting up voice and weeping at grave of Abner all people weeping

DIRGE OF DAVID, WHICH HE COMPOSED
UPON THE UNTIMELY DEATH
OF ABNER BEN NER

Died Abner as a fool dieth?
Thy hands were not bound, nor thy feet put into fetters:
As a man falleth before wicked men, so fellest thou.

During the latter part of her third deposition the Princess Michal grew irritable.

"Have you ever noticed," she asked me, pointing at the royal chief eunuch, "how much he resembles one of his bird-faced gods?"

I stayed discreetly silent.

"And you, Ethan, annoy me just as much, forever scribbling away! What the Wisest of Kings, Solomon, wishes to hear I can say to his face."

I put my wax tablet aside; and Amenhoteph bowed, saying, "If you had rather have us leave, madam..."

"Stay," she said sharply, "I might as well tell the whole story." She rose, her black robe stressing her haggard shape. "I remember his head. Only his head: not his figure, not his hands, not the way he moved, nor anything he ever said. On that day, in Hebron, David sent unto me in the women's house, saying, The King wishes your presence to his face. I wondered; but I followed the servant. And in the royal hall sat David between the Cherubim, and Joab stood by his side with numerous other mighty men; and I bowed before David, saying, Your handmaid has come before you as you desired, my lord. He raised his hand to point at a thing which lay on a small table, under a dark cloth, and he said, Behold, your brother Ish-bosheth. A servant lifted the cloth, and I saw that head: its hair twisted in a loop to carry it by, the eyes like two grey pebbles, beard and gullet one blood-caked mass."

The Princess took a sip of scented water. Then, with that stiff gait of hers, she walked over to Amenhoteph, rapped his knuckles with her fan, and said, "If the tale is too much for your tender Egyptian nerves, you may now leave."

"Madam," he answered, "it was not by tender nerves that we persuaded your forefathers to pile the rocks for some of our finest pyramids."

"But we survived," said the Princess. "We are a durable race." She paused, frowning at me. "Where were we? Ah,

133

yes—my husband, King David, then turned unto two men standing before him and said, Now, Baanah and Rechab b'nai Rimmon, kindly repeat your story to my wife Michal the daughter of Saul and sister of Ish-bosheth. And Baanah and Rechab paled and lost some of their swagger, and they said, If it please you, madam, we came about the heat of the day to the house of Ish-bosheth, and entered easily, because Ish-bosheth had charged us with various duties concerning Abner ben Ner, and the servants of Ish-bosheth knew he expected us. We entered into the midst of the house, into the bed-chamber of Ish-bosheth, who lay on his bed at noon, snoring, with the flies flying about his face. And we slew him, and took his head, and got ourselves away through the plain all night. And we brought the head of Ish-bosheth to Hebron, unto your husband, King David, and we said unto the King, Here it is, here is the head of Ish-bosheth the son of your enemy, who sought your life, and the Lord has avenged our lord the King this day of Saul, and of his seed."

The Princess sat down on her cushions and clasped her hands about her knees. I saw the expression about her mouth and the lines of her face, and I thought of David and his monstrous sense for the spectacular.

"But David rose from between the Cherubim," the Princess went on, "and he said, Now you sons of Rimmon, hearken to me, and you also, Michal daughter of Saul. And he spoke of the young man of Amalek, who brought him Saul's crown and the bracelet that was on his arm, and who thought he would receive a reward for his tidings, and whom he slew in Ziklag. Then, raising his voice, he said unto Rechab and Baanah, and unto me, and unto all who were about him, As the Lord lives, who has redeemed my soul out of all adversity: how much more so will I act, when wicked men have slain a righteous person in his own house upon his bed? shall I not therefore now require his blood of your hand, and take you away from the earth? And as Baanah and Rechab cried out unto him, and there was tohubohu, David commanded his officers, and they slew the two murderers and cut off their hands and feet and hung these up over the pool in Hebron."

The Princess spread her hands. "I do not know what morbid thought caused David to have the head of Ish-bosheth buried in the sepulchre of Abner in Hebron. Was not Ish-bosheth the victim of Abner as much as of Baanah and Rechab his murderers? Or was this adjacence in death meant symbolically, a parable whose purport remained a secret between David and the Lord?"

15

Notes and observations of Ethan ben Hoshaiah on David's foreign wars and various other occurrences in his reign, as discussed during their session on the subject by the members of the Royal Commission on the Preparation of *The One and Only True and Authoritative, Historically Correct and Officially Approved Report on the Amazing Rise* and so forth.

Everything comes to him whom the Lord has chosen, but those destined to fall are trod underground.

As beth follows upon aleph, so the anointment of David had to follow upon the murder of Ish-bosheth. The elders of Israel came to David and spoke, saying, Behold, we are your bone and your flesh; also in time past, when Saul was king over us, you led out and brought in Israel, and you shall be captain over Israel. And King David made a league with them in Hebron before the Lord: and they anointed him king over Israel.

After the pains and the passions, the scheming and killing, the marches and countermarches, the final act must have seemed insipid to David.

An address by King David to his assembled host, preparatory to the assault on the stronghold of Zion; as submitted in session by Benaiah ben Jehoiada and read by him to the members of the Commission.

"Now, you sons of Israel, and of Judah, hearken to the

Chosen of the Lord. Our priests have slaughtered the male of the sheep, and enquired of the oracle of Urim and Tummim; they assure me there never was a more propitious day to storm the city of the Jebusites, Jerusholayim, and take it from the heathen. Furthermore I have dreamed a dream in which Yahveh the Lord of Hosts appeared to me, saying, Behold, I have led Israel out of Egypt, and gone before them by day in a pillar of cloud and by night in a pillar of fire: thus I will go before you and your men as they move against the walls of Jerusholayim."

(*Calls of Hurrah.*)

"Ah, my brave ones, whose sword strikes terror in the heart of the enemy: I want you to prostrate yourselves before the Lord and thank him that he chose you to see this day. For you will be envied throughout the ages because of all the men in Israel you were selected to scale the stronghold of Zion and conquer it for the Lord God of Hosts and for David, your King, thus immortalising your names and also gaining great spoil, each and every one of you."

(*Loud calls of Hurrah.*)

"Now there have been voices, and I have a very good ear for voices, asking, Why does David want this place, Jerusholayim, for his city? It is but a pile of rock, hot in the summer, cold in the winter, and altogether unpleasant. But in that dream which I had occasion to mention, Yahveh spoke to me further, saying unto me, David, you are King of all the children of Israel; therefore your city should not be in Judah, nor in Benjamin, nor in Manasseh, nor in any of the tribes but should be your own, David's city, and centrally located; furthermore I, the Lord your God, shall personally come and reside in Jerusholayim to the great benefit of its citizens and of all Israel. From which you see, my lion-hearted ones, that Yahveh the Lord of Hosts has great plans for the role of Jerusholayim in history, and all we have to do is take the city."

(*Calls of Hurrah.*)

"Also it has been said, and I have a very good ear for what is being said, that the stronghold of Zion and the wall of Jerusholayim are so impregnable that even the lame and the blind can hold them. This is nothing but a rumour noised about by the enemies of David. For in that dream to which

I have repeatedly referred, Yahveh spoke to me still further, saying, David, there is a conduit leading from a well outside Jerusholayim to a gutter within its walls, and he who goes up that conduit will emerge in the rear of the city's defenders and do what is pleasing in the eye of the Lord."

(*Surprise. Calls of Hurrah.*)

"Therefore I say unto you, my invincible ones: God do me so, and more also, if the city, Jerusholayim, be not ours by this night. And whosoever is first to go up the conduit, and gets to the gutter, and smites the Jebusites, including their lame and their blind, he shall be chief captain. Trumpeter, blow to attack!"

(*Extended calls of Hurrah. The trumpet blows to attack.*)

Benaiah ben Jehoiada having finished reading, the members of the Commission sat in obvious discomfort, some studying their nails, others scratching their noses. The source of their discomfort clearly was Joab, for it was he who first went up the conduit, and first got to the gutter and smote the Jebusites; but concerning Joab David was said to have charged his son Solomon, Do therefore according to your wisdom, and let not his hoar head go down to the grave in peace.

But Jehoshaphat the son of Ahilud, the recorder, pressed his palms one against the other, saying, "Why is there doubt in the hearts of my lords as to the treatment of Joab in our report? Is not the serpent openly talked of in the Book of Creation, and mention made therein of Cain the slayer of his brother Abel? In books which are published in certain foreign lands, word about those who displease the eye of their king is frequently reduced from several pages to one miserable line, or stricken out, so that the person thus treated becomes an un-person and his sons are the sons of nobody. But these be the ways of the uncircumcised, and also unwise, for a complete perversion of fact fools but complete fools and renders the entire book unbelievable; and as soon as another king ascends the throne, he orders the book rewritten, whereby the previous king's un-persons are resurrected and his favourites correspondingly demoted, so that the history of a people comes to depend on which edition of it you read. But the Wisest of

Kings, Solomon, would prefer that this Commission mark a man discreetly when he needs being marked, and bend the truth gently where it needs bending, and altogether follow a more subtle policy, so that the people believe what is written; for the King fondly hopes that *The One and Only True and Authoritative, Historically Correct and Officially Approved Report on the Amazing Rise* and so forth shall outlast all other books of its kind.

I noticed the knitted brow of Benaiah ben Jehoiada. He blew fiercely through his nose, and said, "That does it. God do me so and more also, if I won't have Joab tried in a public trial. I have enough testimony against him and enough signed confessions to have him hung twice over, and his head cut off, and his body nailed to any convenient wall; and at this trial he will tell the truth so beautifully that it will not need any bending, gently or otherwise."

At this Jehoshaphat ben Ahilud, the recorder, smiled sweetly. The initiation of legal proceedings, he said, was well within the province of my lord Benaiah, King Solomon concurring; but that hanging a man was one thing and writing about him another.

Behold King David in his splendour.

His hair has turned to the colour of rust, his beard has begun to grizzle. Constant wariness has cut grooves about his eyes, and much of their radiance has dimmed.

(*My lord Jehoshaphat:* Mention somewhere that the Lord has established David king over Israel for the people of Israel's sake.)

David dwells in Fort Zion and calls it the city of David. He adds to its fortifications. He treats with Hiram King of Tyre, who sends him cedar trees and carpenters and masons for the building of his palace.

He takes unto himself more concubines and wives out of Jerusholayim. He needs fresh women, he needs more sons, and hopes that the addition of local damsels to his family will win him acclaim.

(*My lord Elihoreph:* At this point insert names of sons born to David in Jerusholayim.)

He is manifestly the Chosen of the Lord. Unlike Saul's

house which collapsed upon the death of its founder, his is to outlast him for generations. In his hands, power is sanctified by a higher purpose. His poetry deals extensively with the subject; explicit instructions to the royal chief musician go with the texts. But he searches for a more tangible token of his divine mission.

And remembers the ark.

(*My lord Nathan:* Include here brief chapter on the hauling of the ark of God to Jerusholayim.)

The ark of the covenant on which Yahveh is thought seated between two cherubim: carry it to Jerusholayim and you carry with it Yahveh the elusive, migratory tribal God; and God in one place means power in one place.

But where was the ark? A quick quest establishes that its last public worship took place during the judgeship of Samuel the prophet, after the Philistine kings captured it in battle but, plagued by Yahveh with boils in their secret places and with emerods, returned it to Israel. Since then the ark has been gathering dust in the barn of one Abinadab, in Kirjath-jearim near Gibeah.

(*My lord Zadok:* Omit anything apt to arouse doubts in the sanctity of religious objects.)

While the ark is being cleaned of cobwebs and repainted, David approaches with thirty thousand people to fetch it from the house of Abinadab. The ark is set on a new cart, and Uzzah and Ahio the sons of Abinadab are chosen to drive it.

David knows what he owes the Lord: this parade will be the greatest ever, with numerous bands that play away before the Lord on harps, on psalteries, on timbrels, on cornets, on cymbals, enough to scare any oxen. When the procession reaches Nachon's threshingfloor, behold, the oxen do shy and shake the cart, and Uzzah puts forth his hand to the ark of God to steady it. By which the anger of the Lord is kindled against Uzzah, and God smites him for his error; and there Uzzah dies by the ark of God.

(*My lord Zadok:* Word carefully, so as to avoid arousing doubts in the everlasting justice of the Lord.)

David is shocked: if Uzzah was struck dead for a small thing like upholding the ark, what is in store for him who plans to use it for his own purposes?

So David acts to rid himself of the hazard. The body of Uzzah is left lying. The ark of God is carried into the house of Obed-edom, a Gittite, to be left there for observation: should the Lord's anger prove to be lasting, Obed-edom would visibly be stricken.

(*My lord Ahiah:* Stress the choice of a foreigner for this test, thus showing David's great love for his people Israel.)

After three months the findings are unanimous: not only has Obed-edom failed to develop dropsy, or open lesions, or a putrid discharge, but the Lord has visibly blessed his house and all that pertains to him.

David now decides to try again. To be entirely safe, he has oxen and fatlings sacrificed as soon as the bearers of the ark have gone six paces. Then he girds himself with the brief linen garment of the priests and dances in ecstasy before the Lord, to the great joy of the people, who admire his ample appurtenances, and to the disgust of Michal, who observes his capers from a window as the ark is being carried to the tabernacle.

(*My lord Elihoreph:* to show David's generosity, add that on that day he caused to be distributed among the whole multitude of Israel, to women as well as men, to every one a cake of bread, and a good piece of flesh, and a flagon of wine.)

List of David's victories over diverse foreign enemies, as compiled by Benaiah ben Jehoiada, and submitted by him for inclusion in the King David Report.

FIRST PHILISTINE CAMPAIGN:

The Philistines invade through the valley of Rephaim. Acting on advice of the Lord, David beats them by a frontal assault at Baal-perazim. The routed Philistines leave behind them the images of their gods which David orders burned.

SECOND PHILISTINE CAMPAIGN:

The Philistines return, again through the valley of Rephaim. The Lord advises a flanking movement followed by an assault on the enemy's rear, the Lord to give the signal for attack by a wind in certain mulberry trees. Pursuant to the Lord's command, David smites the Philistines on a front from Geba to Gezer.

Mopping-up operations:

The resistance of scattered Philistine troops is broken; David occupies the cities of the Philistines; the five kingdoms cease to exist.

Moab subdued:

The Moabites are attacked by David and smitten. He has two out of every three able-bodied men killed, the rest made tributary.

Great north-eastern campaign:

Hadadezer, King of Zobah, threatens to expand his rule beyond the upper Euphrates river. David marches against him and smites him, capturing twenty thousand foot troops, seven hundred horsemen, and a thousand chariots. The golden shields of Hadadezer's officers and exceeding much brass from Betah and Berothai, cities of Hadadezer, are brought to Jerusholayim.

Damascus occupied:

The Syrians of Damascus come to succour Hadadezer King of Zobah. David slays twenty-two thousand of them, places garrisons in Syria of Damascus, and makes the people tributary.

Edom crushed:

On his march back from Syria, in the valley of salt, David smites the host of Edom, eighteen thousand men. He places garrisons in Edom and makes the people tributary.

Great trans-jordanian campaign:

Stung by King Hanun of Ammon, who forces the ambassadors of Israel to walk bare-bottomed and has one side of their beards shaved off, David dispatches Joab and the host of mighty men. In a double battle before the gates of the city of Rabbath-ammon the Ammonites and their Syrian auxiliaries are beaten in turn. The Syrians regroup and are reinforced by troops from King Hadadezer. David gathers all available Israel forces, crosses over Jordan, and at Helam smites the combined Syrian host under Hadadezer's field captain, Shobach. David slays forty thousand horsemen and the crews of seven hundred chariots; Shobach is wounded in battle and dies. The various Syrian kingdoms withdraw from the war; Ammon is laid waste by Joab, its capital, Rabbath-ammon, besieged and destroyed. The people are put to forced labour; the royal crown of Ammon, weighing a talent of gold and set with precious stones, is placed on David's head.

General comment:
In all these battles and campaigns, the Lord preserved David whithersoever he went.

"And now, my lords," said Jehoshaphat ben Ahilud, the recorder, "the last point on today's order of business: Although he brought the ark of God to Jerusholayim, why did King David fail to build the temple in which to house it, thus leaving the pious work to Solomon his son and heir?"

I was afraid that Jehoshaphat would drop the question into my lap. The construction of the temple, whose costs kept mounting, was a constant source of popular dissatisfaction; and many people praised David over Solomon, because the old King had wisely refrained from building the holy monstrosity.

Jehoshaphat smiled at me. "Ethan?"

But I knew, and Jehoshaphat knew, that every one on the Commission knew the answer. It wasn't avarice. David spent money on his own palace, and he never pinched shekels when it came to displaying his royal splendour. The sorry fact was that he shied away from complications with the clergy. The ark in his Jerusholayim tabernacle had aroused enough rancour because it drew away income from the temples at Shiloh and Shechem and from the thousand-and-one shrines that dotted the countryside, each feeding its band of priests; David feared that a royal temple resplendent with cedarwood and marble and copper and precious stones would turn the resentment of these priests into open enmity, adding to the troubles that plagued him despite the victories of his armies.

I therefore said that the temple of the Lord and all that pertained to it were a matter for the men of God to speak on, and that I was but a modest receptacle waiting to be filled by their words of wisdom. Whereupon Zadok the priest and Nathan the prophet each begged the other to precede him, until Benaiah ben Jehoiada asked if the Commission was to sit all night.

So Zadok began, saying, "If it please my lords, King David did prepare for the building of the temple, iron aplenty, and nails for the doors and the joinings, and brass, and cedar trees. Then he called for Solomon, who was young and tender, and said to him, My son, as for me, it was in my mind to build a house for the Lord God of Israel that would be exceeding magnifical, of fame and of glory throughout the countries. But the word of the Lord came to me, saying, You have shed blood abundantly, and have made great wars, therefore you shall not build a house unto my name. Behold, a son shall be born to you who shall be a man of peace; and I will give him rest from all his enemies round about: for his name shall be Solomon. He shall build a house for my name; and he shall be my son, and I will be his father; and I will establish the throne of his kingdom over Israel forever."

There was great clapping of hands, and Jehoshaphat said the story was most pretty, and its point well taken, especially as to its bearing on the Wisest of Kings, Solomon. But Nathan the prophet raised his brows, and enquired if the members considered it wise to turn the public attention to the abundant blood on the hands of King David.

Thereupon Jehoshaphat said, "Perhaps my lord Nathan has other knowledge and will be good enough to let us share it?"

And Nathan said, certainly; furthermore his knowledge was incontestable because he had it straight from the Lord. It was contained in the book of remembrances which he was writing and which he planned to call *The Book of Nathan*; he would gladly read from the chapter in question to the members of the Commission.

Jehoshaphat thanked Nathan, saying that surely the members would joyfully accept the kind offer; and Nathan snapped his fingers, at which two servants carried in a basket filled with tablets, and he reached into the basket and began reading from the chapter entitled, *The Dream of Nathan.*

It was a fine dream, and very informative. The Lord of course appeared in it and spoke to Nathan at length: of the exodus of the children of Israel from Egypt, and of the settlement of the tribes, and of the period of the judges. In all that time, the Lord went on to say, he had dwelled in tents, and in tabernacles, and had been perfectly satisfied, so that a few more years of discomfort did not matter.

Then Nathan raised his voice mightily, quoting the words by which the Lord commanded him in his dream, "Go and tell my servant David, When you shall sleep with your fathers, I will set up your seed after you, which shall proceed out of your bowels. He shall build a house for my name; I will be his father, and he shall be my son, and your house and your kingdom shall be established forever."

Nathan paused.

Then he concluded, "According to all these words, and according to all this vision, so I did speak unto David."

Again there was great clapping of hands, and Jehoshaphat said the dream was most extraordinary, and its point well taken, especially as to its bearing on the seed proceeding out of David's bowels. But Zadok the priest shrugged his shoulders and remarked at the miracle of it: for in the story *he* had told the Commission the words of the Lord were almost literally the same as in the dream which Nathan the prophet had read from his book of remembrances.

Jehoshaphat ben Ahilud, the recorder swallowed. Then he turned to me, saying, "As an expert, Ethan, which of the two would you advise us to place in the King David Report: the tale of Zadok or the dream of Nathan?"

"The likeness of the words of the Lord in both stories," I said after some thought, "proves the divine origin of either. So only God can judge. It seems to your servant that you will have to draw lots or put the matter to a vote."

"Vote," said Benaiah, "and be done with it."

And it came to pass that the tally was three to three, Benaiah ben Jehoiada and Ahiah the scribe and Zadok voting for Zadok's story, but Jehoshaphat ben Ahilud and Elihoreph the other scribe and Nathan for the dream of Nathan. Therefore the question was referred for decision to the Wisest of Kings, Solomon.*

* Solomonic judgment, handed down after several months: *Include both.*

16

It was a long march, and hot, and the roads dusty; also my dancing before the Lord had been strenuous. After all that, may not a man expect to be welcomed in his own house with kindly words and a cool drink and a basin of water in which to wash his feet?

But Michal the daughter of Saul stands in the doorway and greets me with that derisive expression she has, and to my question as to the whereabouts of everybody she replies, My lord will find them in town, I suppose, or at the gates of the city with the storytellers and street singers and jugglers and sword swallowers, for it is not every day that the King supplies a feast for the people and such a spectacle. Then why did you stay home, I say. I am a king's daughter, she says, I do not mix with the rabble; furthermore I saw enough from my window. Oh did you, I say, and was it a fine sight?

So she looks at me. And I see her breasts rising as she pulls in breath, she still has those fine firm breasts, and she inveighs, How glorious was the King of Israel today, who uncovered himself in the eyes of the handmaids of his servants, as one of the vain fellows shamelessly uncovers himself.

Lord God! The anger rose from my bowels to my brain,

and I thought of the two hundred Philistine foreskins I paid for her by the wish of her father, and the way she looked at those, and I say unto her, It was before the Lord, you understand, who chose me before your father Saul and before all your father's house to be ruler over the people of Israel: therefore I danced before the Lord. And I will yet be more vile than thus, and will be base in my own sight, and display myself before the Lord; and as for the maidservants you spoke of, I am not ashamed for what they might see, for it has served many a maid; but you shall be passed by and shall be childless to the day of your death.

As though you had approached me in love even once, she says hoarsely, after you took me from Phalti and kept me in your Hebron house, and now in Jerusholayim.

Whereupon I say, Why should I add by my own seed to the blood of Saul which is my enemy?

Oh David! she exclaims. And then, The Lord God knows that your heart is but a clump of ice which freezes those who love you and is deadly to your soul; the day will come when you will feel its cold spreading through you, and all the ministering to you of all the daughters of Israel will not infuse you with warmth...

The players and dancers in the gates of the cities play a piece that tells of the hanging of the seven sons of Saul at Gibeon, and how Rizpah Saul's concubine, their mother, stayed under the gallows from the beginning of the barley harvest until the rains came, and suffered neither the birds of the air to attack their bodies by day, nor the beasts of the fields, by night, and thus defeated King David.

Now five of those seven were not properly sons of Saul out of Rizpah, but his grandsons, out of his daughter Merab, who died young; and they were raised by the Princess Michal, Merab's sister, who became to them as a second mother. Thus it came about once more that Michal's hand held the light by which to discern the shapes of the past; but my way to her was blocked.

And I took counsel with Esther my wife, and I resolved to avoid further involvement with Amenhoteph, preferring to address myself to Jehoshaphat ben Ahilud, the recorder, with a request to be permitted to see the face of the Princess. But after several days, Jehoshaphat had me called unto himself, and he said, "Ethan, the lady Michal is indisposed; the Wisest of Kings suggests you submit your enquiries to me."

At which cold fear permeated my bowels, for it was plain that the King mistrusted me and his advisers doubted me; but I kept my wits about me sufficiently to express my concern over the Princess's health; whereupon Jehoshaphat desired to know, what did I want to enquire of her?

"My lord," I said, "as certain plants grow one out of another, so it is with my questions: each is engendered by that which precedes it."

"I fear you overrate the part assigned to you, Ethan," he replied. "A scribe should write, not think; and he who is learned and has knowledge of matters should limit himself to his learning."

"Your servant enquires not for enquiry's sake or out of impudence," I parried. "Has not the Wisest of Kings, Solomon, placed me in my place and promised to help me whenever I should falter or be undecided as to where lies error and where truth? Why, then, am I not being helped? Why is so much being hidden from me which is of essence to my search? Truly, I had rather return to Ezrah and live in peace than torture my soul with Yes and No and Perhaps and But."

"So ask," he said.

"About the dancing in ecstasy of King David before the ark of God, which displeased Michal as she saw it from a window . . ."

"Ah, yes," said Jehoshaphat, "mention was made thereof during the Commission's last session. Do you really feel that a quarrel between two married people is worth including in a serious work of history?"

"The dance of the King before the ark of the Lord is a holy rite requiring mention in a serious work of history; and if the King's wife quarrelled with him over his dancing, it is to her shame."

Jehoshaphat sighed, saying that he had foreseen my question and was prepared for it; and he handed me a few tablets of clay. These appeared to contain personal notes, written in

149

the hand of a man versed in letters, the script well-rounded, with many abbreviations.

I felt as if my brow was being brushed by the wing of the Angel of Fate, and even though I knew what the answer would be, I enquired, "Are these in the hand of King David?"

Jehoshaphat affirmed, "From my files."

He gave me time to read. Later on I was permitted to copy the contents of the tablets, and I have inserted these above. When I had finished reading, Jehoshaphat said, "What do you think?"

I answered, "God alone knows what passes in the hearts of a man and a woman that were as wondrously tied to one another as were David and Michal."

"And that is all you glean from what is written there?"

I remained silent.

"Do you not sense the fear, which speaks out of David's words, and the ghosts rising from between the lines? And the ghosts all carry the same face: King Saul's."

I asked myself, why Jehoshaphat's sudden confidence? Had the decision been made that I was not to live long enough to be able to misuse it?

"If my lord will forgive me," I said, "but it seems to me that David was not the man to traffic with ghosts; he dealt with angels, and with Lord Yahveh himself."

Jehoshaphat smiled. "Then view it in the light of the sun. Himself having usurped power, David would tend to suspect that others might plot to do likewise. The state which he was erecting was needed and therefore pleasing to the eye of the Lord; but by curtailing their power it galled the tribal elders. David's wars were expensive, his ever-growing body of officials consumed the substance of the people; soon the children of Israel longed back to the days of Saul when the King walked behind his own plough and a man could keep the larger share of his produce. What is more natural than that the hopes of the disappointed and dissatisfied, of the distressed and dispossessed should cluster about the spirit of Saul and about Saul's last surviving descendants?"

And how long, then, I continued Jehoshaphat's thought, how long until even a cool mind sees a faction in every chance gathering, a conspiracy in every chance whisper? How long, then, until the state, erected in the name of the Lord, becomes like the god Moloch, who must be fed with the flesh of the innocent?

"My lord would not indicate," I said, my audacity frightening me, "that it was David who caused the hanging of the five young sons of Saul's daughter Merab and of the two sons of Rizpah, his concubine?"

"Would your mind be troubled thereby?"

I hurried to assure Jehoshaphat that I was aware of the fact that the seven young men were hanged not by David but by the people of the town of Gibeon, who are not of the children of Israel, being aborigines, namely remnants of the Amorite people; yet I could scarcely imagine, I added, that anyone in Israel could have been hanged by a band of half-starved natives, unless it be with the consent of King David.

"And now you suspect," said Jehoshaphat, "that David's quarrel with Michal, and all that pertains to it, must be seen in context with the hanging at Gibeon."

I probably paled, for he glanced at me strangely. "My lord," I said, "I fear that evil-minded people and such as bear ill-will towards the Wisest of Kings, Solomon, might read that sort of thing into the story; yet I do not see how we can omit the hanging from the King David Report, since even the dancers and players in the gates of the cities draw on the subject for their performances."

"Why, Ethan," he said, "despite the work you have done you seem to know little about David ben Jesse, the Chosen of the Lord; for has not King David himself supplied our answer to all who want to slur him?"

My startled face seemed to amuse him, and he went on, saying, "There was that famine in the days of David, remember? It was not a big famine, having lasted a mere three years. But it was big enough for people to begin muttering about God punishing Israel for the blood that was on the hands of King David. And word reached the ears of King David, for the King had his ears in the smallest village, and he said to me, Jehoshaphat, the blood which is on my hands I have shed in the name of the Lord and for good purposes; therefore the Lord will not be punishing the people Israel for my sake. But if you will think of someone else's debt of blood which has remained unpaid, and for which we could

151

atone, we might be able to put an end both to the famine and to these ugly rumours."

Jehoshaphat poured some wine into his cup.

"It then occurred to me," he continued, "that when King Saul was new in office he had gone out and in his fervour had slain a great number of the people of Gibeon, notwithstanding the covenant of peace which the children of Israel in times past had sworn unto them. I reminded David of the incident, and David closed his eyes and inclined his head as though he were hearing voices. On coming out of his trance, David told me that the Lord had just spoken to him; he knew the voice of the Lord from a thousand voices; and the Lord had advised him as to the famine, that it was for Saul, and for Saul's bloody house, because Saul slew the Gibeonites."

Jehoshaphat frowned at his cup as though he feared that the wine therein had soured, and he said, "The King then commanded me to have the elders of what was left of the Gibeonites called to Jerusholayim and to pass the word among them that the King had it in his mind to atone for the wickedness of Saul. Thus the Gibeonites came unto David, and he asked them, What shall I do for you? and wherewith shall I make the atonement? And the Gibeonites said, We will have no silver nor gold; but the man who consumed us, let him now be consumed; let seven men of his sons be delivered unto us, and we will hang them up unto the Lord."

Jehoshaphat drank and smacked his lips. Then he said, "Of course there were those in Israel who remarked on it that the Gibeonites asked David for the lives of seven of Saul's male descendants when it so happened that there were just seven of them left aside from Mephibosheth the son of Jonathan, who was crippled and therefore could not become king. But those were evil tongues, and the multitude of the people felt that David had better accede to the demand of the Gibeonites, because of the famine."

"But how did the Princess Michal respond to the grievous matter?" I asked.

"She bore it with dignity," stated Jehoshaphat, "as she bore everything. It was the other one, that Rizpah woman, who created the trouble."

"Under the gallows?" I said.

"They were put to death in the days of the harvest," said

Jehoshaphat after some thought, "in the first days, in the beginning of the barley harvest. And Rizpah took sackcloth, and spread it for her upon the rock under the bodies that hung there, and stayed with her two sons and with the five sons of Merab from the beginning of the harvest until the rains came, and suffered neither the birds of the air to attack them by day, nor the beasts of the field by night..."

His voice trailed off. After a while he resumed in anger, "Ah, Rizpah was a sly one, Saul's concubine. She knew the people, and she knew the soft heart of David, which would take pity as soon as rumour spread of this mother in Israel who sat there repelling the vultures and the jackals from the bodies of her children. And David feared that from the un-buried bones of the sons of Saul might yet rise the ghost of the dead King. But he also knew that next to a noisy pro-cession and a sumptuous feeding the people Israel love noth-ing as much as a fine funeral, such as he had given to Abner ben Ner and to the bloodied head of Ish-bosheth. Therefore David ordered the bones of Saul and of his son Jonathan dug up, which had been recovered from the Philistines and lay buried at Jabesh-gilead; and the bones of the seven hanged were also gathered; and all of those bones were taken to the land of the tribe of Benjamin, to Zelah, and were laid to rest in the family plot, in the sepulchre of Kish the father of Saul. And King David himself selected the funeral music, and he commanded me to be at the head of the mourners; but the funeral oration was delivered by Zadok the priest. And the people cried out and wailed and lamented, and everyone agreed that David had behaved most handsomely."

"As always," I attested, "as always."

FROM A POEM BY DAVID ENTITLED
David's Song of Thanks for Deliverance

The Lord rewarded me according to my
righteousness; according to the cleanness
of my hands has he recompensed me.
For I have kept the ways of the Lord,
and have not wickedly departed from my God.

153

For all his judgments were before me,
and I did not put away his statutes from me.
I was also upright before him,
and I kept myself from my iniquity.
Therefore has the Lord recompensed me according
to my righteousness,
according to the cleanness of my hands in his eyesight.

"You look unwell, Ethan my husband," said Esther to me as I returned to No. 54, Queen-of-Sheba Lane. "Was the talk unpleasant that you had with Jehoshaphat ben Ahilud, the recorder?"

"We spoke of a hanging."

She took my hand into hers. "Who is David ben Jesse that your neck should be itching because of him? God has created both kings and beggars, he assigns them their time under the sun, he cuts them down and makes them fall like grass before the reaper. How would it be, Ethan, if we returned to Ezrah, to peace and quiet?"

"Why, Esther," I said, "we are as a lamb that is hedged in; wherever it may turn, it stays imprisoned."

And Esther said nothing more.

17

I HAD LONG DREADED having to deal with the story of Bath-sheba.

It was even more difficult to treat than the hanging of the seven surviving sons and grandsons of King Saul, for it directly concerned the Wisest of Kings, Solomon; moreover Queen Mother Bath-sheba is very much alive.

All Israel knows that Uriah the Hittite, Bath-sheba's husband, died just in time for David to marry the widow and make their first-born a genuine prince of the blood. The matter was noised about everywhere as those involved in it behaved with a strange lack of discretion; but the facts of it are hard to separate from fable.

Nathan the prophet has written about it at length in his book of remembrances, and I am inclined to believe much of what he says: he watched the dangerous relationship develop, and he interfered in it according to his lights. Speaking as a historian, I feel we are fortunate in having Nathan and his book; it is most useful if one keeps in mind his official rank and the kind of person he is: self-important, self-righteous, self-seeking.

So I went out and came to Nathan the prophet and found him in his house doing nothing.

"Why, Ethan ben Hoshaiah! I was just thinking of you, and there you are."

"My lord's gift of prophecy is one of the miracles of our

155

time. It is not everybody that God favours with second sight and with dreams full of significance, which should be of great help in the writing of books."

"True. Other writers must strain their minds and look up reference work and struggle with logic; I merely wait for the flow of intuition to come from the Lord."

"Aren't remembrances rather based on fact?"

"What are facts without visions and reflections? Do not confuse these, however, with the stammering and caterwauling found in the works of some contemporaries, for that sort of thing stems not from God but from the simple lack of ability to write down a consecutive thought."

"I presume that in your remembrances, provisionally entitled *The Book of Nathan*, you concern yourself also with the story of that heart-warming, tender love of King David and the lady Bath-sheba, that sweet and blessed union of two sympathetic souls from which sprang, after much travail, the person of the present incumbent of the throne."

"I have taken care to tell that tale in all its glorious particulars."

"May your servant count on you to make available for the King David Report the facts as you have gathered them: of course you will be duly named."

"I have only one set of tablets. You will understand that I cannot let these leave my hand."

"Could I peruse them here?"

"When the words of the Lord come down to me, I am able to note these only by using symbols and abbreviations which would be undecipherable to you. But I can read to you and answer questions..."

READING BY NATHAN THE PROPHET FROM HIS BOOK
OF REMEMBRANCES, WITH QUESTIONS BY ETHAN BEN HOSHAIAH
AND NATHAN'S ANSWERS SET IN BRACKETS

King David had asked myself and some intimate friends to come to his house, that night, to converse with him on questions of state, and to have me prophesy if necessary. Much against his wont, the King was late for supper, and seemed distracted, so that I felt moved to enquire if during his

afternoon nap a dream had come to him which needed inter-
preting.

The King looked at me as though I had spoken to him
from the other side of the world, and said, A dream? Why,
Nathan, it was truly a vision!

Abiathar the priest, and Seraiah the scribe, and several
others enquired as to the vision: had the King had it in his
sleep, and had it been more of an angel or more of a human,
and suchlike questions; so there was tohubohu. But the King,
David, stroked his beard, saying, he would have thought it
an angel but for the fact that it was doing its ritual ablutions
as he saw it from the roof of the palace, against the setting
sun, after he had risen from his bed. Whereupon Seraiah the
scribe said that certainly it must be Bath-sheba the daughter
of Eliam and wife of Uriah the Hittite, who was captain of a
thousand and serving under Joab in the siege of the city of
Rabbath-ammon, for she and her husband had recently moved
into the army officers' houses located to the west of the palace.
If the King so wished, added Seraiah, he would go there
and knock at her door and tell the woman that she was found
pleasing to the eye of the King; and the rest would be simple.

Not quite so simple, said the King.

But Seraiah asked, did not all the daughters of Israel belong
to the King, including those married to foreigners like Uriah
the Hittite?

All, replied the King, excepting the wives of soldiers who
serve in the field. These may not be touched, neither by an
elder of the tribe nor by the King; for how could a man be
moved to go out and fight the Lord's battles, unless he knew
his house protected and his wife?

And Abiathar the priest confirmed this, saying it was a law
of the Lord which the uncircumcised call taboo, and that
King David was exceeding wise and equitable.

But the King hit the table with his fist, and he cried out,
Shall I then have this fire consume my bowels and not quench
it?

Abiathar was so startled that the morsel in his mouth slid
into his windpipe, and he had to be helped. Having regained
his breath, he said, The fire which consumes the bowels of
the King must be quenched, for the well-being of the Chosen
of the Lord is the overriding law. Moreover, did not Lord

157

Yahveh plainly denote his will by his timing of the woman's washing herself and of the sun's setting and of the King's entering upon the roof?

And Seraiah the scribe said that the taboo did not apply in this case because Uriah the Hittite would not be deprived of a thing by the King's lying with Bath-sheba Uriah's wife; on the contrary, Uriah would be honoured and enriched by the relationship.

(At this point I thought it was time to break into raptures, and I said that never in my days had I heard anything written in so exciting a manner, and so true to life! But as a guest at the King's supper table, that night, had not my lord Nathan given an opinion on the question of the taboo?

Nathan smiled, and said modestly, "I rarely have an opinion unless and until Lord Yahveh instructs me as to my words."

And he resumed.)

And David sent messengers, and took her; and she came in unto him, and he lay with her; for she was purified from her uncleanness: and she returned unto her house.

(Again I interrupted to say, "Since from the couple in question issued the Wisest of Kings, Solomon, we would not want the reader to assume that there was only the crudest form of copulation. Has not King David ever hinted at some tender dalliance, some words of endearment which he and the lady Bath-sheba exchanged in their first night?"

"King David once remarked to me he never found a male or female more capable than Bath-sheba the daughter of Eliam. As for what was said between them that night, Ethan, I fear you will have to enquire of the Queen Mother in person."

"You know her well, don't you?" I enquired sweetly.

"If it weren't for my advice," Nathan paused, "and for Benaiah's Cherethites and Pelethites, her son would not now be sitting between the Cherubim but in some dank and dismal dungeon."

"Then my lord could easily ask the Queen Mother to let me see her face for just a few questions?"

Nathan raised his faded brow. "You would find her most uncommunicative."

158

And he resumed.)

But the woman conceived, and sent and told David, and said, I am with child.

And it came to pass that I attended the King, that day, for the purpose of delivering some minor prophecies. The King turned to me, saying, You know, Nathan, I think she planned that. I asked what made him think so. And he answered, The Lord knows, Nathan, for the Lord sees not as man sees, the Lord looks on the heart; but I just feel it.

I told the King that to have another son was always a blessing, provided the child was his seed.

Of that he was fairly certain, he replied; he had seen the woman perform her ablutions, and she had come unto him within hours thereafter, clean and purified, and Uriah her husband being four days' fast riding away under the walls of Rabbath-ammon.

I said, So it seems that the Lord speaks unto his servant David by words as well as by actual blessings.

But the King frowned, saying, And what about the law of the Lord, which the uncircumcised call taboo? A man can hide a woman, but a child cannot be hidden; and such a thing as immaculate conception may one day happen in our family, but it has not occurred as yet.

So I said unto the King, Did I understand my lord to say that it was four days' fast riding to Jerusholayim from the walls of Rabbath-ammon which is besieged by Joab, with Uriah the Hittite serving under him?

The King said that this was true.

At which I said, Then it is four days' fast riding also from Jerusholayim to the walls of Rabbath-ammon?

The King said, Why, of course.

And I said, Thus within eight days altogether Uriah could be in Jerusholayim and lie with his wife Bath-sheba and become the father of her child, for who is to say to the day how long a suckling has stayed in the womb of his mother?

But King David jabbed his elbow into my ribs, saying, Nathan my friend, if I did not know you for a prophet, I would say you were a rascal.

Through the courtesy of my lord Benaiah I was permitted

access to several letters found in the files of Joab, who commanded the siege of Rabbath-ammon.

The first of these reads as follows:

> To Uriah the Hittite, Captain of a Thousand, at present
> under the walls of Rabbath-ammon, from his Loving Wife
> Bath-sheba, the daughter of Eliam.
>
> May Yahveh grant my husband long life and spoil aplenty.
> Your loving wife is wasting away, pining for the embrace of
> your arms. Do come! The feel of your loins is unto me
> like paradise, I melt under you like snow in the sun. Do
> come! King David has heard of your name and wishes you
> well; you will sit at his table and grow mighty in his sight;
> but at night you will lie with your little turtledove. Do
> come! May Yahveh cause you to hear my sighs.

This letter was apparently accompanied by a note which
Uriah sent to Joab his commander, and which follows:

> To Joab ben Zeruiah, twice Hero of Israel, commanding,
> from his servant Uriah the Hittite, Captain of a Thousand.
>
> May Yahveh cause the sword of my lord to be invin-
> cible. As the attached shows, there is some trouble at home
> which needs my personal attention. Since the siege is pro-
> ceeding as planned, my services may be dispensed with for
> a brief period. I therefore respectfully request a ten days'
> leave of absence. Upon reaching Jerusholayim, I shall
> report at headquarters.

Uriah's application coincided with a communication to
Joab from his royal supreme commander.

> From King David, the Chosen of the Lord, the Beloved
> of Israel and Lion of Judah, to Joab, who is over the host.
>
> May Yahveh endow you with strength. I have heard of
> one Uriah the Hittite, a goodly man, and brave, and a
> capable officer. You would oblige me by dispatching him
> to Jerusholayim for a few days, as I may want to look him
> over.

The best-laid plans of man are as chaff in the wind unto the Lord. And who would have thought that Uriah the Hittite would turn out to be such a paragon of virtue, such a model of temperance, such a stickler for principle?

Uriah rode into Jerusholayim and reported to the palace; but King David bade him to come to his face, and demanded of him how Joab did, and how the people did, and how the war prospered. Then David said to Uriah, Go down to your house and wash your feet. And Uriah departed out of the King's palace, and there followed him a mess of meat from the King.

But Uriah slept at the door of the palace, with the officers of the guard, and went not down to his house.

I was with King David when a servant came from Bath-sheba, saying unto him, Uriah the Hittite was seen riding into Jerusholayim, and my mistress has readied water for his feet, and has baked the meat which the King sent, and also the bed is prepared for Uriah to lie with her; but he has not gone down to his house.

And the King sent, and was told that Uriah slept at the door of the palace; and he had him fetched to his face. And the King said unto Uriah, Was not that a pretty hard ride you had from under the walls of Rabbath-ammon to Jerusholayim all in four days? Why then did you not go down unto your house?

But Uriah bowed his face, saying, If it please my lord, I may be a Hittite, but I have embraced the true faith, so that I set principle above pleasure. The ark, and the host of Israel and Judah, abide in tents; and my lord Joab and the officers of my lord Joab are encamped in the open fields; shall I then go into my house, to eat and to drink and to lie with my wife? As you live, and as your soul lives, I will not do such a thing.

King David frowned at me; but to Uriah he said, Most honourably spoken, my friend, I shall not fail to mention it to Joab your commander. But tarry here a day or two, I shall invite you to my table, and you shall sit to my right,

next to Nathan the prophet, who is a man of great sagacity.
(Nathan paused in his reading to look at me.

I said that his description of the confrontation of the
King and Uriah was masterly and of great value to the
King David Report, and his casual mention of his own
sagacity a fine touch.

Nathan nodded. "There are a few surprises yet to
come!"

And he resumed.)

So Uriah abode in Jerusholayim that day, and the morrow.
But King David said to me, Nathan, we must get this man
drunk; it is our one hope; for the Lord created wine as an anti-
dote to principle.

And when David had called him, Uriah did eat and drink
with us, and we plied him from the right and from the left,
and the King praised Bath-sheba and advised Uriah to make
use of his opportunity, for when we were old and cold and got
no heat, it would be too late. I also nudged Uriah, and made
him drink with me, until I thought he would fall flat on his
face.

But he did not. He rose to his full size and, his tongue
somewhat heavy, announced it was past his bedtime, for he
was to set out on the morrow to do four days' fast riding
unto the walls of Rabbath-ammon. After which he tottered
out without a by-your-leave.

The King sent a servant after Uriah to see him safely
home to Bath-sheba. The servant returned soon, and he
prostrated himself before the King and said that Uriah went
out to lie on his bed with the officers of the guard, but went
not down to his house.

And the King threw his cup at the servant; then he called
Seraiah the scribe so he might dictate to him. But myself
and the others, we went every man his way.

It might be well to include here a few more documents
from the files of Joab, to which I was permitted access by the
courtesy of my lord Benaiah.

The one is a letter given to Uriah to transmit.

From King David, the Favourite of the Lord, the

Provider of Israel and Protector of Judah, to Joab, who is over the host; by Uriah the Hittite.

May Yahveh reward your loyalty by new victories. Set Uriah in the forefront of the hottest battle, and retire from him, that he may be smitten and die.

The second is a brief entry in the daily report of Joab.

And I commanded Uriah the Hittite to lead a small troop in the direction of Gate 5, for the purpose of luring the enemy into making a sortie, so we might take prisoners and learn from them concerning matters within Rabbath-ammon.

The third document, being a later entry by Joab in his daily report, contains the gist of his instructions to a messenger he dispatched to King David.

When you have given my situation report unto the King, and if so be that the King's wrath arise, and he says to you, Wherefore approached you so nigh unto the city when you did fight? knew you not that they would shoot from the wall? did not a woman cast a piece of millstone upon Abimelech ben Jerubbesheth that he died? Then you shall say, Uriah the Hittite died also.

A final notation, in the hand of Seraiah David's scribe, appears to be a record of the King's reply to the same messenger.

Thus shall you say unto Joab, Let not this thing displease you, for the sword devours one as well as another: make your battle more strong against the city and overthrow it.

READING BY NATHAN FROM HIS BOOK OF REMEMBRANCES
CONCLUDED, WITH QUESTIONS BY ETHAN BEN HOSHAIAH
AND NATHAN'S ANSWERS SET IN BRACKETS

When the wife of Uriah heard that her husband was

dead, she mourned for him. And Eliam her father came, and her mother also, and the whole family came, even the cousins and nieces, and they sat in mourning and tore their clothes and wailed and yammered, so it reached the ear of the King.

The King said unto me, Now I am all for honouring the dead, but Bath-sheba seems to be overdoing it, and I fear the evil tongues saying, Has the wife of Uriah not cherished her husband in life that she carries on so at his death? has she by chance had a lover? Therefore, Nathan, go you to the widow and console her, and tell her to send away the countless relatives who clutter up her house.

I did as King David commanded; and I found Bath-sheba in torn clothes, and her hair in a simple knot, and looking altogether very striking. And she said, Why should I not weep, and wail, and mourn Uriah, and have my relatives lament him? Do I not carry a child inside me which will be born an orphan and have neither father nor inheritance, although it is of royal blood? It is one thing to have a poor helpless soldier's wife come unto the King, and have her lie with him and minister to him topwise and bottomwise, but another to stand by her in her distress and fulfil the royal promise. And she held her hands to her face, and cried out loud, and said how too terrible it would be if Eliam her father and all her family were to learn of her predicament.

So I informed the King of the words of the lady Bath-sheba, and I enquired as to what royal promise he made her, if any. David replied, How should I remember: a man says this and that when he lies with a woman.

I felt great misgivings, for the Lord says, You shall not lie carnally with your neighbour's wife to defile yourself with her. But the King said, Go you, and tell the woman that when the time of mourning is past she can move into the palace, and I will marry her, but without ado, for enough has been noised about this among the people.

And after her time of mourning Bath-sheba moved into the palace, with all her coffers and rugs and earthenware and silver, and with her servants; and all Jerusholayim talked of the wedding on which the woman insisted, for she was big with child when she walked with David under the baldachin, and she waddled like a duck.

("But why did the King behave so meekly and give in to

164

the lady Bath-sheba in all that she demanded of him?" I asked.

Nathan shrugged, saying that the Queen Mother would impress me as a forceful enough personality.

"Does that mean that my lord will try to let me speak to her?"

Nathan seemed annoyed. "We now come to my famous parable," he said, "and my rebuking the King, and my prophesying the future, and none of your common prophecies either that you can buy for next to nothing from any little prophet at the gate of the city, but one that is pertinent and true in all ways."

And he resumed.)

Shortly after the wedding Bath-sheba bore King David a son. But the thing David had done displeased the Lord.

And the Lord sent me unto David. I came unto him and said to him, There were two men in one city; the one rich, and the other poor. The rich man had exceeding many flocks and herds; but the poor man had nothing save one little ewe lamb, which he had bought and nourished up: and it grew up together with him, and with his children, and lay in his bosom, and was unto him as a daughter.

And there came a traveller unto the rich man; but he spared to take of his own flock, nay, he took the poor man's lamb and prepared it for the man that was come to him.

And David's anger was greatly kindled against the rich man; and he said to me, As the Lord lives, the man that has done this thing shall surely die, and he shall restore the lamb fourfold, because he had no pity.

I said to David, You are that man.

But the King said, I thought there was something surreptitious about your story; now, therefore, tell me: did the Lord truly appear to you, or have you been fibbing?

My knees trembled greatly, but the spirit of the Lord was upon me, and I said, Thus speaks the Lord God of Israel, I anointed you King over Israel, and I delivered you out of the hand of Saul, and I gave you plenty of wives, and I gave you the house of Israel and of Judah: and if that had been too little, I would moreover have given unto you such and such things. Wherefore then have you despised the commandment of the Lord, to do evil in his sight? You have killed

Uriah the Hittite with the sword of the children of Ammon and have taken his wife to be your wife.

But the King said, Either the Lord is truly speaking through you, Nathan, or you are the most insolent man this side of Jordan, for have you not been part of this from the beginning, and where was your fine righteous voice then?

My bowels were filled with fear, but the Lord went on speaking through me unto David, saying, Now therefore the sword shall never depart from your house. Behold, I will raise up evil against you out of your own house, and I will take your wives before your eyes and give them unto your neighbour, and he shall lie with your wives in the sight of this sun. For you did it secretly; but I will do this thing before all Israel, and before the sun.

I surely thought that the King would strike out at me, and that I should lose my place at his table and my emoluments and title. But the King bowed his face and said, Nathan, I have sinned against the Lord. But it is mostly Bath-sheba's doing, I don't know how and I don't know why, I am like clay in the hands of that woman.

Thereupon I pleaded with the Lord; and the spirit of the Lord once more came down upon me and spoke unto David, saying, The Lord also has put away your sin; you shall not die. Howbeit, because by this deed you have given great occasion to the enemies of the Lord to blaspheme, the child that is born unto you shall surely die.

After which the spirit of the Lord departed from me. But as the King said nothing and seemed thoughtful, I left quietly and went my way.

(Nathan sighed deeply and put aside the last tablet of his chapter.

I rose and gripped his hand, and in a voice deep from the chest said unto him, "Great! Just great! Shattering!")

18

PRAISED BE THE NAME of the Lord our God, who has made man in his image; but his image is of many hues.

When I was done with the documents from the files of Joab and came to return them to Benaiah ben Jehoiada, he had me called unto him and enquired whether I was satisfied with what I had learned. So I said that these letters and notations were of great value to the King David Report, and that they supplemented in the most curious manner the story of the heart-warming, tender love of King David and the lady Bath-sheba as related in the book of remembrances of my lord Nathan.

"What precisely has he written on the subject?" asked Benaiah.

I told him in brief.

"And you believe all that?" Benaiah grinned, displaying his teeth. "Especially the part about the timely death of Uriah the Hittite?"

"But for overly stressing the importance of his own person," I said, "my lord Nathan seems largely to have recorded what he saw with his own eyes and heard with his own ears."

"Which shows," commented Benaiah, "that man should use not only his eyes and ears, but also the bit of brain which the Lord gave him. Hasn't it struck you that Uriah behaved most strangely? Behold, a man comes home from the war. He was encamped in the field, he has ridden four days, he is tired and dirty but full of juices—and he refuses to go to his young wife who has sent him a letter such as you saw?"

"If my lord will forgive his servant: there must have been many witnesses to the fact that Uriah slept at the gate of the palace, with the officers of the guard, and went not to his house."

"And the reason he gave for his abstemiousness?"

"That was a bit high-flown."

"But what if Uriah did see his wife, Bath-sheba?"

"When?"

"Before he came unto the face of King David, to deliver himself of his noble utterances?"

"My lord seems to forget that the woman sent a servant to King David, to enquire as to Uriah, saying that the water was readied for his feet, and so forth, but Uriah had not gone down to his house."

"That is no proof that he didn't."

Benaiah was right.

"Let us suppose, Ethan, that Uriah went to his house and learned from Bath-sheba that she was with child, and by whom: what would he have done?"

"Killed her."

"Really?"

"Surely he would have turned her out."

"Put yourself in his place."

I thought of Lilith, and of the loss that was threatening me because King Solomon wanted her for a handmaid to his Egyptian wife-to-be. "My lord means to say that Uriah would have gritted his teeth and suffered?"

"Let us suppose, Ethan, that Bath-sheba spoke to her husband as follows: Uriah dear, you know there was little I could do but lie with the King. But now, behold, the old lecher wants to renege his promise and make the child which I carry appear as your child, so that we have no claim on him. But if you behave wisely, Uriah dear, and do not go home tonight to lie with me, then the child will indubitably be David's, and you will rise in the service of the King and sit at his table, among the mighty of the kingdom; and the little prince, who is inside me, shall be King over Israel."

I grudgingly admired Benaiah, whose ears reached into the far corners of the country and whose mind wove a clever web of various threads, and I said, "This would explain Uriah's high-sounding talk before the King and his protestation of unselfishness. But did not Bath-sheba foresee that David, if pressed, might have Uriah destroyed?"

"And suppose she foresaw it?"

My mouth went dry.

Benaiah laughed. "Remains the question as to why Uriah carried the King's letter for four days and nights and never read it. Would you have done so?"

I said I hoped I would never disappoint the trust of the King or of any of his mighty men.

"But suppose Uriah did read it?" asked Benaiah.

"He would have disposed of it."

"Another, similarly worded letter would have reached Joab by another messenger."

"Then he would have fled as fast as his horse would carry him, to any of the Syrias, to the land of his fathers. Anywhere."

"Fled from that glorious future which Bath-sheba his wife had painted for him, and which was his if only he survived until the birth of the child?"

"A dead man has no future."

"I see you never served in the war, Ethan, for you do not know what Uriah assuredly knew: that neither Joab nor even King David in person could set him in the forefront of the hottest battle unless he wanted to betake himself there. It is common soldiers like Abimelech ben Jerubbesheth who must go to the forefront of the hottest battle, where a piece of millstone will be dropped on their head; but a Captain of a Thousand can always contrive to stay out of range."

"Yet Uriah died that day together with Abimelech."

Benaiah clapped his hands, and a servant came and set before me a pitcher of scented water and a few tablets of clay. "Read these," urged Benaiah. "They are Joab's own words, from one of his confessions. I have him confessing daily. It eases his heart."

CONFESSION OF JOAB BEN ZERUIAH IN REFERENCE TO THE DEATH OF URIAH THE HITTITE, UNDER QUESTIONING BY BENAIAH BEN JEHOIADA

Question: And Uriah the Hittite handed you King David's letter?

169

Answer: Yes.

Question: What did you do?

Answer: I obeyed the instructions contained therein.

Question: Did it not strike you as odd that the King would command you to sacrifice one of your best captains?

Answer: King David was the Chosen of the Lord.

Question: So you set Uriah in the forefront of the hottest battle?

Answer: I sent him to lead a small troop to Gate 5, from which I expected the enemy to issue forth and give battle.

Question: Was that all you did? You have confessed to so much, why not confess all.

Answer: I commanded a group of archers to hold themselves in readiness.

Question: And Uriah died with an arrow in his back?

Answer: That is how he died.

Queen Mother Bath-sheba sat languidly on her cushions, observant eyes peering from between her veils now at Nathan, now at me.

I wanted to lead her gently to the point that interested me: had she been just the helpless soldier's wife coerced to quench the fire in the bowels of the King, or was she the moving spirit of the crimes which followed upon the original sin, using her body and the fruit of her womb to beguile the King until it was her son that sat on the throne—not Amnon, not Absalom, not Adonijah, not any of the older sons from wives of longer standing—but her Solomon, the late-comer, out of a junior wife?

I tried every way. I spoke of the misfortune of her first husband's untimely death; she said, as did David, The sword devours one as well as another. I spoke of the kindness of the Lord, who caused Uriah to come to Jerusholayim to see her one last time; she said that the ways of the Lord were beyond our power to discern.

But when I spoke of the child that had to die because David by his deed had given great occasion to the enemies of the Lord to blaspheme, her lids began to flutter. "It was so tiny," she said. "It never had a chance."

"The King loved it?"

"He besought God for the child, and fasted, and lay all night upon the earth."

"King David loved all his children," corrected Nathan.

"The child was dying for him and in his place," Bath-sheba said, "so why shouldn't David have loved it?"

"He besought God to let it live," amended Nathan. "For seven days and seven nights he prayed, and the elders of his house went to him, to raise him up from the earth; but he would not, neither did he eat bread with them."

"The child was dying," said Bath-sheba. "And David was undecided: should he thank God for accepting the child's life in token of his own, or curse himself for this barter with the Lord; and his feeling of guilt waxed great."

"It was no barter," objected Nathan. "It was preordained. For David was the Chosen of the Lord."

"And that is why the child had to be punished?" asked Bath-sheba.

"But the Lord blessed you with another son, madam," Nathan reminded her. "And this son was destined for greatness, even for the throne of Israel."

Her mouth had thinned. "David came unto me that night. He had changed his apparel, and was washed and anointed, and seemed altogether at peace. I said, How can you sit there, wiping the mutton grease off your lips, as though not a thing had happened? David answered, While the child was yet alive, I fasted and wept: for I said, Who can tell whether God will be gracious to me, that the child may live. But now he is dead, wherefore should I fast? can I bring him back again? I shall go to him, but he shall not return to me."

She nodded heavily. "In a way David was right. I stopped weeping, and I said to him, The Lord may have cancelled your guilt in that he took the child's life against Uriah's. But what about your promise to me which you made before God: that your son and mine shall sit upon your throne? Is that also cancelled by the death of the child?"

She gazed at the costly rings on her fingers. "And David said unto me, Be of good cheer and prepare your bed. And he went in unto me and lay with me and I bore him a second son, whose name we called Solomon, for the peace that the

Lord made with David and for the atonement: and the Lord loved Solomon."

She had obviously ended. I thanked her; but she frowned moodily and soon retired to her rooms.

Nathan kept shaking his head. "A veritable miracle," he exclaimed. "I never have heard Queen Mother Bath-sheba talk of these matters, and so minutely! But the story surely needs sifting."

A few days thereafter, a royal messenger came to the house and handed me a summons to appear before the face of the Wisest of Kings on the morrow, after the hour of the public audience, and to bring with me all materials pertaining to the story of the heart-warming, tender love of King David and the lady Bath-sheba, up to and including the birth of their second son whose name was called Solomon for the peace that the Lord made with David.

Also the man gave me a small disc of copper, which was embossed with the royal seal; I was to hand this to the guard upon my entering the inner part of the palace.

But Shem and Sheleph my sons admired the disc of copper greatly, and they told me that Cherethites and Pelethites were now placed in many buildings of the city, and that servants of Benaiah ben Jehoiada had been to their school to enquire of teachers and students on such matters as the wisdom of the Wisest of Kings, Solomon, and the price of corn, and the temple that was being built unto the Lord. And Shem and Sheleph asked if it was true that King Solomon was sick with fear so that he shook and two servants, one on his right and one on his left, were needed to hold him; and if the damsel Abishag of Shunam, who had ministered to King David, was now lying with Prince Adonijah; and if Zadok the priest did not cause the best of the sacrificial meats to be sold on the market; and if Jehoshaphat ben Ahilud, the recorder, did not receive a share of the profits being earned by the use of forced labour in the construction of the temple; and if the Royal Commission on the Preparation of the *Report on the Amazing Rise* and so forth, for which I worked, was not a cabal of falsifiers and prevaricators; and if, in brief, the whole kingdom of Israel was not going to the dogs.

172

At this my anger was kindled greatly, and I cried out at the wickedness of my sons, who concerned themselves with rumours and evil thought instead of learning the law of the Lord as handed down by Moishe our Teacher. But deep in my mind I was troubled: if all this was the gossip of the streets and the talk of the young men, it might well come about that those who walked in the ways of the Lord would find themselves with their heads cut off, for when the mighty feel threatened they strike out at the just.

But on the morrow, after the hour of the public audience, I went to the royal palace, and was ushered into the presence of the King, and found with him Jehoshaphat ben Ahilud, the recorder, and all the Commission members but Benaiah ben Jehoiada. And as I rose from prostrating myself before the King, I could not help looking at him to verify if he shook in the manner described to me by Shem and Sheleph.

The King, however, was merely tapping his foot and toying with the breasts of the cherub to his right, and he asked, "Why do you set your eyes upon me as though I were an ill man? Am I like Saul whom David my father was called in to heal?"

I bowed, saying that my eyes were filled with awe at the splendour that was about the King's countenance by the spirit of the Lord.

"I thought I looked rather poorly today," he scowled. "I lay awake most of the night thinking of the design for the decoration of the temple. I shall have the whole inside overlaid with gold, and all the walls round about carved with figures of cherubim and palm trees and open flowers, and within the oracle two cherubim of olive tree, each ten cubits high, and their wings stretched forth so that the wing of the one touches the one wall and the wing of the other touches the other wall, and their wings touching one another in the midst of the house."

He glanced about as though he were waiting for something, and I hurried to assure him that I thought the design gorgeous, and that it certainly would turn out to be one of the wonders of the world.

"Ethan," he said, "you are as transparent to me as the pools of Heshbon, by the gate of Bath-rabbim, in which you can see the worms that wriggle at the bottom of the water. In truth you are thinking, Is not King Solomon building this

173

temple for his glory rather than God's, and so that people might flock to it from everywhere and speak, Behold the magnificence of the temple of Solomon? But I tell you that the King's fine raiment means more to the ordinary man than a pair of trousers for his back, and a temple resplendent in gold more than a coin of copper in his hand; for thus has Lord Yahveh fashioned the mind of man."

He ceased toying with the cherub and dug his nails into the flesh of his palm. I declared that his knowledge of human nature was beyond compare, and that ill-advised was he who tried to conceal anything before the wisdom of the King.

"Also you are thinking," he continued; "Why does King Solomon meddle in all matters as a fool sticks his nose into every pot? But I tell you that a leader who wishes to preserve his neck must trouble himself not only about war and peace and general obedience to the word of the Lord, but also about such things as what flower should be carved on which wall and which story be told in what manner. For power is indivisible: one stone broken out of its edifice will bring down the whole structure."

He rose and stepped down from his throne as though in search of someone; then his gaze fastened on me. I hastily avowed that an edifice propped by the Lord would withstand even the quaking of the earth.

"How is Lilith your concubine?" he asked. "It appears that I shall have to marry the daughter of Pharaoh and build a house for her and give her servants, for I cannot lodge her with the other royal ladies."

I averred that all Israel would be overjoyed at the King's marriage with Egypt, but surely there was between Dan and Beer-sheba an abundance of handmaids who were prettier, and more graceful, and better suited to serve Pharaoh's daughter than Lilith my concubine.

The King jabbed his finger against my chest. "But it is you, Ethan, whom I wish to honour. Jehoshaphat the recorder and Nathan the prophet and Benaiah ben Jehoiada are as one man in their praise of your zeal; therefore..."

There was the sound of voices at the door, Benaiah's among them, and the clank of weapons. The King turned and rushed towards Benaiah, enquiring, "It is done, then?"

"It is done," said Benaiah.

"You fell upon him?"

"I fell upon him."

"And he is dead?"

"Quite dead."

"Praised be the Lord!"

"Amen," said Benaiah.

And my heart filled with dread as I surmised whose name had been struck off the list which King David on his death-bed had given to his son; but the Wisest of Kings, Solomon, seemed much relieved as he returned to his throne, and delicately sat down on it, and proclaimed, "The entire Commission on the Preparation of *The One and Only True and Authoritative, Historically Correct and Officially Approved Report on the Amazing Rise* and so forth being assembled, including Ethan our redactor, let us begin."

Thereupon Jehoshaphat ben Ahilud commanded me to outline to the King the story of the heart-warming, tender love of his father David and the lady Bath-sheba, as I had gathered it. I did so, omitting the more sordid features or at least palliating them, and concluding my discourse by saying, "And David comforted Bath-sheba his wife, and went in unto her, and lay with her, and she bore a son and he called his name Solomon." Then I added for good measure, "And the Lord loved Solomon."

The King smiled.

And the thought came to me what I would feel, and what I would do, if a man told me before witnesses that my father had had my mother's husband murdered, and that I was the issue of something worse than adultery.

But the King still sat there, smiling.

Finally Jehoshaphat stepped forth and said unto the King, "My lord is acquainted with the position taken by the members of this Commission on the inclusion of undesirable matter in works of history, which is: tell it, but discreetly, and make it appear pleasing to the eye of the Lord our God, from whom stems all wisdom. But in this case it is the considered opinion of all of us, excepting Benaiah ben Jehoiada, that the story, however discreetly told, would cast a doubtful light on the Chosen of the Lord, David, and on Queen Mother Bath-sheba. This leaves us with little choice on so important a matter as the birth and legitimacy of the Wisest

175

of Kings, Solomon: we either leave it untold, and why then do the whole King David Report? or we invent a new and expurgated story of the heart-warming, tender love, suggesting that Uriah died by a distemper of the bowels or a poisoning of the blood and that David saw Bath-sheba from the roof of his house *after* she was widowed. Unfortunately these occurrences do not date back to ancient history; they happened within the memory of thousands of people who are still alive, so that both our silence on the subject or even the best of fables would be scorned by many in Israel. Therefore we respectfully petition the Wisest of Kings to render a decision as sagacious as his judgment in the litigation of the two harlots over the child."

The King turned to Benaiah. "You were not agreed?"

"These men overrate the importance of the word." Benaiah snorted. "If the King wishes to claim that he is the son, say, of an untouched virgin and a dove that came fluttering from the skies, I will send out six hundred of my Cherethites and Pelethites, and on the morrow all of Jerusholayim will swear that he is."

At which the King blinked, and assured Benaiah of his favour, and asked me for my suggestions.

I said it was my sense that a man as wise as King Solomon and endowed with so many gifts, and enjoying the devotion of the people Israel, and blessed with riches and with power, and a prince of peace, was a living manifestation of the love of the Lord and of the esteem in which the Lord held the King's parents.

"Why, Ethan," the King exclaimed, "that is in essence what Mamma always told me. Solomon my son, she always said, your father has sinned in the eyes of the Lord in that he took the poor helpless wife of a soldier and lay with her, and also had her husband killed. But who is to judge the ways of the Lord, she said, who put temptation before your father, for I was not as shapeless then as I am now, and my face a horror; I was of handsome build, and graceful, and my skin like the petals of a rose of Sharon; furthermore he saw me in the light of the setting sun as I was washing myself. So the Lord chastised your father by taking away that poor little child, your elder brother, though he was scarcely six weeks old and innocent of all evil. But you, Solomon my son, were

176

begotten after the sin of your father was paid for and forgiven, for it is said, eye for eye, tooth for tooth, life for life; thus you are not a child of death, but of life; and your name is Peace, and you are blessed by the Lord and beloved by him."

The King swallowed: he was visibly moved by the words of his mother and by the thought of his good fortune in that he was born second.

Then he suggested, "So why don't you write it in accordance with Mamma's wisdom. Or do you pretend to know better than an old woman in Israel who has become the mother of a king?"

And thus it was written in the King David Report, and the story of David and Bath-sheba is contained therein.

19

AFTER THE SESSION King Solomon continued most affable and asked if the members of the Commission, including myself, would break some bread with him at his table. There was much joy at the royal invitation; only Benaiah ben Jehoiada claimed urgent business with his Cherethites and Pelethites and asked to be excused.

Whereupon the other members of the Commission exchanged meaningful glances and adjourned to the royal dining room, the walls of which were inlaid with images of grapes and pomegranates and other delicacies. The King bade me to sit at his side on the cushions, and he tore a luscious morsel from his piece of fattail and graciously stuffed it into my mouth. I chewed, and I thanked him, saying that the King's wrath was as the roaring of a lion, but his favour as dew upon the grass.

"That sounds like a good adage," said Solomon, pleased. And to Elihoreph and Ahiah b'nai Shisha, the scribes, "Mark it down well, for I am planning a collection of pithy proverbs to evidence my exceeding wisdom."

I said I was deeply honoured by the King's wish to include my poor saying in his collection; also, whenever another occurred to me that was of the proper spirit, I would joyfully let him have it.

This gladdened his heart, as he would receive something for nothing, and he enquired about the progress of my work, and which was the next item to be dealt with in the King David Report.

"The Absalom revolt," I said.

"Absalom..." The name appeared to grate on his ear as anything must that pertained to the overthrow of established power. "And where would you begin?"

The roots of the tree are hidden from the eye, I thought, but they reach down to the waters. However, I had to answer the Wisest of Kings, Solomon, in a manner that kings will understand; therefore I said, "It might be best to begin with the story of Tamar, Absalom's sister."

The King took an eye of the lamb, dipped it in pepper, bade me open my lips, and popped it onto my tongue.

I swallowed and thanked him for his exceeding kindness. Then I said, "But Tamar seems buried as in a pit of silence, and your servant is at a loss whether to enquire concerning her from the royal chief eunuch or the royal chief grave-digger."

"Tamar," said the King, "has gone insane, and the family have placed her in the temple of Beth-shan, far from Jerusholayim, where the priests feed her and wash her and do unto her what is necessary."

The room was suddenly very quiet. I thought of the Tamar that was, in her garment of divers colours: these were the robes worn by the King's daughters that were virgins.

"You will not elicit much from her," said the King. "Men of God and conjurers and also doctors have examined her and have tried to learn from her what took place between her and my brother Amnon; but she babbles nonsense."

"The key to wisdom lies in the listening," I advanced, "for does not the spirit of the Lord speak frequently through the ravings of the mad?"

And a debate ensued on insanity and prophetism between Nathan the prophet and Zadok the priest, and both of them grew very vexed. But King Solomon said, "Every way of a man is right in his own eyes; the Lord ponders the hearts."

On that note the meal was ended.

God!

It wasn't the same city, Jerusholayim.

The guards at the gate of the palace had been tripled; the streets rang with the crash of wheels and the stamp of hooves;

armoured chariots were placed at public buildings and important crossings.

Among the uncircumcised, a display of such power would have emptied the streets: not so with the children of Israel, who thrive on excitement. They shouted, and enquired, and waved their hands; they got under the horses and between the Cherethites and Pelethites; thieves and purse-snatchers were everywhere, upsetting the stalls of the merchants and making off with the goods, and the servants of Benaiah ben Jehoiada moved among the crowd and listened, and suddenly a man would be taken by the armpits and led away.

One name was on everyone's lips: Adonijah the son of King David out of Haggith, prince of the blood, who had been slain.

Some said that no man in Israel was safe if a son of King David could be murdered inside his house and his body thrown on the street like a dog's; others maintained that King Solomon could not possibly suffer it, and that Benaiah had overreached himself; a priest raised his hands, proclaiming that Adonijah had brought his end upon himself for his whoring about and his refusal to walk in the ways of the Lord. But a cripple who was clad in tatters shook his fist, crying out that they were all scoundrels and whoresons, Adonijah and Benaiah, and King Solomon the wickedest of them; so he was led away.

And the fear of things to come waxed big in my heart, so that I shrank at hearing my name called.

But it was Shem and Sheleph my sons who emerged from among the people, waving a smudged rag and shouting, "We have seen it! We have seen it all!" And Shem came and gave me the rag, saying, "That's his blood!" And Sheleph added, "There was a great puddle of it!" And Shem declared proudly, "I tore this from my robe and dipped it in his blood as a gift for you and a remembrance."

The food I had eaten at the table of the King rose from my stomach and stuck in my gullet. But Shem and Sheleph were thrilled, and they told me it had been noised in their school that something was to occur concerning Prince Adonijah; whereupon they and others of their fellows sneaked away to the house of Adonijah; but the house was surrounded by men who ambled hither and thither, or observed a crack in the wall, or picked their teeth. And numerous runners came carrying white staffs and shouting to make room for Benaiah ben Jehoiada who was over the host; and Benaiah drove up in his chariot; and he entered the house.

"And behold," said Shem, "he looked sinister."

There was the sound of voices from the house, and a piercing cry; a man came staggering out who was covered with blood from a gash in his face, and collapsed.

"And behold," said Sheleph, "he looked gruesome."

But as the men who had ambled hither and thither were about to pick up the body, a damsel hastened near, wailing and calling out to the Lord and the people. When she perceived Adonijah lying there in a pool of his blood, she threw herself upon him, and tore her clothes, and kissed his mouth and his one eye, for the other had been gouged out by the sword. Then the men who had ambled hither and thither took her by the armpits and led her away.

"And behold," said Shem, "she looked sick."

The body of Adonijah was carried into the house. A while later Benaiah stepped forth, spoke briefly with the men who had ambled hither and thither, mounted his chariot, and drove off.

"And behold," said Sheleph, "he looked as though nothing had happened."

Whereupon I sent Shem and Sheleph home, advising them to stay out of mischief the rest of the day.

The counsel of a brother is like balm upon the heart; but a word from the wise may cure the ailment.

Therefore I bethought myself of Penuel ben Mushi, administrator third grade in the Royal Treasury, who had taken pity on the newcomer of Jerusholayim and, made loquacious by some wine and a slice of lamb, had initiated me into some of the secrets that were whispered about among the knowledgeable.

I reached the Treasury through byways and back streets, and treated the guards at the entrance to a wave of the hand, as do men of high rank who will not be challenged. The hallways of the building were like the insides of a sepulchre;

for great events excite the people, but the servants of the King wait in trepidation.

And I found Penuel ben Mushi in his chambers; he jumped up at seeing me and spread his fingers.

"Friend," I said, "I am not an evil spirit of the Lord; I am Ethan ben Hoshaiah, redactor of the *Report on the Amazing Rise* and so forth; and since I know you as a man well informed on matters public and not so public, I have come to learn from you concerning the end of Prince Adonijah."

But Penuel ben Mushi hammered his forehead, and cursed the day on which I had entered his life, and pleaded with me to leave his chambers and not to let on that I knew him, as the ears of Benaiah ben Jehoiada were everywhere. Nor would he listen to my entreaties; he took me by the sleeve and pulled me to the door and pushed me out.

I left the Treasury as in a daze: what sort of leper had I become, and why, and since when? I walked the streets, a lone man among the crowds and frightened. But as a dog returns to his vomit, so my thoughts always returned to the warning which Benaiah ben Jehoiada gave me on the occasion of his meeting me at the house of Joab, saying. If you know as much as I think you know, Ethan, I think you know too much.

There was nowhere to go but home.

The house was dipped in pink by the light of the evening, and before its door stood the green and gold litter with the red tasselled roof.

I thought of turning away to spend the night in an inn, or a shed, or even a doorway. But I felt too tired and discouraged, and went into the house like a sheep on its way to be slaughtered.

And there was Amenhoteph the royal chief eunuch greeting me at his most guttural and enquiring as to my health and why I was holding myself aloof from him. Lilith my concubine came forth with a basin of water, and she washed my face and hands and feet while Amenhoteph beamed at her graceful movements; and Huldah the mother of my sons brought in wine and bread and a dish of goat cheese which was mixed with minced olives and grated nuts. But Esther my wife sent in, begging to be excused: it had been a long day, and her heart was feeling the strain.

The women left. Amenhoteph ate in silence, daintily placing bits of cheese on his bread. Finally he wiped his hands on a cloth of fine linen, saying, "After a day such as this, a man thinks of his soul and seeks out his friends."

The fear was back in my bowels.

"Death is a quick reaper." He nodded. "How long ago is it that you and I saw Adonijah do unto the damsel Abishag in the manner of he-goats, and in other manners; and now he was fallen upon by Benaiah, and is dead."

He looked at me significantly, and the fear in my bowels increased.

"As a historian, Ethan, you may find assassination a common enough device; but this one has its special aspects, and one of these concerns you. I take it you know what happened?"

I shook my head.

"Adonijah must have lost his last bit of reason over the damsel," said Amenhoteph, "for he chose of all people Queen Mother Bath-sheba to speak to King Solomon on his behalf, and he was so imbecile as to remind her, You know that the kingdom was mine, and that all Israel set their faces on me, that I should reign; howbeit the kingdom is turned about, and is become my brother's."

Amenhoteph tilted his hands in the most delicate manner.

"You can imagine how that pleased the old lady. Had he forgotten that it was Bath-sheba who by her influence on King David had turned the kingdom about? Had he forgotten that Abishag, though no heat passed from her to King David, was nevertheless David's woman, and that to claim any of the King's women meant claiming his power?"

I thought of Adonijah going in unto Abishag and her writhing and clawing at him; and my fear grew hot within me and rose to my heart.

"But Bath-sheba agreed to speak to King Solomon for Adonijah. And King Solomon rose up to meet her, and bowed himself unto her, and caused a seat to be set for his mother; and she sat at his right. Then she said, I desire one small petition of you; I pray you, don't say no to your mother. And the King said, Ask on, Mamma: I will not say no to you."

There she was again, Bath-sheba the wife of Uriah: butter would not melt in her mouth, but the tip of her tongue carried death.

"She said, Let Abishag the Shunammite be given to Adonijah your brother to wife." Amenhoteph's hands moved like the heads of two snakes about to attack one another. "I noticed the faces of Jehoshaphat ben Ahilud, the recorder, and of Benaiah ben Jehoiada: they were as stone. But the countenance of the King waxed yellow as lemon, and he said, Why do you ask Abishag the Shunammite for Adonijah, Mamma? ask for him the kingdom also; for he is my elder brother; even for him, and for Abiathar the priest, and for Joab ben Zeruiah."

Solomon saw a conspiracy, of course. As power is born of conspiracy, the mighty cannot but think in its terms: Bath-sheba was wise in the ways of the mind.

"Then the King cried out at Benaiah," Amenhoteph went on, "and also at me, saying, what good servants were we, and how great our vigilance, that his brother Adonijah and the damsel Abishag were able to consort under our very noses? And where were the friends of the King, and all his counsellors, seeing that he must learn from his Mamma about the affairs of his kingdom? God do so to me, he said, and more also, if Adonijah has not spoken this word against his own life. Now, therefore, as the Lord lives, who has established me and set me on the throne of David my father, Adonijah shall be put to death this day."

I remembered the piece of rag with the dark spots on it that were the blood of Adonijah, and in a shaky voice I asked Amenhoteph which were the aspects of the assassination that concerned me?

Amenhoteph gazed at me, his red-veined eyes protruding slightly, and said, "Is it not the duty of every son of Israel to walk in the ways of the Lord and be an informer unto the authorities? Did you not know of this, that, and the other thing concerning Adonijah which might have been of interest to the servants of the King?"

"Didn't you know, too?" I replied.

"Indeed I did." He tilted his hands and turned his head, so that he looked like one of those figures which the Egyptians

carve on the columns they call obelisks, and smiled as
enigmatically.

Thoughts of Ethan ben Hoshaiah, as he sat in his study
after the departure of Amenhoteph the royal chief eunuch,
meditating

On the nature of rulers
You see a man diligent in his business? he shall stand
before kings.
The heaven for height, and the earth for depth, and
the heart of kings is unsearchable.
When you sit to eat with a ruler, consider assiduously
what is before you: and put a knife to your throat, if you
be a man given to appetite.
The fear of a king is as the roaring of a lion: whoso
provokes him to anger sins against his own soul.
A stone is heavy, and the sand weighty, but a fool's
wrath is heavier than them both.

On conditions in the kingdom
Where there is no vision, the people perish.
If a ruler hearken to lies, all his servants are wicked.
Their heart studies destruction, and their lips talk of
mischief.
The bloodthirsty hate the upright.
The Lord has made all things for himself: yea, even
the wicked for the day of evil.
For a just man may fall seven times, and rise up again:
but the wicked shall fall into mischief.

On becoming involved in the affairs of state
Can a man take fire in his bosom, and his clothes not
be burned? Can one go upon hot coals, and his feet not be
burned?
Put not forth yourself in the presence of the King, and
stand not in the place of great men.
A prudent man conceals knowledge; but a fool's mouth
is his destruction, and his lips are the snare of his soul.

A whip for the horse, a bridle for the ass, and a rod for the fool's back.

A fining pot is for silver, and the furnace for gold: but the Lord tries the hearts.

ON THE ADVISABILITY OF LEAVING ON THE KING'S BUSINESS

The wicked flee when no man pursues: but the righteous are bold as a lion.

Pride goes before destruction, and a haughty spirit before the fall.

A prudent man foresees the evil, and hides himself: but the simple pass on and are punished.

Discretion shall preserve you, understanding shall keep you: to deliver you from the way of evil men, from the man that speaks froward things.

The lot is cast into the lap; but the whole disposing thereof is of the Lord.

ON GOING TO FIND TAMAR THE DAUGHTER OF DAVID AND POSSIBLY SEARCHING AFTER OTHER TRUTHS

Ponder the ways of your feet, and let all your ways be established.

There are many devices in a man's heart: nevertheless, the counsel of the Lord, that shall stand.

The Lord will not suffer the soul of the righteous to famish.

20

"As GOD LIVES," said the captain of the gate, "if it isn't the historian. Have your histories proven worthless, or has the pavement of the city, Jerusholayim, grown too hot for the soles of your feet, for you came with numerous donkeys and are leaving with but one?"

I complimented the captain on his exceeding good memory, saying, "Ah, yes, it's been a long time since I came here with my archives and my family; but I live now at No. 54, Queen-of-Sheba Lane, the King's Houses, and am at present setting out on the King's business." And I produced my credentials.

Meanwhile the beggars had gathered, and such folk as will collect at the gate, and they quipped about rats fleeing the pest-ridden house, and they said that the blood of Adonijah in the streets was but a beginning and that the hills of Jerusholayim would soon bristle with gallows from which hung the parasites who sucked the marrow of the people and the substance of the working man.

The captain let the tails of his whip crack over their heads, saying, "Listen to me, you unkempt rabble and sons of Belial: do your backsides itch for the rod, do you want your tongues torn from your gullets? The Lord has spoiled you by too much freedom, and the bounty of the King has caused you to have excess vigour. But your brains have shrunk to the size of a lentil, for you forget that the kingdom is ruled by the Wisest of Kings, Solomon, through Benaiah ben Jehoiada his favourite servant and through the Cherethites and Pelethites, who see into the heart of each one of you, and who will teach you to keep your lips shut."

And to me he said, "Be gone! Don't you understand that you learned men are an annoyance to the people, and a bother to the servants of the King?"

So I wended my way to the north, towards Beth-shan, on the road past the temple of Nob which was trod by David when he fled from Saul.

And my soul was heavy at the thought of Esther my ailing wife whom I had left behind, and of Lilith my concubine who had been missing at my departure, and of my future which was highly uncertain: for though I might escape an immediate blow by absenting myself from Jerusholayim, I was too old and too set in my ways to learn how to live in the caves and subsist any length of time in the wilderness.

As I rounded the rock from which flows the spring of the boundary, so called because the land of the Jebusites extended up to here before David conquered Jerusholayim and vanquished them, behold, there sat by the spring a small figure entirely wrapped in a white mantle and holding a little bundle.

And my heart jumped, for I saw it was Lilith, and my throat went dry, so I could say nothing as I halted my donkey.

She uncovered her face and came towards me and took my hand, saying, "Do not cast me from you, Ethan my friend. I will walk behind you; where you eat, I will glean the leavings, where you lie down to sleep, I will warm you; for I love you more than my life."

I took her unto me and held her; and I felt how unbearable it would be to lose her to King Solomon and to think of his stubby fingers crawling over her skin; but I also knew that it was unsafe for one man to travel with a beautiful woman on the roads of Israel, for there were marauders about, and soldiers, and all manner of sinister folk, and these might do unto my concubine what in the time of the Judges was done to the concubine of that young Levite by the men of the town of Gibeah, who took hold of her and abused her all the night until morning and then sent her back to him: and the whole of Israel rose as one man and went out to punish the men of

188

Gibeah after the Levite carved his concubine into twelve pieces and sent these to the tribal chieftains. But that was in the time of the Judges; today you could slice your bride into fine shreds and present these to every law enforcement officer in the country, and not a one would bestir himself.

"Lilith my love," I said, "God is my witness that I would like nothing better than to take you with me. The rigours of the journey would turn into joy, and every day would be to us like a honeymoon. But this country is in the throes of unrest; that is why I am trying to vanish; and the road is apt to be perilous."

But she opened her eyes at me, and she said, "I have lain at your feet, Ethan my friend, and I have ministered to you in every way. At first, when you took me from my father in consideration of twelve sheep of good breed and four goats and a milk cow, I saw you as an old man, moody, and smelling of mildew; but with time, as you taught me some of your songs and showed me your kindness, I came to love you, and you were to me as a father and lover and husband all merged in one. Do not think I have come here blindly: I fully realise what it means for a young woman to travel in these times with a man who is a scholar, and gentle, and unskilled in the use of the knife. And if you cast me from your face, I will not go back to No. 54, Queen-of-Sheba Lane, but I will follow you and be unto you as a shadow; and as no man can rend his shadow from him, so you will not be able to rend me from you, unless you tell me that you don't love me and intend lying with other women along the way, with village wenches and whores, in which case I would pray unto the Lord to strike you with boils in your secret places, and with emerods, and with general impotency."

Now the thought of lying with some village wench along the way had been lurking in the back of my mind, for a man in flight is as a bird on the wing, looking about for an occasional field mouse. But the great love of Lilith overwhelmed me, and I felt shame at my whims, and I said, "Lilith my love, why is it that men so rarely perceive the depth of feeling of which women are capable and thus let the blessings pass by which could be theirs? May God do so to me and more, if I ever forget what you taught me and betray your love. Nay, but I will not have you walk behind

189

me; you shall ride on this donkey part of the time, and share my bread; and at night we shall lie under one coverlet, and warm one another, and do unto each other in every manner that is pleasing, and afterwards gaze at the skies and listen to the sighing of the wind."

So we moved on from the rock and from the spring of the boundary, and there was a light on the face of Lilith as from a hundred stars.

On the seventh day of our journey, as the sun was setting like a giant red ball, we saw the walls of Beth-shan that were low, and crumbling in places, and its turrets in disrepair; for the Wisest of Kings, Solomon, spent the riches of the country on the construction of the great temple of the Lord, and the extension of his own palace, and on Fort Millo, and on the walls of Jerusholayim, and on Hazor and Megiddo and all the cities of store that he had, and cities for his chariots, and cities for his horsemen, and that which he desired to build in Jerusholayim and in Lebanon; but the rest of the country went to ruination.

And a man came from the gate who had a rope and was pulling a stubborn old he-goat, and he cried out and cursed the day he was born, and the day the goat was born, and most of all he cursed the priests of the temple of Beth-shan.

"Citizen," I said unto him, "you seem to be sore afflicted with this aged animal. There is no flesh to him and no strength, his horns are decayed and his hair fallen out; he is worth nothing; so why not take pity on him for the sake of the Lord and let him die in peace?"

"Worth nothing?" The man now cursed my mother who had borne me, and the mother of Lilith my concubine, and for good measure also the mother of the donkey on which I sat. Then he said, "Why, this goat is a strapping fellow, and fiery of temperament, and his legs are surely stronger than yours, stranger. But as to his death, he will die soon, and the steam of his blood will rise to the lord from the altar of the temple; for I am taking him to the priests as an offering."

So I praised the man for his exceeding godliness, at which he cried out, and kicked the goat, and explained to me that he had to take an offering unto the priests of Beth-shan on the first day of every month, a goat, or a sheep, or a young calf, as they were keeping his son who was born an idiot; the fee was ruining him, and he and his wife and his other children had nothing to put between their teeth.

We followed the man and his goat going uphill, leaving the town of Beth-shan to our left, and reached the temple at the time of the lighting of the lamps, after the evening prayers. And we turned into the guest house which stood next to the temple, and there were received by a priest from whose face and forearm the dirt was peeling in layers; he stretched out his hand for pay for the night's lodging, saying, "The Lord looks on the heart; but a man who trusts is soon out of pocket."

Later we partook of a morsel of bread and some meat, all gristle and sinews, which must have come from the elder brother of the he-goat whom we had encountered. After which we crawled under my coverlet, and huddled together; but we could not fall asleep for the snoring of the faithful who had come from afar to pray at the shrine and to sacrifice unto the Lord, and for the yowling and caterwauling and yammering that sounded from the huts of the insane, as though all the evil spirits of the Lord were assembled here and braying to the moon. Lilith shivered. She was not afraid of marauders, she whispered, or of soldiers, or of the servants of Benaiah ben Jehoiada; but her heart went cold at the thought of an evil spirit descending upon her and tearing her by the hair, or pinching her nipples, or placing a changeling inside her womb.

"Lilith my sweet," I whispered back, "I know a spell which will keep the evil spirit from you, and I have drawn a charmed circle about us before we laid ourselves down, so that nothing will touch us."

And she sobbed, once, and nestled her head to my shoulder and fell asleep.

On the morrow I paid my respects to the chief priest, who was well-fed and of a rosy complexion, but quite as unwashed as his subordinates.

I could not discern from his face how much he believed of my story or what he thought was my real intention; but when I had finished he said, "We do not keep our dear patients behind bars, or locked up, or under restraint; three things, I always say to my priests, are the key to successful treatment: forbearance, understanding, love. Of course, when one of the dear patients becomes obstreperous, he may receive a sharp blow that will numb him and keep him quiet; but the blow is so short as to be painless; do not hurt them, I always say to my priests, pray with them. We have regular visiting hours: who so wishes may approach our dear patients and see what he can make of their babble; why, I know men of substance who conduct their business by what they glean from the utterings of our dear patients; but no feeding or teasing them. For all these services, and all these kindnesses, you are expected to bring an offering unto the Lord; we have in the yard of the temple a fine assortment of cattle on the hoof, from which you may choose; the Levites will sell you the animal whole or any part thereof; you surely will be satisfied, and the Lord will love you and grant all your wishes."

So I went with Lilith to the yard of the temple, which was crowded with sheep and goats and calves and oxen that had been contributed by the families of the dear patients. Now the creatures were being sold by the priests to the faithful, who bargained for their offerings and cried out unto the Lord at the prices they were being charged. Off to one corner I discovered our old acquaintance, the he-goat, who was more dead than alive; and I took pity on him and said to the Levite to deal him a short, sharp blow and take him to the altar, for I would sacrifice a hindquarter of him if the cost was within reason; and the Levite said he would give me a good price because the Lord had brought me to him, and he was sure he would find other faithful to share the he-goat, so the poor animal might be delivered of his agony and be agreeable in the eyes of the Lord. Whereupon he handed me a potsherd, which served as a receipt, and which would entitle me to visit the insane.

But at the visiting hour I went to the huts of the insane; and Lilith followed me, although she was sore afraid and pale to the roots of her hair.

There were three huts: one for those that had fits and made faces, and one for those that sat as in stupor and were incontinent, and another for various kinds of cases, including those that were violent. In each hut two priests were on duty whose faces showed the indifference of an ox, but whose hands were hard as iron. You could see that the dear patients were in mortal fear of them; for whatever their ailment, they shrank at the sight of the priests and whimpered. But the stench from the huts was so great that it hit you at twenty paces outside; and within the huts you could scarcely breathe, and the dear patients, many of them naked or with their rags half rotted off them, were smeared with their own excrement and with snot and with spittle, and some lay as though dead.

I asked the priests for Tamar the daughter of David. They opened their mouth as in soundless laughter, and one of them said, "What's in a name? We have here a king of Persia, and two Pharaohs, and several angels of the Lord, two of them female, and others more who claim to be prophets and have visions. Shall I show you the goddess of love, Ashtareth? Her breasts are withered, her hair is as wisps of chaff, her toes have been eaten away, her eyes drip pus. Tamar the daughter of David! Why not Eve the wife of Adam?"

I took Lilith by the hand and fled with her from the hut, and out of the yard of the temple, and down the hill, until we came to the fields; and there Lilith fell to the ground and hid her face. But I thought of the ways of the Lord which are winding and tortuous. And behold, a woman came shambling up the path who was dressed in a garment of divers colours such as the robes with which the King's daughters that are virgins are apparelled. Her head was inclined in a strange manner, and she was singing in a small, childlike voice,

> ...*Open to me, my sister, my love,*
>   *my dove, my undefiled;*
> *for my head is filled with dew,*
> *and my locks with the drops of the night...*

And I saw that her garment of divers colours was pieced together of crazy patches, and that her face was old and haggard and twisted, and her eyes stared emptily. Lilith had risen in awe and was saying, "Tamar the daughter of David..."

But the woman walked on unseeingly, singing,

> *I opened to my beloved;*
> *but my beloved had withdrawn himself,*
>   *and was gone:*
> *my soul failed when he spoke;*
> *I sought him, but I could not find him;*
> *I called him, but he gave me no answer.*

And Lilith hurried after her, imploring her, "Tamar, dear sister, dear love..."

The woman shambled on.

"Listen to me, Tamar. Here is Ethan my beloved; he is gentle and good, and his hands are as the wind from the sea that caresses your face..."

Something seemed to be changing in the woman's bearing.

"My heart goes out to you, Tamar. I will hold you. Here is Ethan my beloved; he knows a spell which will drive from you the evil spirit of the Lord..."

The woman stood still.

"He will draw a charmed circle about you, and calm will return to your mind and peace to your soul. Look at me, do you see me..."

The woman nodded.

"Do you see Ethan my beloved, who is wise in the ways of the Lord, and wise in the ways of the people..."

The woman turned. Life had come to her eyes. I took a step towards her. She raised her hands as though to ward off a blow; then she dropped them, and the twist that marred her face began to dissolve.

And Lilith kissed her, as one sister kisses another, and the woman followed us.

WORDS OF TAMAR THE DAUGHTER OF DAVID SPOKEN TO ETHAN BEN HOSHAIAH AS SHE LAY IN THE GRASS OF THE FIELD WITH HER HEAD BEDDED ON THE LAP OF LILITH HIS CONCUBINE

...O God it is not what he did to me or how he did it simply throwing me on his bed and holding me down and tearing my clothes off and hurting me and slapping my face

when I screamed that was wicked but not the worst thing
although I was a virgin I truly was and I knew that no longer
a virgin the daughter of a king lost much of her value I
knew quite a bit we were numerous daughters and all of us
having the hot blood of David so I knew about life by the
time I was eight or nine and had my experiences in that
harem of my father's the girls would visit each other at night
and drink wine and take hasheesh and play with the maidservants and crawl in each other's beds I saw all that and
perhaps I should have come to love women like many of them
but for my mother Maacah the daughter of the King of
Geshur who said to me Tamar I shall whip you if I catch you
in bed with one of those evil ones or find your maidenhead
gone you are of royal blood and not of the blood of those
upstarts and climbers sometimes I wish your father had been
more fastidious in the choice of his other wives and his concubines so that was my mother and I was afraid of her though
my brother Absalom was not he was a wild boy and let his
hair grow and when she reproved him he kicked her with his
feet and bit her so she told my father and he had him flogged
where was I ah yes I was a virgin when Amnon my brother
out of another wife of my father's out of Ahinoam the
Jezreelitess began pursuing me and trying to take me for
walks in the garden and pawing me but I said this will not
do Amnon I don't mind a nice happy brother-sister relationship but none of that slipping your hand down my breast
and rubbing yourself against me also you perspire and have
an unpleasant odour he grew morose then and sulking did
not become him he was sallow-faced and had an ugly pout
so he fell sick or pretended to be which roused the fear of the
Lord in my father who had just lost his infant son out of
Bath-sheba also Ahinoam the mother of Amnon was acting
as though her darling boy were a small helpless suckling
she filled the whole palace with her wailing and drove my
father to distraction so he came to me saying Tamar my
daughter you know the trouble I have been having on account
of the Lord being displeased with some of my doings and now
Amnon has fallen ill and told me he is dying for some meat
cakes as only you know how to make of minced meat and
certain spices rolled in fine dough and then served in chicken
broth if only you would cook it for him he would get well so

I said to my father if that is all he wants I shall be happy to prepare the meat cakes and send them over to his house but he wants you to come and do them in his kitchen said my father and serve them with your own hands so I said why should I he is unpleasant to my eye he should be glad I am willing to prepare any meat cakes for him and not make conditions now now said my father he is a very sick young man sick people have their moods also he is your half-brother so be a good sister and go to his house and dress him the meat what could I do I went to Amnon's house where he lay in his bed looking sick and speaking in a voice hardly audible ah meat cakes and raising his hand to touch mine but his hand drops and the servants click their tongues saying how weak is poor Amnon from his illness and please to hurry the meat cakes or he will surely die and he moaning oh my head my poor head he cannot bear the slightest sound say the servants and rise to leave and there I am with my pots and pans and my meat cakes and broth Tamar dear sister he sighs just a wee bit to start with perhaps I can eat when it is served by your tender hand come here come closer nay do not spill the broth I say but he pulls me to him there you have done it I say what a misfortune and all over your coverlet what are you trying to do suddenly he has regained his strength and drags me down on his bed among the meat cakes saying come lie with me dear sister so I answer nay nay my brother do not face me for no such thing ought to be done in Israel do not you do this folly and I whither shall I cause my shame to go and as for you you shall be as one of the fools in Israel now therefore I pray you speak unto the King for he will not withhold me from you howbeit he would not hearken to my voice but being stronger forced me and lay with me and having finished turned away his face saying why you are not a woman you are little better than a board of wood I am not I say how can you expect passion from one being raped also you have hurt me tearing my maidenhead and also I was lying in chicken broth and meat cakes you should try me another time I will not he says so therefore be gone really I say you rape your own sister and then throw her out like a prostitute rape he says you were quite willing you lay there and let me do as I pleased that was after you slapped me I say I felt faint Tamar he says you knew when you came what I wanted and

196

laughs a woman who spreads herself for any comer is not the wife for the next king of Israel so arise be gone but I said to him this evil in sending me away is greater than the other you did to me he however called for his servants and said put now this woman out from me and bolt the door after her and he threw me my garment of divers colours and the servants put me out I heard the bolt click into place and I cried out and tore my garment and strewed ashes on my hair and a pain rose in the back of my head that spread until it filled my skull and burst through my eyes and ran down my face and pulled it and twisted it and there was my brother Absalom saying has Amnon been with you I looked at him he said hush my sister hold now your peace he is your brother I said nothing he said do not let this thing destroy you I said nothing he took me by the hand and led me to his house and told me I could stay there I said nothing but that pain in me kept spreading and I said nothing . . . nothing . . .

21

A PLEA UNTO GOD FOR MERCY AND FOR HELP IN
DIRE STRAITS
MASCHIL OF ETHAN THE EZRAHITE

Have pity, O Lord, on the creatures of your spirit, on those you have fashioned from the clay of this earth.

You have provided them a mind for understanding, and their tongue to speak with; you give and you take away according to your judgment.

And also the heart you have given them, which can be broken but once; show mercy, O Lord, take note of the suffering and the silence.

There she goes in her garment of divers colours; she has spoken before you, but now she turns and is gone, her misery closed up within her.

See the daughter of the mighty has been humbled: her eyes are dead and her hands grip emptiness.

But I have listened to the voices coming from dark shores and to the babbling of the mad, and I pray unto the Lord on High for my soul.

Make haste, O God, to deliver me; make haste to help me, O Lord.

Let them be ashamed and confounded that seek after my soul: let them be turned backward and put to confusion, that desire my hurt.

But I am poor and needy: make haste unto me, O God;

you are my help and my deliverer; O Lord, do not tarry.

But on the afternoon of the day, behold, there rose a pillar of dust, and a clamour was in the plains, and numerous chariots were sighted and horsemen that moved on Beth-shan.

And Lilith said, "Do not wait, Ethan my friend, until the Cherethites and Pelethites infest the temple and its surroundings; but let us saddle the donkey and journey further."

Therefore we bought salted meat from the Levites, and bread; and Lilith mounted the donkey and drew her mantle over her head. At which the Levite weighing the meat said to me, "A beautiful daughter is as a jewel unto her father; he who hides his treasures from the soldiery, well-advised is he."

Lilith giggled underneath her mantle; but I grew vexed and hit the rear of the donkey with a switch, so that he moved on, and I explained to Lilith that with men it was as with wines: a young wine bubbled and gave you a headache; but a wine well matured was smooth to the tongue, and had strength.

That night we slept by the dried-out bed of a brook, screened by some growth of gorse; and the next day we came to Giloh in the foothills, whence hailed Ahitophel the counsellor of King David, who threw in his lot with Absalom. Ahitophel had had a big house, and the Lord had given him riches of various kind; but he had been of a restless mind. I asked a seller of pickled olives where was the house of Ahitophel; whereupon the man spread his fingers against me, saying, "Ahitophel? You might sooner ask for the house of Belial, who is the embodiment of all evil, for Ahitophel has been struck from memory by decree of the elders of Giloh. Also the street that was named after him has been renamed Street of the Glorious Achievements of David, and the orphanage which he founded and maintained was closed, so that in our day the orphans of Giloh beg for their living and join the marauders, and the girls become prostitutes. But the house of one unnamed stands up there beyond that knoll, you can't miss it, for one wall has collapsed, and weeds grow in the yard; and also there is the tower in which his ghost walks at the new moon."

Following the directions of the seller of pickled olives we came in due time to the house of Ahitophel. The sun stood high on the heavens, not a leaf stirred in the wilderness that once was the garden, and all was still but for the chirping of the crickets. We walked through the rooms that were bare and deserted, our steps echoing hollowly from the tiled walls and from the ceilings inlaid in the manner of Sidon and Tyre. And I thought of the man who had built all that, and who had joined with the rebels against King David, and who had ended his life when he saw that the rebellion would fail and his efforts were thwarted: what manner of man was he? and what were the forces that moved him, and Absalom, and also King David?

A slight cough made Lilith start.

I turned. In the doorway to the garden, outlined against the bright noon, stood a thin little man. He had something wraithlike about him, as though he might vanish again as suddenly as he had appeared. But he stayed, scratched his chin, and enquired meekly as to our purpose, for there had not been a visitor to this place, he said, since the name of Ahitophel was struck from memory by decree of the elders of Giloh.

I said the lady with me and I were travelling, partly for business, partly for pleasure; and that we had seen the house from afar, and found its location attractive and its design of interest, so that we came to look at it.

He stepped closer. The location couldn't be more beautiful, he confirmed, and Giloh and its surroundings were famed for their bracing air. The house might be somewhat in need of repair; but anyone with a few shekels to spare could make of it a veritable paradise, for it had been that until the previous owner was led by an evil spirit of the Lord to cast in his lot with long-haired Absalom and to rebel against King David. Considering the size of the grounds, and the amenities, the property was to be had cheaply; he was almost ashamed to name the amount: it was so much below its value. We might ask, now, why he was willing to sell at such a ridiculous price. He wanted to be honest with us; we looked like God-fearing people; also everybody in Giloh would tell us about the one fault of the house: the ghost of its previous owner which walked the tower at the new moon. But anyone seriously interested need not worry as the ghost was perfectly harmless; it did not rattle or sneeze or howl; it merely appeared, white and silent, at the window behind which the previous owner had hanged himself.

So I thanked him very much for the offer, saying I might consider it at a later date; but who was he, and by which rights was he selling the house, and the grounds, and all that pertained to it?

"I am Jogli the son of Ahitophel," he said, shrugging sadly. "I am the last of the family to remain on the property; and I, too, shall leave as soon as it is sold."

I had a sudden inspiration from the Lord. "Jogli," I enquired, "are the house and the gardens all that was left by Ahitophel your father?"

"There were his robe of state and his chain, made of gold, and his cup and plate and some goodly works of art; but these went to the moneylenders long ago." He bethought himself. "In the back of the tool shed I still have a few barrels filled with tablets of clay. I tried to sell them; but people say that any writings that were in the possession of Ahitophel must be displeasing in the eye of the Lord and subversive of the rule of the King."

"Jogli," I said, "I happen to be a collector of old scriptures. If you would let me see those barrels, and the tablets of clay therein, perhaps I shall buy some. But let me warn you: I may find little or nothing that is worth having, and my means are limited."

Jogli ben Ahitophel did not hear me through. Not heeding the vines that impeded him, or brush, or thistles, he hurried ahead of us towards a crumbling shed which was overgrown with red creepers. Inside it stood three solid barrels. And Jogli took tools and worked furiously; and when he had opened one barrel, he handed me the tablets of the uppermost layer.

The first of these read, *Notes of Ahitophel the Gilonite, Royal Counsellor, on the Rule of King David and on the Revolt of Absalom his Son, also his Thoughts on Various General Subjects.*

I heard the thumping of my heart. Lilith enquired if I felt unwell. I muttered something about the air in the shed being close, and stepped outside. When I could think again

201

clearly, I said, "Jogli, this is not like a piece of lamb, or a cake, which you can judge by the taste of a morsel thereof. If you want me to purchase the one or other of these tablets, I will have to examine them at my leisure, staying in the house, in a room that has four walls and a ceiling, so that the rain does not rain on the young lady with whom I am travelling and the sun does not ruin her skin. Also we shall need food and a pitcher of wine or two. Do you think you can supply us with that?"

Jogli ben Ahitophel bowed, and his hands trembled with excitement. We could have the whole house for as long as we wanted, he said; he would bring us straw to sleep on, and would share with us his bread and his cheese, and if I gave him half a shekel he would run down to Giloh and fetch a skin of fairly good wine.

Thus we had found not only a refuge but also reading matter of pertinence to the King David Report, so it could be said that my journey continued on the King's business.

But as to the apparition of Ahitophel, I assured Lilith that the new moon was several weeks off and that we should be gone before the ghost, white and silent, showed itself at the window of the tower.

From the Notes of Ahitophel the Gilonite

ON THE MAN DAVID

In the beginning we all believed in him.

He was the Chosen of the Lord, he embodied the great change from which the people Israel was to emerge, strong, purified, abreast of the times, so that the promise might be fulfilled which the Lord gave to Moishe our Leader and the people be made plenteous in every work of their hand, in the fruit of their body, in the fruit of their cattle, in the fruit of their land.

This meant to wrest power from the tribal elders and deprive them of their privileges and prerogatives, to limit the priests to the temple, to establish a state which would tax the rich and protect the poor, administer justice, further trade and crafts, and conduct foreign wars. It required the absolute devotion of those sworn to the cause of the Lord.

And we had little by which to guide ourselves. The law of the Lord as given to Moishe our Leader had been promulgated in the old days when there was no landed property and every man did that which was right in his own eyes and peace reigned among the people. But once the land was taken, injustice arose, and one man became the other man's wolf. Therefore we proclaimed, *Every man under his vine and his fig tree, from Dan even to Beer-sheba.*

There are those who maintain that David mouthed these words so as to gain adherents among the people, and that the great change was to him but a means to win personal power, and that no crime was too low for him to stoop to if it served that end.

I feel this is too simple a view. One night, on the roof of his palace, David read to me a new psalm he had written:

I sink in deep mire, where there is no standing:
I am come into deep waters, where the floods overflow me.

They that hate me without a cause are more than the hairs of my head; they that would destroy me are mighty.

They that sit in the gate speak against me; and I was the song of the drunkards.

I am weary of my crying; my throat is dried: my eyes fail while I wait for my God.

Because for his sake I have borne reproach; shame has covered my face.

For his sake I am become a stranger unto my brethren, and an alien unto my mother's children.

Much of David's poetry is cant; these verses are not. This is the language of a man who has demeaned himself in a great cause.

DIFFERENCES OF OPINION ABOUT DAVID

In the beginning we all believed in him. Later, as it grew clear that the Chosen of the Lord had turned into a despot, we chose different parts.

Jehoshaphat ben Ahilud told me, "You expect too much, my friend. Even if David were the man you thought him to be, he could not create the world you want. I am for accepting what is possible and practicable under the circumstances: one Israel, strong and indivisible."

"What does it help us," I said, "to have one great stink in

place of a thousand petty corruptions? Can't you see the strains that will rend the kingdom apart? If we do not change things from the root up, if we allow David to carry on and wax stronger, only one judgment valid, his, only one word that counts, his, your one Israel will splinter like a rotted tree in the storm."

"I doubt it."

"Or it will die of inertia; and all the King's dancing, and all his speeches, and all his prayers and poems will not infuse it with life."

"Chastity of thought is fine in a bride," he said, "but in the struggle of men it may cost you your head."

Joab ben Zeruiah told me, "He is the chief captain. The captain knows best."

"But you have eyes to see," I said, "and a brain to think with in that thick skull."

"I am a soldier," he said.

Hushai the Archite, the friend of David, listened to me with understanding, and said, "I, too, am aware that not everything is as one might wish. Pray, keep me informed on your plans."

THE MALCONTENT GROW MORE NUMEROUS

But I saw that the cause of the Lord required the abolition of the rule of David. For this I needed a league that included every malcontent in the country, and a man to head it who was capable of firing the hearts of the people.

The Lord saw to it that the number of malcontents grew daily by the hand of David. There were the tribal elders with their families and hangers-on, who felt their power and possessions slipping from their hands, while they had to furnish the levies for David's eternal wars; there were the big land-owners and cattle raisers, who with jaundiced eye saw the royal domains encroach upon their preserves; there were the local priests, who heard of the plans for a central temple and trembled for their livelihood; there was the huge mass of peasants, craftsmen, porters, hawkers, drovers, and so forth, who had the tax-collector dogging them and whose debts grew until they had to sell themselves in bondage; and the hands of the royal servants had to be greased when you were born and when you died, when you married and when you moved, at the gates of the cities and at the gates of justice. And there were the young people, who grew up into this and who therefore smirked at the teachings of their elders and at the promise of the great change.

But the idol of the young was Absalom the son of David. The daughters of Israel swooned at his name: from the sole of his foot even to the crown of his head there was no blemish on him; and when he polled his head, which he did once every year at the year's end because the hair was heavy on him, he weighed the hair of his head at two hundred shekels after the King's weight.

WHEN OUT LION-HUNTING DO NOT SET SNARES FOR RABBITS

Absalom was not altogether stupid; but he saw only one move at a time, and was stubborn.

I sought him out to probe his opinions. He had few of these, and hardly any about his father, King David; he resented the King's failing to punish Amnon after the rape of Tamar; but his one great hate was his half-brother Amnon. Absalom would have conspired to bring down God's lightning from the skies, if only it would hit Amnon; in vain I explained to him that you do not set snares for rabbits when you go out lion-hunting, and that he would bag Amnon along with much bigger game if only he thought matters through.

He however concocted his big plan. He did not disclose it to me, but his many hints made me fear the worst. Since I did not wish to be suspected of being an accessory to his no doubt crude and savage plot, I retired for a while to Giloh, to tend to my roses, and learned only later what happened.

It seems that Absalom went to his father the King and invited him and all the King's sons, his half-brothers, to the big sheep-shearing feast at his country estate near Baal-hazor, which is beside Ephraim. He knew quite well that David would be too busy to come; nevertheless the King would appreciate the gesture and might permit his sons to attend. David doubted the wisdom of letting Amnon go; but Absalom explained to his father that it was more than two years since whatever had passed between Amnon and Tamar, and who knew if it had been entirely Amnon's fault, and as for him, he harboured only the friendliest feelings towards his brother Amnon. Well, God bless you then, said David; and all but Solomon, who was still in his swaddling clothes, the King's fourteen sons mounted their mules and rode out to Absalom's place at Baal-hazor.

Absalom had a fine meal prepared for them. He was not stingy; and he wanted their stomachs filled and their minds numbed, especially Amnon's, for he had commanded his servants, saying, Mark you now when Amnon's heart is merry with wine, and when I say unto you, Smite Amnon; then kill him, fear not: have not I commanded you? be courageous, and be valiant.

And those servants went at their business promptly and skilfully: Amnon never had a chance. Then all the King's sons arose, and every man got him up upon his mule, and fled.

And Absalom fled also: to Syria, to Talmai the King of Geshur his grandfather on his mother's side.

But I had lost the head of the league I wanted to forge against King David who had made a mockery of the great change and of the cause for which he was chosen.

THE EDGE OF SORROW DULLS WITH TIME

Amnon was mourned in the usual manner: the King tore his garment, and lay on the earth, and all the King's sons and the King's servants rent their clothes and lifted up their voices and wept. But few felt sorry for Amnon: people knew him for a fool and a knave.

"Ahitophel," David told me, "my heart is sore afflicted. I have tried prayer, and poetry, and planning for new wars, but nothing will help."

"The edge of sorrow dulls with time," I said. "There's a troupe of dancers come from Babel, and everyone praises them highly. Have them appear in the palace: did not your predecessor, King Saul, have you play music for him and sing?"

"It is not for the sake of Amnon alone," he mused. "As I remarked upon the death of that infant, Bath-sheba's first-born: can I bring him back again? But Absalom! I had such great hopes for the boy."

He waited for me to speak. I said nothing; I did not want

to be remembered later as the one who suggested the return of Absalom.

"I thought of obtaining an oracle from Abiathar the priest or also from Zadok," said David, "or a prophecy from Nathan; but I know the ways of the men of God: they will try to divine my mind rather than the will of the Lord."

So I rose and went to Joab and said to him, "You know that the King is still very wroth at your having slain Abner ben Ner."

"But that was long ago!" cried out Joab. "Meanwhile I have stormed Jerusholayim for him, and won him great and important victories, and rid him of Uriah so he might lie with Bath-sheba; furthermore he made me captain of the host."

"That may well be," I answered. "However the King spoke of it only recently, and was much displeased. But I know a way in which you may find grace in his sight."

Joab implored me to tell him.

"It is perfectly simple," I said. "There is a wise woman in Tekoah. If you will go to her, and speak to her thus and thus, as I will presently instruct you, and fetch her thence, I am sure you will not only be re-established in the King's favour, but also you will have done a good deed for the people Israel and for the cause of the Lord."

And Joab listened to my words, and he went and fetched the woman from Tekoah.

ON THE USEFULNESS OF PARABLES

A parable is to life what the model is to the house.

The parable I told Joab to tell to the woman of Tekoah, so she might re-tell it to King David, was clear in its implications. Her story was to be that she was a widow woman and had two sons; but the one smote the other, and slew him. And now the family was risen and demanded of her to deliver the one that smote his brother, so they might kill him for the life of his brother whom he slew; which would deprive her of her last son and heir, and would leave to her husband neither name nor remainder upon the earth.

It was a genuine conflict: the ancient law of the revenge of the blood as against the new property right. And I knew which David would side with.

The wise woman of Tekoah was as good as her reputation. When David had told her that he would not suffer the revengers of the blood to destroy any more, and that not a hair of her son should fall to the earth so there might be an heir to the property and to the name of her husband, the woman raised her hands and spoke, "Now, then, since my lord the King has passed judgment in my case, why does he not apply it in his own and fetch home again his banished?"

David was surprised; and as he saw Joab standing nearby, grinning like a sated cat, he said unto the woman, "Hide not from me, I pray you, what I shall ask you."

And the woman said, "Let my lord the King now speak."

David said, "Is not the hand of Joab with you in all this?"

It was then that the wise woman of Tekoah showed real capability. "As your soul lives, my lord O King," she exclaimed admiringly, "none can turn to the right hand or to the left from ought that my lord the King has spoken: for your servant Joab, he bade me, and he put all these words in the mouth of your handmaid. And my lord is wise, according to the wisdom of an angel of God, to know all things that are in the earth."

You can imagine how David lapped that up: a man turned despot feeds on flattery. Finally he said unto Joab, "Go, therefore, and bring back the young man Absalom."

And Joab fell to the ground on his face and said, "Today your servant knows that I have found grace in your sight, my lord O King."

So Joab went to Geshur and brought Absalom to Jerusholayim.

22

From the Notes of Ahitophel the Gilonite
(Continued)

THE LONELINESS OF KING DAVID

BY THIS TIME King David was filled with mistrust; helpless
against the hostility that surged up wherever he turned in
the country, he felt sure only of his Cherethites and Pelethites,
who were not sons of Israel and therefore not susceptible to
the moods of the people. He saw himself alone in what he
regarded as the cause of the Lord, and he grew bitter and
withdrew into himself; when Absalom, back from Geshur,
came to throw himself at his father's feet, David refused
him, saying, "He has killed his brother Amnon: what would
stay his hand from slaying me?"

But Absalom feared to make any move until he was fully
rehabilitated. "You have heard of the new captain my father
has chosen to set over his Cherethites and Pelethites," he
said to me. "This Benaiah ben Jehoiada is shrewd and has
no compunctions."

"Get Joab to speak to the King for you," I suggested. "He
has done it before."

"As I am still in disfavour with my father," said Absalom,
"Joab has been avoiding me, although I sent for him
twice."

"Do not your fields at Baal-hazor and Joab's adjoin?" I
said. "Now is the time of the barley harvest. Have your men
burn one of Joab's fields."

And Joab arose and came rushing to Absalom's house and demanded, "Wherefore have your servants set my field on fire?"

Absalom answered, "I will pay for your barley. But why did you not come when I called you? Pray go to the King and speak to him in my name, Wherefore am I come from Geshur? Has the heart of the King hardened towards his son Absalom? But I yearn to see the King's face; and if there be any iniquity in me, let him kill me."

So Joab went to the King and told him, and his words must have been very convincing, for David had Absalom called to him.

And Absalom came to his father and bowed himself on his face to the earth before him: and David's heart was moved so that he could not speak. He lifted Absalom up from the ground and kissed him, and sobbed, "Oh my son Absalom, my son, my son."

ABSALOM MAKES HIMSELF BELOVED

I went to Absalom and told him that things in the country were coming to a head; high time, I said, that he established himself also among those in Israel who thought of him as a giddy youth and a hotspur.

"People must begin to see in you their champion," I advised, "a man with a passion for justice and a heart for the small fellow, and with the perspicacity of a mature leader. Learn to shake hands and to kiss even the cheek that is eaten by sores, listen to all complaints, and make promises that will satisfy everybody. Talk the language of the lowly, but wink your eye at the rich. Always smile; and be lavish with hints that they who side with you will prosper."

Absalom was no master of the trade, but he applied himself. He rose up early, and stood beside the way of the gate. And when any man that had a controversy came to the King for judgment, Absalom would call unto him and say, Of what city are you? So the man would answer, Your servant is of one of the tribes of Israel, and I have come in this and this matter. And Absalom would nod understandingly, or cast up his eyes to the Lord; and he would say to the man, See, your matters are good and right, but there is nobody deputed of the King to hear you. Moreover Absalom said, Oh that I were made judge in the land, that every man who has any suit or cause may come unto me, and I would do him justice! And when any man came near him to do him obeisance, Absalom put forth his hand, and took him, and kissed him. But every once in a while he retired into the chamber above the gate, and rinsed his mouth with scented water, and gargled, and spat.

After a while, I heard it said from Dan even unto Beer-sheba, what a goodly man was Absalom, and that the crown of Israel might look very well on his ample hair. But among those whom Absalom had been kissing at the gate were several servants of Benaiah ben Jehoiada; and it was told me that Benaiah was readying to speak on the matter to King David, and also on the purchase by Absalom of chariots and horses, and his hiring fifty men to run before him.

Therefore, after weighing the favourable against the unfavourable, I decided to act.

AS A FIRE SPREADS IN THE BUSH

It was agreed that I would go to Giloh and wait there while Absalom got leave from the King to journey to Hebron, whence David himself had begun his battle for power over Israel. Absalom was to tell his father that he had vowed a vow while he abode at Geshur in Syria, saying, If the Lord shall bring me again indeed to Jerusholayim, then I will serve the Lord at his shrine in Hebron, on the altar built unto the Lord by Abraham our forefather.

And David believed Absalom's words and said to him, "Go in peace."

Absalom took two hundred armed men with him. They were not told in advance as to the why and whereto of the ride, so that none would betray himself to the servants of Benaiah ben Jehoiada; but when they had crossed into Judah they were told, and every one of them stayed with Absalom: thus it was seen how little loyalty King David commanded outside the ranks of the Cherethites and Pelethites, and of the Gittites, who were hired mercenaries from Gath.

In Hebron Absalom offered sacrifices to God; and he sent for me; and he also sent spies throughout all the tribes of Israel and instructed them, As soon as you hear the sound of the trumpet, then you shall proclaim, Absalom reigns in Hebron.

When I reached the town, I found it in the state of tohubohu: people in many parts of the country had heard of Absalom gathering forces; they came streaming into Hebron and camped around the walls and crowded the place; but Absalom continued piling cattle on the renowned altar and praying unto the Lord.

"You will lose this before you ever set out," I told him. "By now Benaiah will have spoken to your father; and have you asked yourself how many of the people that sit in the gates of Hebron were sent by Benaiah and work for him?"

"What shall we do?" he said, binding up his hair that was nearly ripe for polling.

"March."

"March?" he repeated, as though the word were entirely new to him.

"Tomorrow by the break of dawn, march."

So we marched out of Hebron, fifteen hundred footmen, and a few horse, and a dozen or so chariots that were armoured; but as a fire that spreads in the bush we increased with every mile of way. When we reached Beth-zur we were six thousand, and ten thousand in Bethlehem the birthplace of David, where he halted to feed and water and to group our people in hundreds and thousands and to name captains over them; and Absalom embraced me, saying, "Your wisdom, Ahitophel, is as the wisdom of an angel of the Lord."

And I answered, "Pray do not ever forget that you spoke these words."

And ever more people came to join us: both youths and men in their prime, poor men mostly, but filled with hope and with belief in the cause of the Lord.

A ROYAL FEAT

As we approached Jerusholayim from the direction of Bethlehem, behold, there came messengers from the city, saying that David had fled, and that he had passed over the brook Kidron with his wives and his priests and his hangers-on, with the Cherethites and Pelethites, and with the Gittites;

and that he had taken with him the ark of the covenant of God; but that he had left behind ten of his concubines to preserve his house and all that was therein.

I asked the messengers, "As Jerusholayim can be held easily, did not the King make any attempt to prepare for the defence of the city?"

"Nay, nay," they said, "the King saw that the people were rallying to Absalom; and he consulted with Joab, and with Benaiah ben Jehoiada; and they feared greatly, for they would have the enemy without the walls and within."

So I advised Absalom, "Have the trumpets sounded."

Thereupon the gates of Jerusholayim were opened wide, and we marched in to the blare of horns and the beat of drums, and with cymbals and timbrels and cornets and harps. The people came from their houses and greeted us with joy, saying, we were their deliverers; and the daughters of the city embraced our young men.

As we reached the palace, I said to Absalom, "Let us gather unto you those ten concubines that were left by your father King David, so you can establish yourself before the people Israel in his place."

"Do I absolutely have to?" said Absalom. "I am fatigued from the march, and from the welcome, and my buttocks are sore from riding that mule."

"Who possesses the King's women possesses his throne," I replied. "You know the custom."

So the ten concubines of David were brought together. "God!" exclaimed Absalom upon seeing them, for the King had left to his rebellious son only such among his concubines as were elderly and unpleasant to behold; the comely ones, and those of fine shape, he had taken with him. But Absalom was very good about it, and climbed up behind them to the roof of the palace, where a tent was erected in a conspicuous place, near the spot from which David discerned Bath-sheba the wife of Uriah as she did her ablutions.

And Absalom went in unto his father's concubines in the sight of all Israel. As time went by, a hush descended on the multitude; but when Absalom staggered forth from the tent and showed himself to the throng, all the people called out, "Praise be unto the Lord!" and, "May the strength of your heart be as the strength of your loins!"

But Absalom fell down on his face before God and thanked him.

THE ARK OF GOD RETURNED

Suddenly Abiathar and Zadok were back, who had fled with the King, and also Hushai the Archite returned to Jerusholayim, and they did obeisance to Absalom.

Absalom was jubilant. "Behold," he said to me, "they have brought with them the ark of the covenant that my father took with him from the tabernacle of the Lord. The ark of God is as God in person, and the people will be encouraged thereby. Furthermore, Zadok and Abiathar can give us oracles, so we may know when to strike out and in what direction."

"I have my oracle inside my head," I said, "which has spoken true in all things concerning you."

"You are a wise man in the manner of an angel of the Lord," he admitted.

"Moreover," I said, "should you not ask yourself why these two priests have returned, and why Hushai has come back, after they fled with your father? Maybe the King sent them, so they should spy on you and transmit messages to him about your plans and intentions? Or they are to give you advice which is crooked, and which will lead you to perdition."

"I will have a word with Hushai," said Absalom.

And Hushai came to Absalom and greeted him, "God save the King, God save the King."

"You were known as the King's friend," said Absalom. "Is this your kindness to your friend? Why did you not go with your friend?"

Hushai's answer sounded forthright, "My loyalty is not to one man. But whom the Lord and this people and all of Israel choose, his will I be, and with him I will abide."

I saw that Absalom was being swayed.

"And again," Hushai went on, "whom should I serve? Should I not serve in the presence of my friend's son? As I have served in your father's presence, so will I be in your presence."

That persuaded Absalom. He had seen the people flock to him, and he believed he was irresistible.

"The Lord helps those that help themselves," I told Absalom, "but he who sits on his buttocks is soon lost."

"Wherefore are you fretting?" he said. "My father wanders about in the wilderness with a handful of men, and he is cut off from the people, while all of Israel has turned to us and is shouting, Absalom our leader! Absalom our King!"

"A wolf that howls from afar is a wolf nonetheless," I said. "We have wasted precious days by idling about in Jerusholayim; do we want to waste our victory? Now, therefore, let me choose twelve thousand men, and I will arise and pursue after David this night; I will come upon him while he is weary and weakhanded; the people with him shall flee, and I will smite the King only. Once he is destroyed I can bring back his men, and Israel will have peace."

The tribal elders who had joined with Absalom agreed: they feared David and wanted him disposed of quickly. But Absalom had tasted of the sweetness of power; and he feared being left in Jerusholayim without sufficient protection if I moved with twelve thousand picked men after David.

Uncertainly he proposed, "Let us call now Hushai the Archite also and hear likewise what he says."

Hushai came, and Absalom told him of my advice. Then he asked, "Shall we do after Ahitophel's saying? If not, speak up."

Hushai stroked his beard. "The counsel that Ahitophel has given seems wise, but it is not good at this time. You know your father and his men: they are men of war, and they are chafed in their minds as a bear robbed of her whelps in the field. And with his experience in warfare, your father will not lodge with his people but hide in some pit or some other place."

Absalom appeared thoughtful, and the men about him nodded their heads.

"And it might come to pass," Hushai continued, "when some of your people encounter David's mighty men and are thrown back, that whoever hears it will say, There is a slaughter among the people that follow Absalom. Then he also who is brave and whose heart is as the heart of a lion shall melt; for all Israel knows that David is a great captain and those with him are valiant men."

Absalom chewed on his lip, and the men about him looked discomfited.

"Therefore I counsel," said Hushai sagely, "that the levies of all Israel be generally gathered unto you, from Dan even to Beer-sheba, as the sand is by the sea for multitude; and that you go to battle in your own person. So shall we come upon David in some place where he shall be found, and we will light upon him as the dew falls on the ground: and of him and of all the men that are with him there shall not be left so much as one. Moreover, if he be gotten into a city, then shall all Israel bring ropes to that city, and we will draw it into the river, until there be not one small stone found there."

And Absalom said, "Amen, and may the Lord God make it come true"; and the men about him breathed more easily.

In vain I argued that this mass levy would require months to be raised: meanwhile David would establish himself somewhere and gather strength and prepare his counterblow.

But Absalom said, "The counsel of Hushai is better than the counsel of Ahitophel."

And I could say nothing further, for now it was Absalom's word that counted.

THE LORD HAD APPOINTED TO DEFEAT MY COUNSEL

I made one more attempt.

I assembled a number of keen young men, who knew how to move softly, and told them to follow Hushai the Archite upon all his ways.

Soon enough one of my young men returned, saying, "Hushai has gone and met in a secret place with Abiathar the priest and with Zadok, after which a wench came out of the place and left Jerusholayim by the gate and proceeded to En-rogel. There, at the well, she met Jonathan the son of Abiathar and Ahimaaz the son of Zadok; whereupon those two went on towards Jordan; but we are following them."

"You have done well by the cause," I said. "Have you secured the wench?"

"We have," he said.

The wench was brought in. She looked quite bedraggled from the handling she had got, and she was frightened.

"Now what did you tell Jonathan and Ahimaaz the priests' sons when you met them at En-rogel?" I enquired.

She threw herself at my feet, whimpering, "Your handmaid has vowed a vow before God, and before Abiathar and Zadok his priests."

And she was not persuaded either by kindness or by reason; wherefore I called several servants that were of strong build and told them to make the wench talk. They were with her the whole night; but she would not speak, and by the morning her cries ceased, and she was dead.

But by midday another of my young men returned, saying, "We followed the priests' sons unto the town of Bahurim, which is at the border of Judah, where they entered a house. We surrounded the house, and went in and searched it, and found them not; but the woman of the house told us that they be gone over the brook of water. It being night, we waited till morning to look for the tracks of their feet, and saw none, and the people derided us, saying that the servants of David had squeezed them, but Absalom's men were taking their all; therefore we came back to tell you of it."

Later it was discovered that the two priests' sons had hidden in the well of the house in Bahurim, over which the woman had spread a covering and thrown ground corn thereon. Thus the message of Hushai had reached David at Mahanaim, east of Jordan, where he had established himself, and David would conduct himself accordingly; but I had no proof before Absalom against Hushai, nor against Abiathar and Zadok the priests.

And I saw the haphazard way in which the host of Absalom was gathered, and that there was dispute and disagreement, and few supplies, so that the men fell upon the countryside and took from the people, looting and drinking and whoring; and many went home, each to his own tent. And if a man spoke of the cause of the Lord, he was scorned as lame-brained and an asshead, and was laughed at.

By all these signs I knew that the Lord had appointed to defeat my good counsel, to the intent that the Lord might bring evil upon Absalom. Thus, while Absalom at the head of his motley bands slowly moved to cross Jordan, I saddled my ass, and arose, and got me to my house at Giloh. I had a few things to write, a few chores to do, a few dispositions to make before finding me a good stout rope.

I put down the last of the tablets, feeling as though I had lived those days at the side of Ahitophel.

"I see you have finished," said Jogli. "You want to have the tablets, do you not?"

Didn't I! They supplied the answers to much that had puzzled me about David. But the amount of shekels I had with me was limited and would have to last me a good while. And in my delicate situation, how was I to arrange for the shipping of such rare and ticklish matter?

"I will make you a good price," said Jogli. "Two hundred and fifty shekels."

I smiled absent-mindedly.

He hesitated. "Two twenty-five."

I looked towards the ceiling.

"You are robbing me. Two hundred."

"Jogli," I said, "would you safeguard the tablets for me if I left you a small token payment?"

His face fell. "How small?"

"Twenty."

"Twenty! Ahitophel my father may God rest his soul would rise from his grave. Twenty! He would haunt us not only at the new moon but every night of the week except on the sabbath..."

He broke off.

"What was that?" said Lilith.

"Horses," I said. "A troop of horsemen."

Lilith's lips moved in prayer.

"Give me the twenty," said Jogli.

The horsemen were coming closer.

"Give me fifteen. Quick. I will keep the tablets for you. I will cover the barrels so that no one will find them. Give me ten. Give me..."

The horsemen were at the gate, shouting, "Where is Jogli? Where is the son of him whose name was struck from memory by decree of the elders of Giloh?"

"Here I am," quavered Jogli.

Covered with dust, several armed men strode in. "May God do so unto me and more also," the one at the head exclaimed, "if we have not caught the bird that has flown the coop without so much as a peep to his friend Benaiah ben Jehoiada. But my lord Benaiah has charged his servants, saying, Go you throughout the country from Dan even to Beersheba and bring to me Ethan ben Hoshaiah, of Ezrah; and whosoever fetches him shall be rewarded accordingly. So let us go."

He tied my hands behind my back; but the hands of Lilith my concubine were not bound, and she followed after me.

23

PRAISED BE THE NAME of the Lord, who weighs men in the balance, with weights that are grief, and sorrow, and despair.

I was escorted by my captors into the presence of Benaiah ben Jehoiada, and I fell to the earth before him. "My lord," I said, "behold the wrists of your servant that are bleeding, and my feet that are cut to the bone, and my body which is more black and blue than its natural colour. For I was driven and forced to run beside the horses, and was given but a cup of foul water and not enough bread to keep a dog alive, and when I fell down from weakness I was kicked and mishandled and cursed. But Lilith my concubine was placed on my donkey, and she was laughed at and called such names as no daughter of Israel should have to hear, all the way to Jerusholayim."

Benaiah frowned at the head of the escort. "Did I not tell you to deal gently with Ethan, and according to his deserts?"

"Truly," the man answered, "my lord did; and we treated him according to the deserts of a person in the category of a learned man holding questionable thoughts."

But Benaiah bade him to untie my hands. And he told me to rise, and offered me tidbits of meat, and sweets, and scented water, saying, "How easily are the words of the mighty misconstrued by their servants! But let it be a lesson to you, because it is said, Give instruction to a wise man, and he will be yet wiser, teach a just man, and he will increase in learning."

I held my tongue, thinking, An hyena that smiles shows his teeth also.

"Now, then," Benaiah dismissed all the people about him, "take a seat on those cushions, Ethan, and listen, for it was not by a whim that I had you searched after from Dan even unto Beer-sheba and brought back to Jerusholayim."

"Your servant is listening," I assured him.

"I believe I once mentioned to you and to the members of the Commission that I was planning to bring Joab to trial." He paused to grind his jaws. "Adonijah the King's brother having been disposed of, King Solomon has now approved of the undertaking."

"The wisdom of the Wisest of Kings is beyond compare," I confirmed.

"And since in the past you enjoyed the confidence of Joab," he went on, "and since you also took an interest in the illicit relationship of Adonijah to the lady Abishag of Shunam, but forgot to tell me of your observations and thus made yourself punishable, now, therefore, I intend using you as a witness at the trial."

He was watching me as though I were a fly caught in syrup.

"But is not Joab confessing to anything you want?" I asked, trying to appear calm. "Who needs a witness when you have such a defendant?"

"Who needs a witness!" he repeated angrily. "We have had an abundance of confessions lately! You charge a man with harbouring evil thought: he confesses. With denying the wisdom of the Wisest of Kings: he confesses. With deviation, factious spirit, conspiracy, subversion, sedition: he confesses. The people Israel no longer doubt the confessions; they merely shrug at them. Where does that leave the law of the Lord and the whole judicial process? That is why the King needs a witness for this trial whose name has not been bandied about in the gates of the cities, a witness with a reputation of wisdom and honesty."

"Should not a witness have witnessed the alleged crime or have direct knowledge of it?" I enquired meekly. "For it is written, You shall not bear false witness against your neighbour."

"I would not ask you to bear false witness to save my soul,"

221

scoffed Benaiah. "You will hear the full story from me, and you will tell it truthfully as I told it to you: that is all which is required of you."

"And which story would your servant be required to tell truthfully?" I asked.

Benaiah ben Jehoiada called his scribe, and the man came, bringing several tablets of clay, and placed these before me. But Benaiah reached for a piece of aromatic chewing gum, which is made of mastic, and popped it into his mouth, and he settled back on his cushions and said to me, "Read!"

TESTIMONY INTENDED TO BE GIVEN BY ETHAN BEN HOSHAIAH AGAINST JOAB BEN ZERUIAH, WHO WAS OVER THE HOST IN THE TIME OF KING DAVID, AS IT WAS DRAWN UP BY BENAIAH BEN JEHOIADA AND SHOWN BY HIM UNTO ETHAN, WITH THOUGHTS OF ETHAN SET IN BRACKETS

To the court and the people Israel, I hereby bear witness as follows.

When David was come to Mahanaim, he had the people numbered that were with him, and he set captains of thousands and captains of hundreds over them, and grouped his forces in three columns, one under Joab, another under Abishai the brother of Joab, and a third under Ittai the Gittite, who headed the mercenaries from Gath.

And the King said unto his men, I will surely go forth with you myself also.

(A noble gesture, considering the fact that latterly David had been directing his wars from his palace in Jerusholayim.)

But the people answered, You shall not go forth. You are worth ten thousand of us: therefore it is better that you encourage us from the city. So the King stood by the side of the gate as his army marched out by hundreds and by thousands. And he commanded Joab and Abishai and Ittai, saying, Deal gently for my sake with the young man Absalom. And all the people heard the King charging his captains concerning Absalom.

(Even assuming that a man as ruthless as David should at such a moment discover his heart for his rebellious son,

222

why the conspicuous manner of his orders? Is this his repudiation, preparatory to the fact, of all guilt of the death of Absalom?)

Now the court and the people Israel know the outcome of the battle that took place in the wood of Ephraim: twenty thousand of Absalom's men were slaughtered that day, and the wood devoured more people than the sword. As to Absalom, he fled upon his mule, and the mule went under the thick boughs of a great oak, and his hair was caught in the oak; thus he was suspended between the heaven and the earth, and the mule that was under him went away.

And a certain man saw it and told Joab of it. Joab said, You saw him, why did you not smite him there to the ground? I would have given you ten shekels of silver and a girdle.

(The answer, natural enough under the circumstances, appears to be Item One in establishing Joab as the sole culprit.)

The man said unto Joab, Though I should receive a thousand shekels of silver right in my hand, yet I would not put forth my hand against the King's son: for in our hearing the King charged you and Abishai and Ittai, saying, Beware that none touch the young man Absalom.

(David's innocence is once more being stressed.)

Then said Joab, I may not tarry thus with you. And he took three darts in his hand and thrust them through the heart of Absalom, while Absalom was yet alive in the midst of the oak. And ten young men that bore Joab's armour compassed about and smote Absalom, and slew him.

(The armour supplies additional evidence, if such were needed, of Joab's guilt.)

And they took Absalom, and cast him into a great pit in the wood, and laid a very great heap of stones upon him: and Absalom's people fled every one to his tent. But when King David, who had stayed in the gate of the city, was told by the messenger that the Lord had avenged him that day of all them that rose up against him, and that the young man Absalom was dead, he went up to the chamber over the gate, and wept: and as he went, thus he said, O my son Absalom, my son, my son Absalom! would God I had died for you, O Absalom, my son, my son!

(And he seems to have felt it. There is a ring of truth to

David's dirge, though in essence it differs little from the ones he sounded after the death of Saul and of Jonathan, of Abner ben Ner and of all the others who discommoded the Chosen of the Lord and were disposed of.)

Benaiah ben Jehoiada topped his graciousness by having a litter carry me to No. 54, Queen-of-Sheba Lane. And I felt that my eyes had seen nothing prettier in a long time than this crooked little house with its crumbling face and its sagging roof, for which I paid an exorbitant rent to the King.

And there stood Lilith my concubine, who had preceded my coming, and Shem and Sheleph my sons, and Huldah their mother; but Esther my wife was not in the door to greet me.

I enquired after her, and was led to her bedside. She lay there, smiling at me; but how she had wasted away in the time I was gone! The coverlet hardly rose above the bed: so thin was her body.

"Esther," I said, "I should never have left you."

She petted my hand.

"I will go to the tabernacle," I said. "I will take there a ram of the finest breed, with a fat tail, and I will get from the Levites such potions and ointments as are sure to help you."

She motioned for the others to leave us, and for me to sit by her side, and said, "How was it? Tell me."

I made it all sound like a big adventure: the temple at Beth-shan with its subtile priests; the meat cakes that were the undoing of Tamar the daughter of David; the deals which were offered me by Jogli ben Ahitophel; and the discovery I made in his tool shed. But of the trial against Joab, which Benaiah was planning to hold, and of the part assigned to me therein, of this I did not speak. And Esther my beloved wife listened, her eyes showing a reflection of the sparkle that once was theirs. And hope returned to me, as though she could get well and would, too; and I told her so.

"Will I see?" she suddenly said in a small childlike voice.

But this was the tone of voice she used when we were young and playing that something great and wonderful would come to us by the Lord.

"Will I see?" she repeated.

"Yes," I said, "you will."

She wanted to laugh happily, but a rattle sounded instead. The life that was on her face gave way to grey horror; she gripped my hand desperately.

"Esther!" I cried out.

She was fighting for breath. At intervals her head fell sideways; she seemed to be losing consciousness. I felt her pulse: it raced madly.

"Air!" she gasped.

I pushed open the window shutters as I feared to move her to the roof. I sent Shem and Sheleph to fetch a Levite who was reputed to rely more on his knowledge of the body than on ancient prayers. "Make him hurry," I said, "I will pay him whatever he asks in shekels of silver."

Then I waited by the side of Esther, whose love for me was deeper than all the fountains of the great deep; I wiped the sweat off her forehead, and the spittle off her lips, and I watched her trying to fight off the angel of darkness.

The Levite came, a short greasy man, who looked about in the house as though he were taxing the furnishings to determine how much he might safely charge. He tested the motion of the eye, and he pressed his thick ear to her shrunken breast. "She has water on her lungs," he said finally.

"Can you help her?"

"She needs air."

"Will she live?"

"Let us carefully take her outside and support her by placing cushions in her back."

"Will she live?" I repeated.

"You might pray to the Lord," he answered, "and pray hard."

A PRAYER FOR HELP IN GREAT NEED
BY ETHAN BEN HOSHAIAH

Lord my God, who is covered with light as with a garment, who stretches out the heavens like a curtain, who makes the clouds his chariot, who walks upon the wings of the wind:

Incline your ear to your servant, who is bowed to the ground before you.

My heart is sore pained within me: and the terrors of death are fallen upon me.

Fearfulness and trembling are come upon me, and horror has overwhelmed me.

O Lord, hide not yourself from the supplication of your servant, who beseeches you for but a small drop of your everlasting mercy, for but as much as is needed to ease the suffering of your handmaid whose love for me is deeper than all the fountains of the deep, and to help her last through this night.

You are great, O Lord, and your works are great, and you do wondrous things: so why not this thing which is small, requiring but a flick of your finger?

But I will heed my ways, that I sin not with my tongue: I will keep my mouth with a bridle, while the wicked is before me.

I was dumb with silence, I held my peace; and my sorrow was stirred.

My heart was hot within me; while I was musing the fire burned.

But I will speak with my tongue unto him who is menaced by the wicked, and warn him to flee the ungodly, before he is tried; thus I will cleanse myself in the eye of the Lord, and do right, and thwart the work of my enemies.

And now, Lord, what wait I for? my hope is in you.

Hear my prayer, O Lord, and give ear unto my cry; answer to my tears; for I am a stranger with you, and a sojourner as all my fathers were.

O spare the light of the love of my soul, which flickers weakly, and keep it burning; and spare me, that I may recover strength before I go hence and be no more.

But as the first faint hue of rose foreshadowed the dawn, Esther began to breathe more easily, and the beat of her heart slowed and grew stronger, and she fell into a sleep. I bowed myself to the ground and thanked God; and I paid the Levite all of five shekels silver for his counsel, and for the ointment he had smeared about Esther's heart and the drops he had instilled in her mouth. Then I drank some heated milk, and arose, and left the city through the south gate, directing my steps towards the house of bricks of various colours, in which Joab was crawling about. And there was a conflict of voices within me as to my warning him to flee before he was put on trial: was he not as wicked as the rest of them? Moreover I feared the guards at the house and the wrath of Benaiah. But the voice that reminded me of my vow and of the great help of the Lord, that voice prevailed.

As I came near the house, behold there was a commotion, and people running to and fro. I was seized roughly by a servant of Benaiah ben Jehoiada, who enquired as to my name, and what was I doing in this vicinity. I said I was of one of the tribes of Israel, and come to Jerusholayim with some friends; and that we departed yesterday, each to go to his city, but stopped at a wayside inn for a last farewell; and one drink had led to the next, and there was singing and general merriment; but on the morrow I found myself in a ditch, alone and in as sorry a state as I ever was in, for I was of good character, and married, and paying my taxes and tithes as required.

At which the fellow wished me to hell and sent me away; and I went without tarrying. At the south gate had gathered a multitude of people, who were debating excitedly; it was noised that Joab had broken away from his house and that he was seen hastening to the great tabernacle of the Lord, which was erected by King David. And wagers were made as to whether Joab would reach it, or if the servants of Benaiah would lay hold of him on the way.

But I thought gratefully of the wisdom of the Lord, who had accepted my vow and had recalled the angel of darkness from Esther, and who had caused subsequent events to happen so as to spare me unnecessary travail.

Now, therefore, I followed the mass that was surging past the building site of the temple and on to the great tabernacle; and everywhere the workmen downed their tools and the merchants closed their stalls, and they joined the rush.

The doors of the tabernacle stood wide open; and there was Joab hanging on to the horns of the altar, his clothes torn, his hair wild, his eyes as the eyes of a madman; and near Joab tarried Zadok and other priests, and they knew not what to do. And Joab turned to face the people Israel, and he cried out, "Hear, O Israel, the true confession of the cause of the Lord, and who now is but a wreck, and a victim of the rule which he himself helped to institute."

Zadok and the other priests raised their hands and called out to Lord Yahveh, thus attempting to drown the voice of Joab; and I thought of what this would do to the plans of Benaiah for the trial of Joab.

"I was beaten, O Israel," shouted Joab louder even than the priests, "and tormented in mind and body, until I weakened before the Lord, and confessed to the most heinous crimes, and took upon myself the guilt of others, and upon my head the blood that was on the hands of my betters. But now tidings have come to me that I am to be tried in public, before the King, by Benaiah ben Jehoiada, and that false witnesses will appear..."

And there came runners, their white staves beating a road through the crowd; and behind them an armoured chariot that was drawn by white horses. "Whoa, there!" said Benaiah, and climbed off heavily: he wore his helmet, and his breastplate, and his long sword.

At the door he was met by Zadok who pleaded, "Not with the sword! Not inside the shrine of God and before his altar and the ark of the covenant!"

Benaiah seemed to hesitate. Then he called into the huge tent, "Joab! Thus says the King, Come forth!"

And Joab said, "Nay: but I will die here."

There was silence from the door of the tabernacle to the building site of the temple; only the crows cawed that always hover near the places of sacrifice.

And Benaiah turned; and he mounted his chariot and drove off.

But the hands of Joab were still locked about the horns of the altar. "Hear, O Israel," he resumed, "I withdraw all confessions that were extorted from me in the loneliness of my house, under the boot of Benaiah and under the fists of his servants. Assuredly the blood of war is upon my hands, and on my girdle, and in my shoes, and also the blood of those that I killed in the service of the cause as I believed. But all this blood I return upon the head of David, who commanded these murders, and upon the head of his seed forever: for it was not shed in the cause of the Lord, nor in any cause that was noble or necessary, but for the aggrandisement of the man David and so as to seat him upon the neck of Israel and tighten his rule."

By now Zadok had recovered his wits, and he and the other priests were filling the air with invocations, and with entreaties to the Lord, and with general clatter; and the people clamoured to hear Joab and called out to him; and the din was great.

Then the runners were back, letting their staves crack down indiscriminately and shouting, "Move, you bastards! Make way for Benaiah ben Jehoiada, who is over the host, and over the Cherethites and Pelethites, the King's Own!"

Once again Zadok confronted Benaiah, pleading the sanctity of the shrine and the inviolability of the altar of the Lord and of all those that clung to it.

But Benaiah drew his sword, saying, "Did not Joab himself declare, I will die here? I have brought his word to the King; and the King told me, Do as he has said, and fall upon him, and bury him, that you may take away the innocent blood, which Joab shed, from me and from the house of my father. And the Lord shall return his blood upon his own head, who fell upon many men more righteous and better than he, my father, David not knowing thereof, and slew them with the sword. Their blood shall therefore return upon the head of Joab, and upon the head of his seed forever: but upon David, and upon his seed, and upon his house, and upon his throne, shall there be peace forever from the Lord. Thus spoke King Solomon."

Benaiah ben Jehoiada strode past Zadok the priest, and past the other priests. Sword in hand he stepped to the altar of the Lord; but the priests hastened to draw the big curtains, thus shutting the tabernacle and hiding from the sight of the people all that was therein.

24

AFTER THE SLAYING of Joab at the altar of the Lord all Israel fell to trembling. No one knew who was next to be seized, what crimes he would have to confess, or in what manner he would be disposed of: some prisoners were transported to the mines near the Red Sea, whence came the King's copper and his iron ore; others to the quarries, to hew the rock that was used in the construction of the great temple and of the new cities for the King's chariots and horsemen and stores; others again found themselves with their head cut off and their body nailed to the wall of the city.

I could but wait for what would befall me. Benaiah himself had remarked to me that I knew too much: too much, that is, of the ways of the mighty, which these prefer to keep hidden. Also I learned that the royal barge of Egypt was at sea, carrying Princess Hel-ankamen the daughter of Pharaoh, as King Solomon had finally seen fit to grant free passage through Israel to Egyptian goods. The time was near when the King would honour me by taking Lilith my concubine to be handmaid to his imported bride and would solace himself in Lilith's arms for the frigid embrace of the Princess, who was reputed to covet women over men.

And there was the suffering of Esther my wife, whose heart might not last through her next attack.

So I worked till I dropped, seeking thereby to fight off the sorrow of my days and the anguish of my nights. Though I doubted that I would be permitted to finish my work on the King David Report and feared that another, still more corruptible man than I would be called in to add the last touches and strike out what truths I was hoping to convey, I spent most of my hours in that stable that held the royal archives, digging among the confusion of potsherds and tablets of clay and pieces of leather in an attempt to round out my knowledge of the final years of the rule of King David.

MISCELLANEOUS NOTATIONS BY ETHAN
BEN HOSHAIAH ON THE FINAL YEARS
OF THE RULE OF KING DAVID

Suppression of Absalom revolt solves none of the underlying conflicts: resentment of impoverished masses against growing wealth of landed gentry and royal household, tribal and clerical hostilities against growing arrogation of power by royal servants—therefore new uprisings against David, some small and scattered—the biggest one, however, headed by one Sheba (his device: "We have no part in David, neither have we inheritance in the son of Jesse") is for a time supported by all tribes but Judah—David clings to Jerusholayim and holds land between city and Jordan—suffering, as did Absalom, from lack of trained fighting men and experienced leaders, Sheba is forced by Joab to withdraw into walled town of Abel, near Beth-maachah—Joab fills up trenches, throws up banks, batters walls—town is saved by a wise woman who pleads with Joab and offers him Sheba's head—the head is cut off by the townsfolk and cast over the wall to Joab: end of Sheba revolt—David rewards Joab by giving him permanent rank of captain of the host, and balances the nomination by simultaneously confirming Benaiah as chief of Cherethites and Pelethites—David initiates reform of army (up to then depending for its levies on goodwill of tribal chieftains) and of administration (up to then hampered by lack of reliable data on population, property, produce, trade, taxation, and so forth)—his decision to have his subjects numbered confronts him with big taboo (Lord Yahveh, expressing people's age-old desire to protect themselves by hiding in their mass: "The number of the children of Israel shall be as the sand of the sea, *which cannot be measured or numbered*")—David orders army to carry out census—senior captains reluctant;

Joab to David: "My lord the King, are they not all my lord's servants? why then does my lord require this thing?, why will he be a cause of trespass to Israel?"—David persists—after nine months and twenty days census completed for all but the tribe of Benjamin (mountain people, who evade the census-takers) and the tribe of Levi (whose members carry no arms and hold no land)—allowing for minor errors: of Israel, a thousand thousand and a hundred thousand valiant men that draw the sword, of Judah, four hundred three score and ten thousand—David's breaking the taboo calls for divine punishment—minor prophet Gad (Nathan avoids trouble-some affair) with message from Yahveh: "Thus says the Lord, I offer you three things; chose you one of them, that I may do it unto you: (a) seven years of famine in the land, (b) your fleeing for three months, your enemy hot in pursuit, (c) three days pestilence in the land"—David chooses pestilence as likely to hurt the towns worse than the countryside, and the towns (except for his own city, Jerusholayim) are still largely populated by pauperised indigenous Canaanites whose demise would be of small concern to the people Israel—within three days, seventy thousand perish by pestilence from Dan even unto Beer-sheba—but behold, as the angel of pestilence reaches the threshingfloor of one Jebusite named Ornan and (description by King David himself) "is standing between the earth and the heaven, having a drawn sword in his hand stretched out over Jerusholayim," Lord Yahveh repents of the evil and commands the angel, "It is enough, stay now your hand"—enters prophet Gad with new message from God: David is to erect altar on Ornan's threshingfloor —David purchases threshingfloor and surrounding land, the future building site of the great temple of the Lord, for fifty shekels silver according to one entry in archives (eleventh stall of the third row, on the right) or six hundred shekels gold according to another entry (twelfth stall of the third row, on the right: probably a later insertion intended to manifest David's generosity in his dealings with Lord Yahveh as no piece of land in or about Jerusholayim was ever worth six hundred shekels gold)—upon acquisition of temple site, David, like many another despot, develops interest in archi-tecture—he supervises the drafting of the designs for the temple, coerces tens of thousands to hew wrought stones, amasses supplies for construction: cedar wood, iron, brass, nails, joinings—at the same time, further administrative reforms so as to create new loyalties by judicious distribution of offices and patronage—numerous priests and all of the King's servants are sorted and newly assigned (of a total of thirty and eight thousand Levites, twenty and four thousand as clerics, six thousand as district officers and judges, four thousand as door-keepers, four thousand as musicians)—a treasury department is established (under Shebuel ben Gershom), a foreign office (under Chenaniah of Izhar)—the tribal elders and clan heads are replaced by officials called "Chief fathers" who are drawn from David's own tribe, Judah (a thousand and seven hundred under Hashabiah of Hebron for the tribes west of Jordan, two thousand and seven hundred under Jerijah of Hebron for the East Jordanian tribes Reuben, Gad, and half Manasseh)—army reform is completed: David now has available a standing army of mercenaries (Cherethites, Pelethites, King's Own, and so forth) for purposes of inner security and immediate employment in war, and a host of valiant men, divided into twelve courses of twenty and four thousand each, who in peacetime are called up for training one month out of the year—to cover increasing costs of royal splendour, royal domains are extended and made to branch out into various fields of endeavour: wheat, wine, olive oil, cattle (both in Sharon and in the valleys), breeding of camels and asses—David becomes biggest producer and trader of goods in Israel—part of his personal treasury is set aside as a contribution to the future temple: by account in archives (second stall, first row on the right) three thousand talents of gold (of the gold of Ophir) and seven thousand talents of refined silver for candlesticks, lamps, tables of shewbread, fleshhooks, basons, bowls, cups, cherubims at ark of covenant, and for wall decorations—decline of royal health: complaints of fatigue, chills, impotence; also irritability, low spirits—young virgin sought to stand before David, cherish him, lie in his bosom, stimulate his blood— Abishag the Shunammite failing despite all her ministering —David to the Lord: "We are strangers before you, and sojourners, as were all our fathers; our days on earth are as a shadow, and there is none abiding."

* * *

The green and gold litter with the red tasselled roof was set down before the door of the house, and a servant proclaimed the visit of Amenhoteph the royal chief eunuch.

I felt a weakness in my knees as Amenhoteph stepped from the litter, hands outstretched, and announced, "Glad tidings, Ethan my friend, from the Wisest of Kings, Solomon."

He entered, smelling of the finest perfumes of Egypt, and overwhelmed everyone with his gracious enquiries: of Esther, as to her health, of Huldah, as to her joy in her sons, of Lilith, as to her recent journey, of Shem and Sheleph, as to their progress in school; and he exclaimed to all of them as to the great honour which is about to be bestowed on me.

Then he turned to me, saying, "I hear you muttering with eyes downcast: you are praying a prayer of thanks to your god, Yahveh?"

I had indeed been praying: that he should drop dead, as should the Wisest of Kings and the entire Commission on the Preparation of *The One and Only True and Authoritative, Historically Correct and Officially Approved Report on the Amazing Rise* and so forth.

But Amenhoteph placed his arm about my shoulder and steered me gently to my study, where he informed me that in view of the closeness of the arrival of the daughter of Pharaoh it was desired that Lilith my concubine should be delivered unto the royal palace before the sun set another time, so that King Solomon might honour me by accepting her as a handmaid to his wife-to-be. "And now will you tell the damsel of her good fortune," he concluded, "for I have no doubt that this will make her most happy."

I replied that I preferred preparing Lilith gradually, as women were known to have suffered greatly by sudden tidings, some losing their faculty of speech, others developing a twitch, others again becoming complete idiots. But the eunuch tilted his hands in a manner brooking no contradiction, and I arose and went to the door of my study and called Lilith.

And Lilith came, and I took her by the hand and led her unto Amenhoteph, and I said to her in a voice that was the voice of a stranger, "When I took you from your father, Lilith my love, I gave in exchange twelve sheep of good breed and four goats and a milk cow; but you have grown dear to my heart, and are the joy of my loins, so I would not trade you for all the herds in Israel. But now one has come who is more powerful than I, and he wants you. Therefore prepare yourself, my daughter, put ointment on you and myrrh and essence of attar, and close your heart to me, for you and I must part, each to go his way, I into old age, but you to—"

"Ethan!" she called out to me.

"—to the palace."

"Ethan my lover," she said, "when you left Jerusholayim the other day, and I waited for you at the big rock which rises beside the road, I told you I would be unto you as a shadow; and as no man can rend his shadow from him, so you will not be able to rend me from you, unless you tell me that you don't love me. Do you no longer love me?"

I told her of the advantages of living in the palace, enjoying the protection of the daughter of Pharaoh and always being near the face of the Wisest of Kings.

"Do you no longer love me?"

I told her that what she and I had experienced would remain forever within the sight of the Lord and within our hearts, but that life consisted of changes which none of us could hope to avoid.

"Do you no longer love me?"

I told her what it would mean to me, in my situation, to be able to oblige King Solomon, and if she really loved me, she must not think of herself only and of her feelings.

"Do you no longer love me?"

"I no longer do," I said.

"Then I shall kill myself," she answered quietly, "for my life has been given me through you."

"I was afraid of something like that," said Amenhoteph. "There exist such women: not many, thanks be unto the gods of Egypt and to your god, Yahveh, but enough to be a nuisance and to fill barrels of tablets of clay with their tender stories. I shall hold you responsible, Ethan my friend, that nothing untoward happens to the damsel until she is delivered into my hands, at the royal palace."

Thus I was made to guard the victim of my betrayal

235

against her escaping the putrescence thereof. Thus I was turned into a worm that is eating his own dirt.

And what did I gain by it?

And I went to the house of Nathan the prophet, and sat in his door like a supplicant, to be let into his presence.

But the servant said, "My lord is otherwise engaged."

I said, "Tell him I had a dream from the Lord concerning him."

After a while the servant returned, saying, "Come in."

Nathan sat in his room, looking ill; his face, always so smooth, had grown slack; his eyes were as two trapped mice. And I knew that he, too, was fearful of the servants of Benaiah ben Jehoiada.

"What kind of dream was it?" he enquired. "Was there an angel of the Lord in it, and if so, did he enter from the right or from the left, and were his wings spread or folded, and did he carry a sword? For I also had a dream, and in it a black angel of the Lord came down at me from the height, holding a fiery sword stretched forth against me."

"May God have mercy on my lord," I exclaimed, "for such a dream could frighten the wits out of a man. But my dream was a dream of life, and the part of my lord therein was altogether pleasant, for in it you went unto King Solomon with your famous parable."

"Did I, now?" he said dubiously.

"And you told the King as you had told unto David his father: even of the rich man who had exceeding many flocks and of the poor man who had nothing save one little ewe lamb, and how the rich man, having to feed a guest from out of town, spared to take of his own flock, nay, but took the poor man's lamb and roasted it for the man that was come to him."

"And I suppose," said Nathan, "that in your dream the Wisest of Kings, Solomon, was as kindled with anger as was David his father, and spoke, As the Lord lives, the man that has done this thing shall surely die, because he had no pity; whereupon in your dream I replied unto the King that in this instance, fortunately, matters might be set right in good time and that he must only forgo the joys of having Lilith the

236

concubine of Ethan as a handmaid to the daughter of Pharaoh."

I complimented Nathan on his prophetic gift, and on his great insight into the hearts of people.

But Nathan said, "You are a fool, Ethan. Even if I were to invent a parable ten times better and more original than the one of the little ewe lamb, and told it to Solomon, he would send me to the devil. His father, King David, was a poet and had a poet's imagination. Thus it was that he saw himself in a special relationship to God: the Chosen of the Lord, and yet his servant, called upon to wear himself out in the cause. King David therefore could understand the poor man with his one little ewe lamb. But this one?—ptui!"—Nathan spat—"this one is but an imitator, vain, without vision, his dreams mediocre, his verse trite, his crimes growing from fear, not from greatness. He craves recognition. He must constantly show that he is important. Therefore he collects: gold, buildings, armies, foreign ambassadors, women. He needs your Lilith. He must prove to himself not only that he is wiser than you, but that he is the better man."

Nathan had risen, truly a prophet of the Lord. But his fervour did not last. Whatever had driven him to pronounce judgment over King Solomon evaporated and left him deflated. "You will not repeat my words to anyone, Ethan," he pleaded. "For I shall deny I ever spoke them. I shall claim you said them to me. In truth I believe you did. These were your thoughts, I swear, which were transferred by an evil spirit of the Lord into my mind, as my mind is but a receptacle waiting to be filled."

I told him not to disquiet himself, and arose, and went my way.

The daughter of Pharaoh came into Jerusholayim with a very great train, with camels that bore gold, and precious stones, and linen of byssus, and other raiment, and perfumes; and she had her ladies with her that ministered to her. King Solomon met her at the gate of the city, with all his mighty men, and with drums, and trumpets, and cymbals, and timbrels, and with all sorts of horns, so that the noise was heard from one end of Jerusholayim to the other. And the people came streaming to the gate, and they lined the road to the palace, to hail the Princess with joy and to praise the wisdom of the Wisest of Kings and his power: but for all of this they had been rehearsed by the servants of Benaiah ben Jehoiada and also by the Levites.

Esther my wife said to me, "It is time to clothe Lilith."

So Lilith bathed herself, and oiled her skin; but her hair was done by Huldah so that it shone like moonlight on the waters of the Lake Kinnereth. Also her eyelids and her lips were painted, and her cheeks, were daubed with a powder to give them colour. And Lilith placed a bundle of myrrh betwixt her breasts, which were as two young roes that are twins; and she sprayed essence of roses upon herself, and of cinnamon. Then she put on a garment of green and scarlet and sandals of soft leather that revealed the fine shape of her instep and her toes. But withal her face was motionless, and her eyes without expression, so that she looked to me more like a painted corpse than a live woman.

Now Amenhoteph the royal chief eunuch had sent his litter for Lilith, and she seated herself in it and was borne off. I walked beside her so as to spend these last moments with her, and because I had been made responsible for her by Amenhoteph until she was delivered into his hands, at the royal palace.

We wended our way through the mass of people that returned from greeting the daughter of Pharaoh at the gate of the city and at the palace. But I saw neither the people, nor the bearers of the litter, nor the face of Lilith in the window of the litter: I fastened my gaze to the red tassels, trying not to look at Lilith my concubine, who had loved me, and whom I was bartering away for the uncertain favour of the King, and for a period of grace, I felt as though I were walking in a funeral procession. A part of my life was being carried to the grave, along with my dignity as a son of man.

But by the grace of the Lord, praised be his name, I am endowed with the gift of observing myself at times of inner stress, which helps in preserving one's sanity. And though I saw nothing pretty as I watched myself shuffle along beside that litter, I also recognised that I was caught up in my time and unable to go beyond its limitations. Man is but a stone in the middle of a sling, to be slung out at targets he knows not. The most he can do is to try making his thought last a little beyond him, a dim signal to generations to come.

I have tried.

Let me be judged accordingly.

25

But lord yahveh sent a blessed sleep unto Esther my wife; and she slept through the night and awoke on the morrow, saying she was much refreshed and felt almost well.

And I made myself believe that my prayers to God, and the potions and ointments of the Levite, and the valiant struggle of Esther had caused the Angel of Darkness to retire from her altogether. For though we know that it must come, death is inconceivable to us, and no man, however wise, can reconcile himself to it.

Esther spoke to me, saying, "Your work is nearing its end, Ethan my husband, and the *Report on the Amazing Rise, God-fearing Life, Heroic Deeds* and so forth will be finished, so that we may return to Ezrah, to our house which stands there in the shade of the olive trees that were planted by us. I long for a drink from its well, for its water is sweet and healthful and the best of all potions."

I answered that we would soon return there, to sit under the olive trees, and under the vines, and to listen to the rippling of the well.

"I should like to be back in the month of Zif," she said. "That time of the year is so lovely."

Just then a noise sounded as of fists battering the door, and Shem and Sheleph burst into the room, calling out that the servants of Benaiah were come, with swords, and with horses, and with a chariot. Esther's hand, which I still was holding, trembled.

"Open to them," I said to Shem and Sheleph, "I shall be out directly."

I noticed that I was calm of mind, and that I saw everything about me with great clarity: the splotches on the wall, the candlestick, the coverlet that hardly rose over Esther's wasted body.

But as I arose to go, Esther said in a thin voice, "Won't you kiss me a last time, Ethan?"

I turned back hastily. "But this is not the last time, Esther! I will be back presently: the servants of Benaiah that come to seize a man for detention, they come at the break of dawn."

I kissed her gently, feeling a bit guilty at my thoughts having been so much upon myself at this moment of affliction; but Esther raised her hand and stroked my brow and my temples.

Then I went out to meet whatever would befall me.

Now the chariots of the servants of Benaiah drove through Jerusholayim at speeds that exceeded all limits, with whips cracking, and with blood-curdling shouts to make way. And whoever did not jump aside in time was thrown to the ground, or run over, so that each chariot drew behind it a wake of howls and of curses.

Up on the chariot I was held tightly by two men, while we lurched around corners, and rattled downhill, and up again, and finally halted at a side entrance of the royal palace. Thereupon I was rushed by the same two men over numbers of stairs, through passageways, past sullen guards, into a small room which received its only light by a narrow opening near the ceiling. And there I stayed for a long while, or so it seemed to me.

And I spoke unto Lord Yahveh, Hold out your hand unto me, and lead me through the valley, so I may see again your sun and the light of your day. Do not cast me from you; remember not my sins and my failings, but think kindly of me and of my endeavours. For what is man in your sight, and what is his soul but a reflection of your being; in you, O God, we reach our full measure, but without you we are lost as a speck of sand in the sea. Do not forsake me, O Lord, let me not fall to the depths, but raise me up to your hill, and to your holy place, that I may stand under your sky in dignity and sing your praise.

241

There was a scraping sound, and part of the wall moved aside, and a voice said, "Come forth, son of Hoshaiah!"

I found myself in a fairly large hall. I blinked, shaking my head, for it was to me as though I had seen the whole picture before: King Solomon seated upon his throne between the Cherubim; and by his side Jehoshaphat ben Ahilud, the recorder, and Zadok the priest, and Nathan the prophet, and Benaiah ben Jehoiada; and Elihoreph and Ahiah b'nai Shisha, the scribes, sitting further off, with tablets of wax and with stylus, waiting to note down what was being said. This was where and how it had all begun; but the King had become more yellow of complexion, and his eyes more beady, and his mouth more crooked, so that his face looked like one of those masks which are used by the uncircumcised to frighten off the evil spirits of the Lord; indeed, time had left its traces on everyone of us but Benaiah: as it is said, He who feels not, ages not.

But I prostrated myself before King Solomon and spoke, "Behold, my lord, your servant is unto you as a footstool, waiting to be trod on; but do not destroy me utterly, for I have been useful to you, and may be so, again."

As I looked up, I saw that the King and his mighty men were utterly unmoved, and I knew that this was a court, and that I was the accused, and that the balance was weighted against me.

Jehoshaphat ben Ahilud bade me to rise, and said, "Pray do not act simple-minded, Ethan, as the Wisest of Kings, Solomon, has seen through your cunning and your devices. Now, therefore, you had better confess. A full confession, leaving out nothing and disclosing the names of your fellow conspirators, may help your case and may induce the Wisest of Kings to show mercy."

"If it please my lord the King and my lords," I answered, "I should be the very first to confess fully, if only there were something to confess. But your servant is free of guilt, in that I have worked diligently and conscientiously, compiling and writing the King David Report according to the instructions given by my lords and by the Wisest of Kings, Solomon, and in the letter and the spirit of their words."

"Ethan," said the King, "I had hoped for something more original from you: for nowadays all those that are wicked say they would like to confess." And turning to Jehoshaphat, "Read the indictment."

The indictment was a lengthy piece, filled with references to the words of the Lord, and to the wisdom of the Wisest of Kings, and meandering through a wilderness of verbiage, from which jutted a few terms such as Slander, and Subversion, and Calumny, and Innuendo, and Perversion of the Mind, and Literary High Treason.

Jehoshaphat having finished, the King gazed at me from narrowed eyes, and he queried, "Son of Hoshaiah, do you plead guilty to high treason committed by word, and in writing, through the interspersion of doubts, and of evil thought, and of mischievous notions in *The One and Only True and Authoritative, Historically Correct and Officially Approved Report on the Amazing Rise, God-fearing Life, Heroic Deeds, and Wonderful Achievement of David the Son of Jesse, King of Judah for Seven Years and of Both Judah and Israel for Thirty-three, Chosen of God, and Father of King Solomon,* and by clothing said doubts, and said evil thought, and said mischievous notions in a language that pretends to be artless and pleasing to the eye of the Lord: as charged in the indictment?"

"Not guilty," I said.

There was a silence. Benaiah ground his jaws, and Nathan looked at me anxiously, and the King toyed with the noses of the Cherubim. Finally he said to me, "Speak."

I thought, if I was to be hanged, it might as well be for speaking my mind, and I began, "There lived a wise man in Ur of the Chaldees, whence came Abraham our forefather. He was so wise that he could prove all that was on the earth and under the earth and in the skies: the grass, the herb yielding seed, the fruit tree yielding fruit after its kind, the great whales that swim in the sea, the fowl that may fly above the earth, and every living creature that moves. He could also prove that which is not seen: the thought in your mind, the desire in your heart, the fear in your bowels. And there came an angel of the Lord to tempt the wise man, saying unto him, You can prove all that which is? The wise man said, My lord speaks truly. The angel said, But can you also prove that which is not? Can you prove that a thought was never thought, a desire never had, a fear never felt? At this, the wise man fell to the ground before the angel of the Lord, and he cried out, God alone can prove that which is not; may he that sent you have mercy on me, for I am but a man. Now, if it please my lord the King and my lords, how then should a poor son of Israel such as myself do what the wise man of Ur could not do before the angel of the Lord? How should I prove to your satisfaction the doubt never doubted, the thought never conceived, the mischief never plotted?"

"We can read," said Benaiah, "even between the lines."

"The word of the Lord has been my guide," I replied, "as has the wish of the King to have a report written which would establish forever One Truth, thus ending All Controversy, eliminating All Disbelief, and allay All Doubt in reference to David ben Jesse."

"You seem to imply that the word of the Lord and the wish of the King are in contradiction?" remarked Jehoshaphat.

"The word of the Wisest of Kings is law to his servants," I said, "and has not my lord Jehoshaphat advised us in one of the earlier sessions of the Commission that the King desired us to follow a subtle policy, marking a man discreetly when he needed being marked, and bending the truth gently where it needed bending, so that the people might believe what is written?"

"Which you took as your licence to slip in matters detrimental," said Zadok the priest, "thus creating controversy, arousing disbelief, evoking doubt, and in general trying to defeat the stated purpose of the work."

"As my lords well know," I pleaded, "I shaved from the facts much that was rugged, and evil-smelling, and distasteful to the eye of the King. But you cannot entirely divorce history from truth and expect to remain credible. Who can cook without fire? Who can wash you without wetting you?"

"I myself am a historian of sorts," said Nathan, "yet my book of remembrances contains but the noblest and most uplifting sentiments. It is a matter of attitude, and whether the writer's mind be constructive or overly critical."

"Is it not a matter of the mind of the reader as well?" I answered him. "What appears proper to the one may seem evil to the other. He whom the shoe fits will wear it; why hang the shoemaker?"

244

"There is a way of writing," said Jehoshaphat ben Ahilud, the recorder, "which permits of no interpretation."

"My lord speaks truly," I agreed, "but such writings are as foul fish in the market, which no one will buy, and which are cast out; but the Wisest of Kings, Solomon, wanted a book that would outlast all others."

The jaws of Benaiah stopped grinding. "You are ready to swear by the name of the Lord, Ethan, and by the life of Esther your wife, that nowhere in the King David Report can be found a suggestion of things having been otherwise than written therein?"

I thought of Esther lying ill and wasted, and of the great mercy of the Lord; but I also saw these men facing me, and that they were without mercy.

"Well?" said Benaiah.

"As the sun breaks through the clouds," I shrugged, "thus truth will break through words."

"That seems sufficient," said Jehoshaphat.

"His attitude," said Nathan, "is anything but constructive."

Zadok the priest cast his eyes heavenwards, saying, "And we shall have to sit for months like nitpickers, searching this mess for hints of subversion and godlessness."

And Benaiah ben Jehoiada said with a smile, "Knowledge is a blessing from the Lord, but he who knows too much is like an illness that festers, and like a stink from the mouth. Now, therefore, let me fall upon this man Ethan and slay him, so that his knowledge may go to the grave with him."

But I threw myself again at King Solomon's feet and kissed his fat toes, and said, "Hear your servant, O Wisest of Kings, for I am crying out to you not only as to a ruler, but also as to a fellow poet. Pray let me read to you from my psalm *In Praise of the Lord, and in Praise of David,* and then judge of my character, and if I deserve to be fallen upon by Benaiah and slain."

Before the King could say Yes or No, I pulled from my robe a strip of thin leather, on which I had written my verse, and I read.

IN PRAISE OF THE LORD, AND IN PRAISE OF DAVID
MASCHIL OF ETHAN THE EZRAHITE

(The Lord speaking:)

I have made a covenant with my chosen, I have sworn unto David my servant,

Your seed will I establish for ever, and build up your throne to all generations.

I have found David my servant; with my holy oil have I anointed him:

With whom my hand shall be established: my arm also shall strengthen him.

The enemy shall not exact upon him; nor the son of wickedness afflict him.

And I will beat down his foes before his face, and plague them that hate him.

Also I will make him my firstborn, higher than the kings of the earth.

My mercy will I keep for him for evermore, and my covenant shall stand fast with him.

His seed also will I make to endure for ever, and his throne as the days of heaven.

It shall be established for ever as the moon, and as a faithful witness in heaven.

The King politely clapped his hands; so did the other lords; and Elihoreph and Ahiah, the scribes, enquired if they could have a copy of the psalm, to be included with the minutes.

I said I should be glad to ready a copy for them, provided I was left alive to do it. At which King Solomon shoved his gold-embroidered skullcap forward, scratched his pate, and pronounced judgment as follows:

SOLOMONIC JUDGMENT

Where any word displeasing the eye of the King, and of established authority, is inherently treasonable,

And whereas certain words inserted by the accused, Ethan ben Hoshaiah, of Ezrah, in *The One and Only True and Authoritative, Historically Correct and Officially Approved Report on the Amazing Rise, God-fearing Life, Heroic Deeds, and Wonderful Achievements of David the Son of Jesse, King of Judah for Seven Years and of Both*

246

Judah and Israel for Thirty-three, Chosen of God, and
Father of King Solomon, have displeased the eye of the
King, and of established authority,

And whereas the accused is thus proved guilty as charged
in the indictment,

Now, therefore I, Solomon, the Wisest of Kings, by
the power vested in me through the covenant of the Lord,
do hereby sentence said Ethan ben Hoshaiah to death.

"Very good," said Benaiah, drawing his sword.

King Solomon however raised his head and went on to
speak.

SOLOMONIC JUDGMENT
(Continued)

But physical death of the accused, Ethan ben Hoshaiah,
being inconvenient to the King, in that it might cause
evil-minded people to claim that the Wisest of Kings,
Solomon, was fettering thought, or hounding learned men,
and so forth,

And it being equally inconvenient, for the identical
reason, to place the accused, Ethan ben Hoshaiah, in our
mines or our quarries, or with the priests of Beth-shan, or in
another such institution,

Now, therefore, let him be silenced to death; let no word
of his reach the ear of the people, either by mouth, or by
tablet of clay, or by leather; so that his name be forgotten
as though he were never born and had never written a
line;

But that psalm he read us, *In Praise of the Lord, and in
Praise of David,* which is written in the spirit and the
manner of all those that write like the lowest kind of
servants, trite, and full of platitudes, and bare of imagination, this psalm shall carry his name and be preserved
for all times.

"As my lord the King commands," said Benaiah, and
sheathed his sword. "But I still believe in the direct way."

That night the Angel of Darkness entered upon the house,

and he spread his wings, and their shadow fell over Esther my beloved wife.

I saw the change which the angel had wrought on her face, and I cried out and fell to the ground by her bedside, knowing what had come to pass, yet unable to accept it.

My God, my God, I spoke unto the Lord, how can her smile be gone, and the sound of her voice, and the touch of her fingers. How can her love be swallowed entirely by the gloom of Sheol, and the great brightness of her soul be doused as a candle of tallow? Without her I shall be like a brook without water, like a bone sucked dry of its marrow. Take one of my hands, O Lord, take my eye, take the half of my heart, but let her rise from this bed, to live, be it for five days, or three or one. You have created the world and all life within it: what is it to you to return this one life? For I have failed her grievously, in that my love for her was as nothing to the love she bore me: how can I repay her, and in what coin, if she be dead? There is hope in a tree, if it be cut down, that it will sprout again: but this woman, whose heart was as a fountain of clear water, shall she be less to you than one of your trees? Remember, I beseech you, that you have made her. You placed the thought in her mind and the loving-kindness in her heart; why will you reduce her to dust again. You clothed her with skin and with flies, you gave her the light in her eyes, which has lighted my way; why destroy the work of your hands, O Lord, and your own image? If I have sinned, then mark me; do not acquit me from my iniquity. If I be wicked, woe unto me: but why take the life of her who was righteous, and a joy to humankind; why send her to the depths whence no one returns?

Thus I strove with the Lord; but Yahveh wrapped his silence about him, and the face of Esther my wife grew to be as a stranger's.

Then came Shem and Sheleph my sons, and Huldah their mother, and they helped me into my study. I tore my clothes and strewed ashes in my hair. Later the house filled with neighbours and with Levites. They shrouded Esther's face and her poor wasted body, and they wailed; moreover they ate and drank and patted my back and spoke of the Will of the Lord, and that every one of us must go to the land

248

of darkness and the shadow of death; but all this passed me by.

And the next day they took Esther and loaded her on a cart that was drawn by two milk kine, and carted her out of Jerusholayim through the gate, and lowered her into a hole in the ground.

26

THERE WAS NOTHING which held me in Jerusholayim; moreover, the servants of the King were urging me to surrender
the house No. 54, Queen-of-Sheba Lane, saying, You have
no position in the service of the King, therefore be gone. So
I sold what belongings I had, or gave them to people; but as
to my notes and archives, these I secreted away.

And I went one last time to the sepulchre of Esther my
wife, to pray there unto the Lord. As I gazed at the stone,
I thought of the words which David had spoken upon the
death of his first-born out of Bath-sheba; and I whispered,
"You shall not return to me, but I shall go to you."

Then I arose to go to the tabernacle of the Lord. With some
of the few shekels left me I bought part of a lamb and placed
it as an offering on the altar at which Joab had recently been
slain by Benaiah ben Jehoiada. I observed the smoke curling
up to the blue sky, and I knew that Lord Yahveh was accepting my sacrifice, and that he would grant me a safe journey.

On the way back I stopped to view the progress of the
construction of the temple which King Solomon was erecting
unto the name of the Lord; and I saw the huge rocks that
were being hewn to measure and piled one on top of the
other, and the porch of pillars, and the chapiters that were
carved with pomegranates and with lilies; but I also saw the
sore backs of the people that built it, and their thin faces and
tortured eyes.

And the Lord sent an angel that stood by my shoulder and
spoke unto me, "What is stone, and what are iron and brass,
and what are the thrones of the kings and the swords of the

mighty? All this will turn to dust, says the Lord; but the word, and truth, and love, these shall remain."

We carried our possessions on our backs; but at the gate of the city we were held just as though we were come with forty donkeys that were loaded with rugs and coffers and with archives. The Cherethite mounting guard called his captain, and the captain of the gate came out and exclaimed, "Not the historian! And not in this fashion, carrying bundles and walking on his two feet!"

I pointed at my credentials, at the royal seal, at the exit permit, and told him to please let us pass without further ado, as the day promised to be hot, and we wanted to be on our way.

"I see you have finished your work," the captain said less for my benefit than for that of the vagrants and idlers and thieves and other unsavoury folk at the gate, "and you have given these people what they need most in the world: a history." He turned to the crowd. "I want you to thank this man, Ethan ben Hoshaiah, for in addition to your boils and the stink from your mouths you now have by his tireless effort an account of your great virtues."

They slapped their thighs and threw themselves on the ground for joy; and they pressed close to me and Shem and Sheleph my sons and Huldah their mother.

"Pray tell these men," the captain said to me, "did you depict them as the chosen people, who live by the word of Lord Yahveh and by his laws, or did you write of their wickedness and stupidities?"

"The people," I said, "are the source of both good and evil."

"There you heard how fickle you are," said the captain, letting his whip crack over the heads of the crowd, "but the King is from God, and so are the King's captains and all those in his service." He disregarded the muttering that rose around us, and once more turned to me, "What does that make you, then? You are not of the people, neither are you of God. You are not one of the rulers, neither are you among the ruled. You are as the serpent who offers the fruit of the tree of knowledge; and you know that the serpent was cursed

251

by the Lord God to crawl on his belly, and to eat dust all the days of his life, and to have his head crushed by the heel of man."

Hearing those words, the crowd moved in on us, its stench hot and heavy. I saw the hate in the pus-filled eyes, and the stumps that were raised in threat. Shem and Sheleph cried out, Huldah scratched at the faces of those nearest her, and I, knowing my fists to be ineffectual, cast about for help. And I perceived runners that carried white staves, and behind them the green and gold litter with the red tasselled roof.

And behold, the beggars and vagrants and thieves scattered like birds as the Cherethites and Pelethites cleared the gate of people. Escorted by the captain of the gate, Amenhoteph the royal chief eunuch strode across the steps, and he came and bowed before Huldah, and he chucked Shem and Sheleph under their chins; but to me he said, tilting his hands prettily, "I thought I could not let you go, Ethan my friend, without saying farewell. In more than one sense, you and I both were strangers in Jerusholayim. Therefore I have watched you and your doings with sympathy, and now that you leave us, I shall feel the void. If it is a solace to you, I will tell you that Lilith your former concubine has adjusted herself and feels well, ministering to King Solomon and also to his new wife, the daughter of Pharaoh. Furthermore, Lilith sings unto the King the songs of love which you taught her; and the King is much pleased by them, and he has caused them to be written down for a collection to be published under the title, *The Song of Solomon*. Now, therefore, I hope you will accept this parting gift in the spirit in which it is meant, and as a token of friendship."

From the fold of his robe he brought forth a small vial. "It was sent to me directly from the perfumer's," he mentioned, "an excellent house in the city of the sun god, Ra, in Egypt. May its odour always refresh you, and may it remind you that in a world of eunuchs it does not pay to act like a man."

I took the vial, and turned, and went my way.

When we had crossed the brook Kidron and climbed the crest beyond, I stopped for a last look at the city of David. And I saw it lying there upon its hills, and I wanted to curse it; but I could not do it, for a great splendour of the Lord lay over Jerusholayim in the light of the morning.

252

AUTHOR'S NOTE

The King David Report actually exists. It may be found in the Bible, beginning with I Samuel, 6 and ending with I Kings, 2.

As I sometimes read the Bible, it occurred to me that this section of it represented more than a fine oriental fairy tale or an edifying parable. Behind the stories of giants and prophets, of beautiful women and ugly murders, there emerged the account of a revolution which developed according to its inherent laws, and which found its completion in the establishment of the state by David. But here was also a novel. What a character, this David ben Jesse—a killer who maintains close personal ties with God, a brigand who doubles as a poet, a tyrant who from a dozen hardly settled nomadic tribes forges a nation.

A historical novel? But could the Bible be considered ancient history? Didn't its ideas and values influence people even today, particularly today? Which parts of the David legend needed to be re-told in such a novel, which might the reader be expected to know? In general, was one obliged to stick to the biblical report, and if so, to what extent? What language, what literary form did one choose to relate the story?

The answers might be contained in the material at hand. The archaeologists have unearthed witnesses of stone and of clay that inform us of life in the Near East a thousand years before Christ. But only the Bible supplies any evidence specifically referring to David, though its words about the son of Jesse are often contradictory.

Nature and intent of the biblical report about him are obvious: the story is slanted so as to legitimise the rule of David's successor, the wise King Solomon. Whence, then, the

253

contradiction? The reason became clear to me when I got hold of a German Bible translation published in 1909 by Herr Emil Kautzsch, professor of theology at the University of Halle. On the lower halves of page after page of text, this edition analyses the sources of chapter and verse; from this it appears that not long after the death of David the story of his life and royal rule must have been patched together from various source materials, and where the several parts refused to fit together, the seams remained visible.

Now the format offered itself for a new telling of the David story. If one retraced the steps of the editorial Commission which met under King Solomon, if one went back to the sources and let these speak—the royal annals, army records, letters, eye-witness testimonies, songs and myths from which the King David Report was carefully pieced together—one might be able to lay bare the essence of the King and to make the many-faceted man that David was come alive: one—that is in this case one Ethan of Ezrah, author of the 89th psalm and secretary of the Royal Commission, the same Ethan about whom it is said in I Kings, 4, 31 that he was one of the wisest men in Israel; only King Solomon was alleged to have been wiser than he.

Then something occurred that frequently happens in the telling of a tale: Ethan, who was to be a mere narrator, assumed a life of his own. Around the David novel grew an Ethan novel, the story of an intellectual who must face the conflicts of his time and who is tormented by the limitations which are set to his writing the truth.

Whether Ethan is the protagonist of this book or whether it's David as seen through Ethan I couldn't say. Opinions might also differ on the question whether The King David Report *is to be considered a historical novel or a biblical one, or a story of today, charged with political meaning. To me, it is all three.*

Berlin, 1972

Stefan Heym

My thanks are due to Prof. Dr. theol. habil. Walter Beltz, University of Halle, for his good advice and most helpful suggestions.

S.H.